9/17

THE Girl WITH THE Red Balloon

KATHERINE LOCKE

ALBERT WHITMAN & COMPANY
CHICAGO, ILLINOIS

Library of Congress Cataloging-in-Publication
data is on file with the publisher.

Text copyright © 2017 by Katherine Locke
Cover illustrations copyright © by Shutterstock.com
Published in 2017 by Albert Whitman & Company
ISBN 978-0-8075-2933-1 (hardcover)
ISBN 978-0-8075-2937-9 (paperback)

Printed in the United States of America
10 9 8 7 6 5 4 3 2 1 LB 22 21 20 19 18 17

Design by Cynthia Fliege

For more information about Albert Whitman & Company,
visit our website at www.albertwhitman.com.

For my grandfathers,
may their memories be a blessing

Chapter One

LEAVING THE AMERICAN SECTOR

Berlin, Germany, Present Day

Ellie

My first day in Berlin was what my saba would have called a *balloon day*. A crystalline-blue sky without a single cloud, everything so bright that I wondered if I had time to run back up to the hotel for sunglasses. Instinctively, I touched my purse at my side. Passport, wallet, phone. Everything necessary for survival. At home, it was probably still snowing. Here, the air was vivid and crisp, like biting into an apple.

I *chose* to be in Berlin, even though Saba hadn't wanted me to come. The crowd parted around me on the sidewalk, oblivious to the tiny war inside me.

Maybe today wasn't a balloon day. Maybe it was just a day with a blue sky, like any other. In a city where I didn't belong, thinking of my grandfather who hadn't belonged here either. I was taking German because of Saba. Because he was German, the same way he was Jewish, and I didn't know how to tell him that, to me, both of those identities were equal. I tried once, but that was when he could walk away from me. Now he just turned his head and his eyes went vacant. Mom said that was why he used the Hebrew word for grandfather, not the German or Yiddish words.

My mind was getting away from me again. I just needed to let go.

"Ellie Baum!" Mrs. Anderson, my teacher, stopped at the front of our group of sophomore and junior German students. She lowered her sunglasses to the end of her nose so she ended up squinting until her eyes almost disappeared. "You're dawdling. Keep up! Everyone together!"

Keep up, let go. Same things. I grimaced. If I could have wished a balloon into existence, I would have, just to send Mrs. Anderson back to the United States. The rest of us could explore Berlin on our own. Basically everyone we'd met so far spoke English anyway, and the hotel wouldn't know the difference. Mrs. Anderson shook out the map and held it in front of her, like a bullhorn shouting her tourist status.

I rolled my eyes and caught up with my best friend, Amanda. "This is ridiculous."

Amanda handed me our itinerary. "If she has us walk much more, we're going to see the whole city on the first day and we'll have nothing left to do."

Some spring break. I thought it'd be perfect: a chance to use my German, get out of snowy Pittsburgh, and bolster my college applications. It wasn't too early to start worrying about those. What if this wasn't worth it? What if during this entire trip I just felt worse and worse about leaving Saba behind and breaking his heart by coming here?

"You feel okay?" Amanda asked, frowning at me. "You look pale."

I shoved the itinerary back into her hands as we meandered from our hotel toward the U-Bahn subway station. "I'm fine. Going to be a *long* week."

"We'll figure out how to make it fun," Amanda promised, which wasn't quite what I meant. Amanda's idea of fun and mine tended to differ. She probably wanted to sweet-talk her way into some hot dance club tonight. Me? I was always the sidekick.

At home, I knew who I was. Here, I felt a little less like me, and a little more like the granddaughter of a Holocaust survivor. I didn't usually think of myself that way, but I couldn't shake the feeling.

In the suburbs of Pittsburgh, people just drove everywhere, so I didn't know what to expect from a subway, but the U-Bahn wasn't that bad. It didn't smell like pee, at least. Under Mrs. Anderson's dour gaze, we packed ourselves into one car and slipped beneath the wall that once divided the city. And while some of my classmates were loud and obnoxious, no one really paid attention to us. The tunnel lights flashed by us, and my chest tightened. *Deep breath, Ellie.* I distracted myself by scrolling through my phone with Amanda, looking at the photos we'd taken so far.

"Girls, put those away," called Mrs. Anderson.

What was she going to do? Put us on a plane back home because we had our phones out? We both ignored her.

Amanda showed me pictures she had taken of street art she'd seen, including one of windows within windows all the way back until I could see a faint hint of green, like pasture land. "Even graffiti is better in Europe," she said.

I kept flipping through pictures, down to the ones that Saba and I took of his new dog a week ago. We talked about his dog, not about me going to Germany.

When I first signed up for the trip, I tried to tell him that Germany was different now than when he was here. He never returned to Berlin, not after escaping during the war. He didn't want to listen to me. Or maybe he couldn't.

A country never changes, Eleanor. It's not a person. They killed six million Jews. The people you see? They sat. They let it happen.

I swallowed hard and put away my phone, looking up to smile at Amanda and the other girls. I was here. I needed to put guilt away and just figure out how to enjoy my time here.

"Potsdamer Platz!" Mrs. Anderson called out. "Redstone High School, this is our stop!"

There she went again, sharing her neon tourist sign with the rest of us. Apparently, blending in was for other people. The locals on the metro gave us knowing looks as we and a hundred other people with cameras slung around their necks and maps in their hands pushed our way out the door, chattering in all different languages. The subway station dazzled with glossy white tile as we stomped up the stairs.

I seriously regretted not having sunglasses. Glittering, modern buildings formed a protective shield around the plaza. People moved in huge crowds at varying speeds. A woman in a business suit pushed her way through a crowd of hyperblond tourists taking photos in front of the Potsdamer Platz station sign. A ticker sign displayed the international news on one of the buildings.

A memorial to the Berlin Wall stood in the middle of the crush. Mrs. Anderson guided us toward it with waving arms, like we wouldn't be able to find it. Six slabs of the wall rose in front of us, covered in layers of vibrant graffiti, with commentary on plaques between them. It no longer looked like a wall this way, but rather a line of bright, colorful people linking arms. *Red rover, red rover, send a wrecking ball and freedom right over.*

Most people milled around the pieces of the wall, taking pictures of it, taking pictures of themselves with it. I just stood there. I didn't know what to do, but I didn't want to take a picture with the wall. I didn't know why we took pictures of ourselves with symbols of tyranny and oppression. Maybe it was a way of remembering. Maybe it was the only way we knew how to say we recognized the importance of everything that had happened to bring down the wall.

I touched the wall with my forefinger, middle finger, and ring finger, the same three fingers I pressed to the space between my eyes when I said the Shema, the holiest of Jewish prayers. I tried to think of something profound to say, but couldn't. Instead, I whispered, "I'm glad you're in pieces now."

I glanced around nervously, worried I'd been overheard whispering to stone, but no one paid any attention. Next to me, a middle-aged man with rippled scars like burns on the backs of his brown hands studied the wall with a pensive look on his face. He looked old enough to remember the wall when it divided the city. Maybe he had been one of those people who sat on the wall the night it came down, cheering and helping East Berliners climb over. Maybe he had been an East Berliner.

Maybe your imagination's running wild, I chided myself.

Then the man and I watched together as someone leaned past him, pressing chewing gum into the wall with his thumb. It stuck there, a little blue piece of gum and a thumbprint. Enough of a print to identify him.

The gum chewer disappeared into the crowd as quickly as he'd come. All of a sudden, the world felt incredibly small. Like everyone else around us had disappeared and left just the man with the scarred hands and me trying to understand why chewed-up gum and a fingerprint seemed so profound. We are strange, sometimes, in the ways we choose to bear witness.

The man sighed, frowning, and then tipped his face toward the blue, blue sky. He said in a British accent, his voice low, "This is how I want to remember the wall. Like this."

I blinked, surprised that he wasn't German, and looked around to see if he was talking to anyone else. But it was still just the two of us standing at this panel. When I turned, the man was gone, his words lingering in the air.

"Some history must be remembered. The other history, like where we killed millions of Jews, not so much," mocked Amanda, appearing at my shoulder. She reached around for my map, and I relinquished it.

My mind was still stuck on the man and how I wished I'd thought of something to say in response. But what would I have said? I couldn't even think of anything to say to Amanda. Not really. I had seen pictures of Berlin's Holocaust memorial, and it was in no way small, but her words felt too much like trying to compare two different tragedies in Germany's history. The twentieth century hadn't played nice with Europe. Or maybe it had been the other way around. My chest knotted. Did defending Germany now mean apologizing for events of the past? Were memorials apologies?

I tuned back in to catch Amanda saying, "There's a cool club near here. They say that it's been there since 1946."

"Yeah, because a club totally sounds like me." I yanked the map back and rolled my eyes at her. Amanda stuck her tongue out at me. Predictable. She'd be sneaking out tonight, and I'd be covering for her. Always, always the sidekick.

Mrs. Anderson unfolded her tour-guide booklet and read aloud to us amid a sea of tourists about how this had been one of the busiest intersections in all of Europe between the World Wars. It was destroyed in World War II and then bulldozed for the death strip that existed on the east side of the wall. I tried to imagine this shiny, busy, tourist-filled place as nothing but a dirt strip with barbed wire so the guards could shoot those trying to make a run for it—and failed. People had died here on the dirt beneath this plaza, trying to reach freedom.

Places can be victims of history too.

Behind me, I could hear Mrs. Anderson exclaim, "When in Berlin, *ich bin ein Berliner!*"

And some smart-ass classmate of mine said, "You're a jelly doughnut?"

I had to press my lips together to keep the grin off my face as my classmates burst into laughter and Mrs. Anderson huffed at us.

She acted like she didn't know we'd be like this and she hadn't been teaching most of us for at least two years. We were burned out after a red-eye flight across the ocean. I needed a nap. Or caffeine. A vanilla latte, maybe. I began to scan the streets for a Starbucks.

An elbow collided with my ribs, and I turned to glare at Amanda. She giggled and tilted her head to the left, a wide, sparkling grin on her face. "Check *him* out."

Sitting on a park bench was a guy, maybe a few years older than us, with an earring and tattoos. His feet tapped out a rhythm as he strummed a guitar. It was a little cold for stringed instruments outside so he kept trying and failing to tune it. Still, he was cute in a shaggy hipster kind of way. Definitely more Amanda's type than mine. He caught us staring and winked. He sang out a line from a horribly overplayed song from like two years ago, and Amanda practically melted.

"Come on, let's listen to him real quick," she begged me, pulling at my arm. I glanced doubtfully at the group. Not that I wanted to be around Mrs. Anderson anymore, but I really didn't want to get in trouble for falling behind again. Then Amanda, who knew all my weaknesses, said, "You can practice your German *and* tell your mom you weren't shy the whole trip. Two birds, one hot, gorgeous, guitar-strumming stone."

"I've been social," I protested, gesturing over my shoulder at the group.

Amanda snorted. "Get out of your head and live a little, Baum. You're in *Europe*."

I had no suitable comeback so I let her drag me over to the guy on the bench. He laughed throatily and lit a cigarette as we approached. I wrinkled my nose and tried to step upwind of him. He couldn't have been more of a stereotype if he tried. Maybe he *was* trying. It clearly worked. Amanda was blushing before we even said anything. The guy winked at me, and I turned away before I could ask him something awkward like whether his face tattoos hurt. I stared at his shoes as he said, "American girls!"

Amanda giggled, brushing her hair over her shoulder. I snorted. He gave her a patient smile and tossed me a wink. Definitely Amanda's type. It took me a few minutes of helping her with the vocabulary, but she finally managed to ask in very rudimentary German if he lived in Berlin. How she ever got to German II would be beyond me if I hadn't helped her through every group project and homework assignment.

As he went through the motions of speaking like a five-year-old to her, my gaze slid over his shoulder and I watched a red balloon drifting over the grass, the string dragging on the ground. Some kid must have accidentally let it go. It made for a great picture, though, that solitary balloon floating without rising higher, surrounded by all the oblivious people and this beautiful day.

Just like Saba's balloon from his stories. A balloon, on a balloon day.

The balloon drifted closer, and higher. The knot of my heart untangled in my chest. I took a deep breath, relaxing enough to smile for the first time that day. Saba would love this. He'd know it was an apology to him, not on behalf of Germany like a memorial.

I grabbed Amanda's arm and interrupted her conversation with the guy, much to his evident relief. I pulled my phone out of my purse and waved it at her. "Hey, take a picture of me with that balloon."

"What?" She took the phone and my purse, frowning at me. I could practically hear her saying, Baum, you've lost it. Keep it together in front of the hot guy.

"For my grandfather," I called over my shoulder as I stepped toward the balloon. "Just take the photo, Amanda. I'll email it to my mom tonight."

The balloon was small and round and red, and so perfect. I reached out and grabbed its string. I felt a sharp jerk right between my ribs on my left side, and the world spun black.

Chapter Two

BROKEN BALLOONS

East Berlin, German Democratic Republic, March 1988

This night was not my night. First, a Passenger went missing. Then, everywhere I went looking for him, there were Volkspolizei. *Vopos*, crawling all over the city like cockroaches. It was as if—and *scheiße*, I didn't want to believe this—we'd been ratted out by someone. I shoved my hands into my cloak pockets, turning over the key to the workshop and safe houses in my fingers. The metal of the key never got cold, and it kept the fingertips of my left hand warmer than my gloves. In my right, I carried a knife to slash the balloon.

Wasn't right for a balloon to linger.

I'd no way to tell if my Passenger this week, a young guy named Garrick, had made it successfully to the other side of the wall. Usually, we could see a light in the church over there turn on when the Passenger landed. Tonight, no light. He might have landed anywhere along the wall. We just had to pray not inside the Todesstreifen on this side. The death zone was no place for a guy with a red balloon. I turned every corner with a steady chant in my head: Come on, Garrick. Be there.

Sometimes things went wrong with balloons. I had seen it before—a Passenger who let go too early and broke the magic free, making the balloon and the Passenger both visible. Usually that ended well if it happened on the other side of the wall. On this side of the wall, it would be the end if the police found him before I did. The police weren't completely incompetent. They knew we were getting people out somehow, and I was willing to bet a red balloon that they knew it wasn't natural.

I crossed the Karl-Marx-Allee, sticking to the shadows. There was no strict curfew in place, but I was in no mood to be stopped by the police. Even though my German was nearly perfect, they'd know I was not a native. And my ability to hold on to my temper and my secrets was admittedly tenuous. I was just here by circumstance. And circumstance kept me here. Until that changed, I played the best game I could and did the best job I could.

Tonight, it felt like a cursed job.

A few streets over, a car horn blew and tires squealed. The footing was pretty slick, especially where the road crossed the trolley tracks. The slush was accumulating at a steady rate now. Late snow for us.

I searched street after street in my sector, hoping with every block that Mitzi Weber, my partner, was having better luck north of me. Balloons had specific trajectories, and this one's shouldn't have altered too much. I figured if Garrick had fallen from it, he could have run off to hide anywhere. He was a more-than-wanted man by the East German government. Anyone with that target on their back kept their head down. They had one foot in the grave.

Didn't we all.

I was about to give up and go home, find Ashasher and Aurora, and tell them something went terribly wrong when I saw movement down an alley to my left. I paused midstride and backed up to stare into the shadows. My hands gripped the key and the knife as tightly as possible. The wind picked up the snow and blew it in a big, wild way down the alley, and then I saw it. A red balloon. *The* red balloon. It burst out from the shadows, held by its tether, and my heart stopped. Everything around me was in motion, but my heart just…stopped.

The person holding the balloon turned and began to run away from me, very clearly not Garrick. Someone who was not a Passenger was *holding a balloon*, and it hadn't disappeared. *Scheiße.* I lurched into a run after the person and the balloon.

"Halt!" I shouted, glancing behind me. Now would be a terrible time to attract the attention of the police.

But I couldn't let the person get away. Not now. Not with the balloon. They didn't slow down. Didn't even turn around to acknowledge me. Warnings clanged through my chest, outracing the adrenaline in my veins. *Danger. Let it go. Safer.* I nearly stopped pursuing them. Then a car backfired behind me, followed by rhythmic footsteps and a single shout. Vopos.

Nothing to lose now. Cursing under my breath, I ran as fast as I could on the slippery cement. I grabbed the person's elbow. "Will you hold up? I just need to ask you about this blasted balloon!"

She—oh *fuck*, a girl, it was definitely not supposed to be a girl—twisted against my grip, threw her head back, and let out a scream that couldn't have *not* been heard by the exact people we needed to avoid. I shoved her back against the wall, covering her mouth. I glanced back up the alley to see if anyone saw us. Turning my head was a nearly fatal mistake. Her knee jerked up, slamming me between the legs. Stars slashed across my vision. My fingers closed instinctively on her cheeks as I gasped.

She bit me, and I yanked my hand from her, cursing.

The Vopos had definitely heard her scream. Voices stormed down alleys all around us, the wet stone making their distance from us hard to calculate. She hadn't let go of the damn balloon. In the streetlights, I could see the double A stamps for Ashasher and Aurora, the two balloon makers. She had Garrick's balloon, this girl who was trying to decide what direction to run—like it mattered.

Didn't she know? In East Germany, wherever you ran, they followed you. I caught her arm and shook it a bit, trying to get her attention. I spoke slowly, because I wasn't sure if she was firing on all cylinders. "Who are you? Why do you have Garrick's balloon?"

What came out of her mouth was far worse than I could have imagined. It wasn't her words—"I don't know Garrick. It's my balloon. Let me go!"—but her terrible German and her American accent. She was American. Perhaps she'd forgotten to go back to the checkpoint. I could get her there, trade safety for the balloon. That'd untangle this particular snarl in this messy night.

"What checkpoint did you come through? Where are your papers?" I asked her, trying to keep my voice low and steady. "Where did you find this balloon?"

"I don't understand," she said, trying to yank away from me. "I don't have any papers. My passport's in my purse. I don't even have my phone on me. I have to find Amanda."

She could be playing me—and doing a good job because I couldn't believe this confused girl with a terrible accent could be a spy or have gotten so lost she didn't know what "papers" meant. Or something had gone unbelievably, terribly wrong. Worse than even a stolen balloon and a missing Passenger. I ran my eyes over her, her thin canvas-cloth shoes, her skirt and short-sleeved shirt. The way she shivered. She wasn't dressed for this weather.

Footsteps behind us, shouts echoing off walls, and her second scream restarted my heart. In times of panic, focus either completely dissolves, or sharpens to the point of pain. My brain chose pain. There were worse choices.

"No time," I said. To her or to myself, I couldn't tell. I grabbed her hand, pushing off the slippery ground into a run. I dropped the German because all the saints in the Catholic Church couldn't save her if she didn't listen to me now. "Run. Do not let go of that balloon."

I'd dragged a screaming toddler through a market a time or two. Running with this girl away from the police who wanted to beat, torture, and imprison us was similar. Exasperated, I stopped and dropped her hand suddenly. She landed with a splat in the wet snow. The streetlights reflected off the tears streaking her cheeks.

I crouched in front of the girl and pulled that damn red balloon down between us so she couldn't see anything but the balloon. The reason we were out here after curfew, running around in the snow. The balloon bounced between us, the magic still clinging to it, sticky and sparkling and making my nose itch.

"You can stay here," I said in German, as slowly as I could, trying to remember how Mitzi soothed anxious Passengers, "and get caught with this. And they will torture you. They are Volkspolizei, and you do not want to know what it is like in their prisons."

Confusion flickered across her face, and she asked in German, "*Was?*"

I didn't have time to explain. I blew out softly, and the balloon bounced against her face. She wiped tears off her cheeks with the backs of her stiff, red hands. I said, "You don't have any reason to trust me."

Her eyes bounced up to me, like I had hit on something she had thought was a big, terrible secret. Of course she didn't trust me. I didn't trust her. Trust was a commodity, and neither of us had traded a damn thing for it.

"You stay and take your chances with the police, girl with the terrible German accent," I said, moving the balloon to watch the panic crisscross her face. "Or you come with me and stay safe."

I stood and offered my hand again. *Take it. Take it, lost American girl.* If she said no, I'd have to take the balloon from her by force and hightail it out of there. I couldn't risk my life, and our work, for some lost tourist.

She wiped her face all over her sleeve and took my hand with the one not clutching the balloon string. I pulled her up off the ground, and nearly into my arms. I jumped back, startled by her proximity, and then by the sound of banging doors, shouts, and someone crying. Lights went on in the second-story windows of the houses farther down the street. We were about to lose the small advantage we had. I pressed the balloon into her chest, wrapping the string around her wrist, and she folded her arms around it, closing her eyes for a split second. Her hand squeezed the string, not letting it go. Not letting the balloon float back up to window level, where other people or the police could see it.

"*Komm*," I told her. And that she understood.

This time, she did not struggle. I checked a street sign as we passed. I was a little turned around, even in a city I was paid to know like the back of my hand. I was dizzied by the wall, police, and a strange American girl clutching a balloon. My life was always a juggling act. Tonight felt like the dark kept lobbing balls straight at me with no warning.

We didn't slow down, no matter what we heard. The Vopos were looking for us. They had been tipped off, either about me or a failed balloon, or maybe they'd found Garrick. This thought made my heart constrict. I'd get him out of prison if I had to. He was my Passenger, and for whatever reason, it seemed like half the Volkspolizei were after us tonight.

I just needed to find Mitzi. She would know what to do.

We'd keep the girl safe and then figure out how to get her back to West Germany. Clean, simple, back to business. We could probably just shove her at the border patrol at the wall. Even if there wasn't a record of her coming in at that gate, if she acted like she had head trauma or something—or if we gave her legitimate head trauma—they might not worry too much. She was just a kid, after all.

I reached the rendezvous point and dropped the girl's hand. The small park between two apartment complexes had been risky—anyone could be watching—but we'd found a corner that was largely shielded from the view of the residents. A short garden wall led to an alley running along the back side of one apartment complex, giving us another exit if needed.

I moved around her to peer into the shadows, looking for Mitzi. The girl with the balloon stood stock-still, her eyes running down the alley like she was considering leaving, but her feet didn't move. I could run her down if I needed to, but for some reason, I didn't think she'd leave.

Finally, a flash by the corner of the apartment building, a flip of blue hair, and I relaxed. "About time you showed up."

Mitzi came out of the shadows, waiting until she was past the trees and the light of the windows before she pulled off her hat so her hair showed bright and blue, a beacon in the night. She tended to stand out in a place made of gray, black, white, and red. She was the antithesis of the East German regime. It'd taken a lot of cajoling to get her to wear the hat, but she'd been picked up twice already by the police. The next time she might not get so lucky.

"You brought a friend," she said, swaying her hips a little like she did when she thought she could tease me, or maybe irritate the girl. Mitzi and I weren't like that. She was probably the only person in the whole world I actually trusted, and one of only two people I gave a shit about. I wasn't exactly her type, so as much as we played with each other like a cat and a mouse, we were friends, and friends alone.

"Thought you might want the company," I replied dryly.

She ran her fingers across my chest, her eyes sharp and sparkling. "Hello, handsome."

"Not in the mood," I said, cutting the game short. I tipped my head toward the girl. "Worse than we thought. That's his balloon."

Mitzi turned to the girl who was shaking—from cold or from nerves, I couldn't tell, and now that Mitzi was here to take charge, I couldn't really care. I was tired, and I wanted to check the radio waves to find out if Garrick had been picked up by the police.

"Streets crawling with the Volkspolizei," Mitzi muttered, taking in the girl. "Think they're looking for her?"

That had not occurred to me, and I instantly felt ashamed for not thinking of it myself. I scowled sideways at the girl, who was looking at us, eyes wide. She looked like a damn deer in headlights. It'd be hard to believe, but Mitzi was right. She could be a criminal. She could have done something to Garrick and taken his balloon. She could be…I swore sharply, stuffed my hands in my pockets, and stomped a few steps away from Mitzi and the girl while I tried to gather my thoughts.

Everything was supposed to be so simple. They'd protect my sister, and I'd do this job for them. For two years…That was the deal. Two years of only minor incidents with my Passengers. Other Runners had all sorts of screwups, but I didn't. I was good at this. And just like that, it unraveled into a pile of useless threads. All because some American girl had to grab the damn balloon. Wherever she'd found it.

I didn't have the time or the energy to handle this, but I didn't have the option not to handle it. That was one of their rules. Once they gave us the balloon, it was our responsibility. We ran the balloons; we dealt with the Passengers; we dealt with any balloon and Passenger problems. They only had to make the magic and identify the Passengers. We were the ones getting the Passengers over the wall.

Or, some days, not.

Complications were not supposed to exist on this side of the wall. Nope. This was not happening—except that it absolutely was.

Mitzi was asking the girl the same questions I had, but of course Mitzi was succeeding where I'd failed. "Why do you have Garrick's balloon?"

The girl frowned, her eyes going over Mitzi's teal hair to meet my eyes. "I don't know who Garrick is. I saw the balloon, and I grabbed it. And then I was here."

The words punched the breath right out of my body.

And then I was here, she said. Like she couldn't remember coming to East Berlin. How come she hadn't mentioned that yet? How come she hadn't asked us to take her to the American checkpoints?

The balloon only made Passengers invisible when it carried them. It didn't render them unconscious. She should have remembered coming over here.

Mitzi was so still that I was sure she had stopped breathing. I gripped the key in my pocket so hard it dug into my palm and burned me. The pain cleared my mind, kept me from shaking. "Where are you from?"

The girl didn't seem to care that I'd switched into English, though Mitzi's head snapped around and she growled, low and deep in her throat, an implicit threat in how she stepped toward me. There was nothing to be done about it though. I knew I couldn't—shouldn't—use English, not on the streets, but I also couldn't risk the girl not understanding me.

The girl peered around the alley and said, "Pittsburgh. If I could borrow one of your phones, I can probably figure out how to get home. Or to the hotel, I mean."

Phones. Like we were going to take her to our safe house. I said to her, the tension so high that it walked the distance between us on a tightrope, "But why are you *here*? This is not a joke."

Childish fear burned from her eyes, replaced by sparks and anger. She let the balloon go from her chest and yanked the string, making the balloon bounce in the air. I glanced around quickly, hoping no one's curtains were pulled back to see the commotion on the street. "Why would I joke about this? We're here on a school trip to Berlin. I was walking in a park when—"

Better, I thought, though my heart tripped when she said Berlin. I guess for people who didn't live in East Berlin, there was no need to clarify. Why would she willingly go to East Berlin? No one came here willingly.

Mitzi jumped in, her English rough and her accent thick. Her eyes stayed on the balloon, red and simple, the long, white string, the faint double *A* imprinted on the side. "What park?"

The girl's eyes jumped back and forth between us quickly. "I don't know. I can't remember. It was near a subway station. There were a ton of huge glass buildings." She scanned our surroundings and added sourly, "Not here. Clearly."

"Not helpful," Mitzi said to her. Or to me. Both of us, maybe. I glared at her.

"I've only been in Berlin for, like, four hours," the girl said, emphasizing her sentence so strangely that my brain spun to keep up, even though we were using English, my second language.

"East or West?" Mitzi asked the question we'd been dancing around for far too long now.

The girl's face contorted, puzzled. "Uh, I don't know? I mean, I guess it used to be the East. Yeah, it must have been the East. There were old pieces of the wall there."

I almost fell to the ground.

Instead, I dropped into a squat, pressing my forehead against my knees and closing my eyes. Snowflakes landed on my cheeks and the back of my neck, but I was too busy trying to breathe to care about the cold. Thoughts of her words *used to be the East*, the lost look on her face in the alley, and her clothes made for sunnier and warmer days ran around my mind, lighting me up and electrocuting me, battering my mind with their implications, complications, hopes, and dashed futures. *Futures.* I'd heard about this particular magic, this possibility, when my sister had first dabbled in magic, but it was forbidden.

Mitzi's hand closed around one of mine. "Focus. We have to keep her safe—"

"Did you hear her?"

"I heard her," Mitzi said softly. "Kai—"

"Someone tampered with a balloon, Mitzi." I pressed my palm into the snow. "I got it straight from Aurora. I didn't leave it, not once. Did you hear what she just said? That's the only way it could happen, right?"

"I want to go home." The girl's voice was strong and clear, like she could coax us into returning her to where she belonged. She hadn't pieced it together yet. Sure, she might realize that this wasn't a dream and she was damn cold and wet. But she hadn't figured out the biggest problem.

Her chin lifted while Mitzi and I studied her, and I had to give her a little credit for that. She was gutsy, even if she didn't know it. To survive time travel, I guess you'd have to be.

"We're not even sure how you got here, kid," Mitzi said in German. I shuddered and covered my face with my hands again. It was bad enough that she was American. It was worse if what she was saying was true.

"Balloons are only supposed to go over walls. This is different, isn't it? Something went wrong." The girl looked at me, and then she glanced around us, then toward the street from which Mitzi had come, toward the hope of streetlights and the wall and wherever she came from.

My training said this was the part where I put the knife into her gut. *Kill her. Let the secret of the balloons go with her to the grave.* But the training was for people who cared about the cause. I didn't. I was here for Sabina, and she was safely tucked in bed. Hopefully. And for all my faults, it was curiosity that I was sure would kill me like a cat. I wanted to know where the girl came from, how she got here.

"What do you know about balloons?" Mitzi's English sucked, but she knew how to rise to an occasion.

"Nothing," the girl said too quickly, wrapping her arm around herself. We said nothing, and finally her mouth thinned into a pressed line. She exhaled hard through her nose, a puff of white air in front of her face. "I've heard a story, okay?"

"What story?" This time, I found my voice.

Her eyes dropped to her feet, a strange expression flitting across her face. It took me a breath to recognize it as surprise and regret. "My saba—I mean, my grandfather—he told me about the balloons. I mean, it could be a story."

But her hand gripped the balloon string. It wasn't a story. She knew that now, if she hadn't before.

Mitzi's eyes shifted to me, and she repeated. "A story about the balloons."

And sure enough, the girl said carefully in German, "He said there were balloons, magic ones. They saved people."

"Oh my god," Mitzi said, unable to hold on to the revelations from a girl standing in front of us shivering and clutching a balloon. "Kai—"

"Mitzi," I said, trying to press a warning into my voice. I didn't want her to speak the truth, for our sake, and for this girl's sake.

"*Kai,*" Mitzi repeated, never taking her eyes off the girl. "This is above us. This is for the Council. We're just Runners."

"I know." I shoved my hands in my pockets. "But don't you want to know?"

She shifted, uncomfortable. "It's not right."

She wasn't wrong. The magic that involved time travel was so illegal that it was blacklisted. The balloon makers could be stripped of their magic for it. And to be stripped of magic wasn't a pleasant experience. But before they found out who did this and sent this girl back to where she belonged, I had to know.

"The wall," I said. Mitzi hissed. She liked rules much more than I did. I just needed to be careful. If the girl thought this through, she'd realize that it wasn't the year she thought it was. "What year did it come down?"

"I knew you weren't German," the girl whispered. "Your accent. It's weird."

"Oh my god, we are in so much trouble. This is so bad," Mitzi murmured. She shook her head as if to clear it and shot me a sharp-edged look. "Enough questions. Where are you taking her?"

"I'm not letting you take me anywhere but home." The girl's voice pitched wildly, nearly screaming the words. She backed up from us. She yanked the balloon. It made a small sound of stress, wobbling above us, then straightening again.

"Oh, shut up," Mitzi and I said at the same time. Then all three of us fell silent, listening to the cars approaching on the road. Headlights splashed against the walls.

"Go," Mitzi told me, her eyes moving back and forth between the girl and me. She squeezed my arm with a thin hand. "I'll lead them elsewhere. Take her to the safe house."

I gripped her coat as she started to step away from me. "See you in an hour."

She stepped back and rose on her tiptoes to press a kiss to my cheek. "One hour, and we'll make a plan."

As she gave us a wave and a smile, dancing off through the shadows to draw away the attention of the police, I shouted after her, "I'm not getting your ass out of jail again!"

She yelled back over her shoulder, "I got myself out, you asshole! Don't forget that!"

I grinned, relieved, because there was something a little frightening about letting your best friend dance off to keep the police from getting you. I offered my hand to the girl, who took it, but didn't move at first. She twisted, looking over her shoulder.

"They're going to catch her."

"She's fine," I said, which was a nonanswer that the girl didn't seem to catch. "Come on. The farther away we are, the better chance we give Mitz."

I didn't drop her hand as we walked through the city into a nicer neighborhood with housefronts in pale pastels with shutters and window boxes full of snow. We were both so cold that we had stopped shivering, never a good sign. I dropped her hand to get the key out of my pocket, and then her head dropped to her chest, her eyes closed, and she shook so violently that the balloon was waving in the air. I shoved the key in the lock. "Don't die before we can get you home."

"Can you get me home?" she asked me. And finally, she sounded as tired as I felt.

I opened the door and gestured her inside. "We're going to try."

The safe house was one of three we had in our sector of the city for Passengers. This was the one Garrick had been in, so it hadn't been cleaned up yet. Dirty dishes sat on the table, the smell of stew lingering in the air. Garrick's balloon had been tricky, I remembered now. Aurora had struggled with the magic, and Garrick had been in the house for ten days, instead of the typical seven. I shut the door behind us and locked it again with the key. Mitzi had her own. It'd be impossible for anyone without the heavy key to open these safe houses. Otherwise, we couldn't guarantee the Passengers' safety.

The balloon bumped against the ceiling, and the string hummed in the girl's hand, like the balloon was speaking to us, like it was confused. Balloons were meant to go over walls, just as the girl had said. I had never seen a balloon inside a house. I had never heard a balloon hum. I'd moved through the sparsely furnished house to the kitchen before I realized the girl remained in the hallway, looking stunned.

She said to me, "It's impossible. This is the weirdest dream I've ever had."

"I'm not sure you're dreaming." I didn't want to talk to her about it until Mitzi was back and she and I could figure out what the hell we were going to do with this girl from—wherever. "Come upstairs. You can stay here. We'll get you home in the morning."

I was glad to have my back to her when I said that. I was a terrible liar. Not that she was all together right now, her eyes all vacant and confused as they slipped around the house, but I didn't need to be questioned on that.

She jerked the balloon. "And what about this?"

I hesitated. I didn't want to see what happened when she let the balloon go, but then again, I did. If the balloon was truly dysfunctional, if its magic had been tampered with or written incorrectly, it shouldn't do anything if she let it go. It could take the next person's bare hand and yank them somewhere else, perhaps, but a normal balloon disappeared when the person for whom it was written let go. No bare hand, no skin on the string, then the balloon was gone. Theoretically. Balloons shouldn't do what this one did.

I leaned on the railing. "Let it go."

She stared up at it. "Can I get home without it?"

An astute question. And that was a bit of a shame. It'd be easier to lie to someone who wasn't so quick to catch on. I said, "We can make you another one."

She let go of the balloon. It floated to the ceiling, collided with the plaster, and rolled sideways. We both held our breath, but the balloon remained.

I glanced at her and found her studying me with careful blue eyes. Now that she was in the house and the light, I could see she was quite pretty. Her long, curly brown hair crept out of her hood on either side of her face and tangled at the ends where it looped into her scarf. She was underdressed for the weather, but that I understood. We didn't usually get blizzards in March, that was for sure.

"In the morning," I found myself saying, "I promise you. We'll have a plan to get you home."

She sagged, defeated, and nodded. She followed me upstairs and went silently into the room I showed her. I shut the door behind her and slumped back down the stairs. So much for sleep.

Chapter Three

LEADING BERLIN

Berlin, 1941

Benno

The morning air clung to our jackets and cheeks, damp and hungry like our empty stomachs. My tongue stuck to the roof of my mouth, and Ruth's hand kept slipping out of mine. Her hand was fat and chubby, like it had no bones in it, and I kept holding it too tight. When she cried, Mama glared at me. Papa didn't look at us. Not once. He just kept his arm around Mama's shoulders. I scanned the crowd, looking for Rebekah, but I couldn't pick out her short, dark, curly hair in the crowds. My heart beat low in my chest. She knew how to keep Ruthie happy. I was never good at this.

Papa rubbed Mama's shoulder and said, *"B'ezrat HaShem,* we will be safe there. There will be only Jews. It will be safer than Berlin."

Mama leaned her head on his shoulder and said, "Maybe Ernst is there."

Papa didn't say anything to that. None of us did. A few months ago, the Gestapo came to the house and demanded my brother, Ernst. They took him away for questioning, and he never came home. They turned him into a ghost at the snap of their fingers. Mama went to the police station to ask where he was, but then the Gestapo came around with a few questions about Papa. Mama stopped asking questions, but I heard her crying at night.

Papa used to tell her that Ernst was fine, wherever he was. "He's a strapping boy," Papa would tell her. "He can take care of himself wherever he is. He's got a good head on his shoulders. He got that from you."

The day by the trains, Papa told her nothing. He just tightened his hand against her shoulder and stayed silent. He did not think that Ernst would be waiting for us, wherever we were going. I could tell by the way he'd rather be quiet than lie to Mama. They told us they were taking us to a ghetto, a place for Jews to live separate from others. I was lucky, Mama said. They had turned a lot of the Jewish boys my year into ghosts. Like Ernst. Disappeared. I guessed Ruthie and I were lucky. At five and sixteen respectively, we stayed with our family. They moved us as a unit first to the staging ground at the synagogue on Levetzow Street and then to the train station. They'd taken Ernst only a few days after his eighteenth birthday. All alone, and he'd never come home.

"Benno," Mama had said as we were packing. She whispered, so Papa wouldn't hear. "You must be good there. You know how Papa is. If we listen to all the rules and we stay together as a family, G-d willing, we'll come through this."

G-d willing. B'ezrat HaShem.

I never thought I'd miss school, but I did. A fraying yellow star clung to the jacket I used to wear to school. It was too small for me now, but we didn't have money or fabric to make me a bigger coat. We were trying to keep Ruthie warm, since she was growing like a weed. She was at that age where her hands and face were all soft and round, but her legs were longer than all the rest of her. In pictures, you couldn't tell the difference between

Ruth and me at that age. We had the same dark, curly hair, the same round faces, the same dimples. Ernst had been more like our father with his chiseled jaw and strong chin. Girls loved Ernst. I didn't get much from girls, but I had Rebekah.

If it weren't for Hitler, I'd be walking with Rebekah home from *schule*, not waiting in line for a train.

"Is there going to be school there?" Ruth asked, tugging my hand. She hadn't even gone to school yet. She knew all her letters though. Sometimes she forgot who Ernst was. It didn't take long. Like forgetting what ice cream tasted like.

"No, Ruthie. No school. Mama will teach you, just like always." I squinted up at the gray sky, full of so many clouds that they no longer had shapes but stretched out for as far as I could see like gray blankets. The sky was sad. The air inside my chest was heavy. I shivered. Mama had made us wear all our winter clothing, but I still couldn't get warm.

"Benno," whispered Ruth, tugging my hand. "Can we play a game?"

I didn't want to play a game. I wanted to go home. I didn't want to be out here in the damp, miserable November cold. And I wanted to know where Rebekah was. *What if we're sent to different places?* But then Mama gave me a look over her shoulder, and I swallowed back my resentment. Ruth was just a child. She didn't know any better.

So I bent my head to her and sang a Yiddish alphabet song to her, followed by a song about two poodles. She sang along to the first and jumped up and down, splashing in the mud, to the second. Her joy, despite the fear and exhaustion and uncertainty around us, made me smile. I picked her up, even though she was too old for that, and swung her around in a circle, making her shriek with laughter. Around us, the families smiled at us, but then one of the Gestapo shouted at me—at us, and Papa hissed. I landed Ruthie back on her feet.

Putting my mouth right next to her ear, I said, "New game, be as serious as the soldiers."

She giggled and stood ramrod straight as we began to walk forward, being loaded onto trains like animals. She was the happiest girl getting onto that train.

We'd heard that the first train from Berlin had been a nicer train. Everyone had seats, and though there'd been a guard, they'd stopped overnight to let people relieve themselves on the side of the tracks. Something had changed then, because that wasn't our train.

This train smelled like ass and sweat, like the gym where I used to watch Ernst box, like sickness. There was a baby who hadn't stopped crying in the corner, and I could hear people coughing. Someone whispered *tuberkulose*, and someone started to wail. It took a few shouts from some of the men in the car to calm everyone down again.

I couldn't see Papa's face, but he never shouted, never turned around. He just kept us in his own little world. Maybe he could not hear them. Maybe he couldn't feel the heat of too many bodies in too small a space. Maybe he couldn't feel the weight of the tears when the baby stopped crying on the other side of the car. The piss and fever, hopelessness and fear, they rattled like the wheels of the train against the tracks.

The train went on forever. I didn't let go of Ruth's hand. Not once. Through the cracks in the side panels, we breathed in fresh air and watched the world whip by, turning from gray to green to darkness and then to green again. In the morning, as the sun rose—sending slivers of light slashing through the train and cutting our skin, lighting up the sweat drying in patterns across our arms and faces—I saw a glint outside the train.

"Look, Ruthie," I whispered, shaking her.

She climbed up on my knee, pressing her eye to the crack, her fat fingers pushing against the wall. "What?"

"A balloon," I whispered. "A *luftballon*."

A red balloon, alone, without even a string, and then, just a glint. It was gone before we could even gasp. But Ruth and I whispered stories about it the whole way to the ghetto.

Chapter Four

ZEITREISENDE

East Berlin, German Democratic Republic, March 1988

Ellie

I woke and breathed in slowly. It took me a moment to realize I didn't recognize the sheets or the pillow or the crack in the plaster alongside my bed. I was somewhere else. It was the only way I knew how to tell myself what had happened. It wasn't a kidnapping or an elaborate ruse or a head injury. I had just ended up somewhere *else*. The room was the same as it had been the night before. I was still in the bed, still under a quilt, still in the world that couldn't be real.

A thin line of sunlight crossed the room carefully from behind the curtain, the way Kai had moved in the alley the night before. I sat up, rubbing at my eyes. My body moved like I had to slog through honey, and every motion from my eyes felt like a hammer inside my skull.

The quiet, dimly lit room let the memories of the previous day trickle in, slow and unsure and cautious. I remembered Amanda wanting to talk to the guitar guy and finding the red balloon. I remembered falling down in the snow and Kai running into me. We ran away from the police and into…Mitzi. That was the blue-haired girl's name. Mitzi. Teenagers without phones. A world, maybe, without phones. Was that possible?

Something went wrong. This can't be real. But I had the same feeling I had whenever Saba told me his stories: that somewhere, somehow, the impossible had happened and things that couldn't be real were.

My skin was lined with the marks of the folds and seams of my skirt and the wrinkles of my shirt, still damp against my skin. My hands felt pruney. My hair was a knotted mat of brown curls. I badly needed a brush, and a shower, and to get out of here. To get home. *Get home.* Like I could find it at a store. Like it's something that could be gotten. I shook my head a bit, trying to clear the unsettled, restless feeling clouding the space behind my eyes.

It didn't help.

The room was plain, with plain furniture set against gray walls. The light switch shocked me when I flipped it. I opened the door. The house was silent. Mitzi had called it *versteck*. Safe house. It was messy, but not in a lived-in way. I half expected to find someone sitting in silence around every corner, but the house was empty. I crept downstairs, my hand sliding along the banister, and stepped into the hall. The short hall led to the living room and the kitchen, an arched doorway between them. The couch and armchair were a muted shade of orange, with dark wood for legs. Like I'd walked onto a movie set.

The kitchen felt like a morgue. Kitchens should have photos on the fridge, postcards, and reminder notes. There should have been oranges in a bowl on the center of the table, and homework from the night before. But everything was cold and clinical, smooth and metallic and too clean for a place where people lived.

There was bread in a cabinet and butter on a shelf in the fridge. I quickly pressed some frozen butter into the soft brown bread. I washed the knife off in the sink, then thought better of putting it back in the drawer. I tucked it into the waistband of my skirt and pulled my shirt down over top of it. I didn't know how to use a knife as a weapon, but it couldn't be that difficult. Pointy end should go into the person I wanted to stab.

I'd imagined a thousand different things happening when I went to Germany. Whatever was happening—and I couldn't even begin to unravel everything around me—hadn't been on my list. I was beginning to regret listening to Amanda, complaining about my teacher, or worrying about what my grandfather thought. I mean, none of that mattered if I didn't get home.

I knew I should go back upstairs to the room, where I had been told to stay by someone who hadn't yet done me harm. Something solid and quiet inside me told me to trust Kai and Mitzi. Besides, they had said they'd get me home this morning. Any trouble I'd be in—weeks of grounding, my car taken away, maybe even my phone taken—would be worth it.

"You say that now, Baum," I said aloud, because Amanda wasn't there to say it for me. "But you can't live without your phone."

At least for now, I'd have to. Amanda had it—and my purse, including my passport and my emergency credit card. Everything that could prove where and what home was before I grabbed that balloon.

The balloon floated in the hall by the entrance to the living room, and I grabbed it on my way to the armchair by the window. This was my ticket out. Somehow. Just like I felt like I could trust Kai and Mitzi, I wanted to keep my balloon close. *My* balloon. It was good no one was here to witness this. My friends and family would never let me forget it.

I idly bounced the balloon, tugging its string and watching the street outside from around the corners of the thin, white curtains. People tromped down the street, heads bowed against the cold, and a woman walked by, holding the hand of a small child who stomped his feet hard into every slushy puddle. For the most part, the street was quiet. It seemed nice enough. It just wasn't my street.

The row houses were all the same plain off-white stucco, but inside the windows, I saw a few flowers, stacks of books, people moving from room to room. The world existed, but it was not my world. Today it was not snowing, but it must have been cold enough, even in the middle of the day, because the snow remained, sticking and glittering to everything within eyesight. The small boy clutching his mother's hand stopped to make a snowball and threw it at a house, making me smile.

I came all the way to Germany to escape the snow and found it anyway.

Then a flash of teal made me tense in my seat. Mitzi walked right by the house without even looking at it, her hands stuffed in her pockets and most of her hair stuffed under a wool cap that looked like something my grandfather would have worn. A stray, bright-colored lock hung by her cheek. Her cheeks glowed red, and her breath blew out soft gray from between her lips. I was sure she would see me, but she never even turned to look at the house.

Without thinking for a second, I grabbed my coat and the balloon. Time to go home. How had it taken me this long to figure that out? I had the balloon, and they had left me alone. If I could find that same park, maybe I could get home. Click my heels three times and think of home? Was that right? I almost felt bad about leaving without saying good-bye. Kai had shouted at me, but he'd been kind too, when he realized I had no idea what was happening.

But I didn't have time for sentimentality for people I barely knew. A set of keys hung by the door beside a coat, and I grabbed one, twisting it in the lock and yanking open the front door. I peered cautiously around the corner. Mitzi walked on, oblivious to the sound of the door behind her, or me, standing in the door-way with the red balloon. Worst game of Clue ever.

I set off down the street after her. The balloon remained bright and cheerful, strangely and magically unaffected by the weather or time. *Time.* Around me, tiny cars, all the same, in varying colors, parked against the curbs. Signs in German reassured me I was still in Germany—at least the balloon hadn't taken me far—but nothing seemed familiar. Everyone's clothes were really weird—boxy shirts, oddly fitting jeans, and way too many stripes. *Holy crap.* They looked like pictures of my parents when they were younger.

I shuddered. Time. *It can't be. There's a mistake.* I held on to the word *mistake* until I felt the shape of it rolling around on my tongue as I made my way down the street. Balloons and time and Walls and snow. Pieces of a puzzle, and I didn't have the big picture to start finding the straight-edged ones to put it together. And I didn't want to put this puzzle together. I just needed to not be here anymore, wherever here was.

The sidewalks grew more crowded and the streets wider as I followed Mitzi. The boxy shirts and baggy pants gave way to office clothes, suits and skirts. *Rush hour.* I didn't blend in with my wrinkled skirt and shirt. I could feel eyes judging me, heard people scoffing at me. Panic and frustration ran together through my veins, colder than the snow and the ice seeping through my shoes again. I began to push my way through the crowds, not caring if that drew more attention to me. A man shouted at me when I pushed past him, making him step into a puddle.

Ahead of me, Mitzi stopped to ask about a long line outside a store. For a moment, I thought she'd get in line and disappear into the store—and then where would I be? But she kept moving. I glanced at the sign over the heads of the people: The Stronger the Socialism, the Stronger the Peace. My brain started to run down that crooked path marked *time* again, but I stopped it immediately. I couldn't get distracted by any remnants of East Germany that might linger in this corner of Berlin.

I crossed against lights and nearly got hit. A policeman yelled at me, his German harsh against my mind. I couldn't translate and still follow Mitzi. And I knew what my priority was. I kept my eyes trained on the teal hair and the brown tweed hat weaving in front of me.

Then, suddenly, she was gone.

Like she had walked into thin air. I stopped in my tracks, breathing heavily and frowning at the crowd ahead of me. I turned slowly. Good job, I told myself. I had no idea where I was, or where Mitzi had gone, or how to get back to the house. If I could remember the park's name, I could maybe ask someone for directions. I mouthed the words slowly, trying to remember the proper conjugations before I made a fool of myself.

"Halt!" snapped an authoritative voice. A hand grabbed me by my arm and twisted me around. I spun around, opening my mouth to snap something back, and shut it immediately. A severe face, blue eyes, and an olive-green uniform. My brain pieced the person together slowly, but when it did, Volkspolizei echoed against my skull. Kai had used that word before, last night, and *Polizei* was close enough to English for me to catch on. *Police.*

He asked me something in German. I couldn't breathe. Couldn't swallow. What had Kai said? They'd lock me up in prison, and I'd never get home. I shook my head, trying to clear the fog and panic. *Think, Ellie!* But his German might as well have been Ancient Greek.

"Oh," said a warm and familiar voice, and Kai's hand closed around my elbow. I looked up at him, and in the light, I saw him clearly for the first time. His brown skin, so unlike everyone around us, and his deep-set eyes. His shoulder-length hair pulled back in a low ponytail, his nose a little too big for his face, his jaw twitching as he gritted his teeth. His shirt stretched tight across his chest, his jacket ending a few inches higher than his hips.

He said something smoothly to the officer whose eyes narrowed.

Don't arrest me. I don't want to die here.

The officer dropped my arm and said something about home, the only word I caught in his long sentence. Kai's voice was low and soft, submissive and not at all like the scowling and demanding guy I remembered from last night. He didn't know what fashion was, but he did know how to sweet-talk the officer into releasing me. Kai took my hand, walking me quickly away and toward a tree-lined avenue. I flushed at the sudden contact and started to pull my hand away, but he gripped harder.

"Don't. Do not turn around," he said out of the corner of his mouth, his lips barely moving. Like last night, he spoke in English, and I knew it was for my benefit. "Do not stop moving."

"Thank you," I whispered as quietly as I could, keeping my eyes straight ahead of me. Adrenaline pounded through me like a fierce pulse. If he had stopped, I would have collapsed. But he didn't stop.

We didn't look like the other couples walking by though. We were too tense, too purposeful. Did I want to look like everyone around us? This world—this place, this part of Berlin, wherever I was—had more questions than answers. In my mind, I mentally asked Kai why he always showed up at precisely the right time, but I could already feel his answer. *Bad luck*, he'd say in that low, guarded way of his. I didn't know why he didn't trust me. I was the one who didn't know what was happening.

A bright-blue flash of color caught my eye and I turned, thinking it was Mitzi, but it wasn't. A boy ran through the park ahead of his mother, his chubby fist holding the string of a blue balloon. I half expected him to disappear or start floating or *something*, and I sucked in my breath.

"Not ours," Kai said, this time in German. "We use red only. Breathe."

I exhaled, hard, and my balloon bounced between us. My hand shook in his, but Kai didn't seem to notice. We jogged against the light, across the street, and jumped together over a slushy pile. And then a man stepped out from behind a tree. A thousand feathers swirled around his head like a moving crown. Individual feathers, distinct and sharp and all different, like he'd plucked a raven. He wore a black shirt and black pants, and he was thick and strong, like a weight lifter. I screamed and yanked the balloon string, turning to run.

"Shut up!" snapped Kai when I collided with his chest. His arm wrapped around me, as he looked over my head. "What are *you* doing here?"

That was his question? The man had feathers whirling around his head, and Kai wanted to know what he was doing here? Seriously? I peeked out from around Kai's arm, trying to see if the feathers were part of the man's hair, or maybe a hat from a street fair. But the feathers seemed to be suspended in air, unattached to anything. I shuddered.

"I am fond of her balloon," said raven man with a deep, gravelly voice, like the kind wizards had in movies. "She can see me?"

"You scared her!" Kai cursed. I twisted out of his grip, away from him. My cheeks felt hot even though it was cold today, and I didn't like feeling so exposed. But I didn't want him to think I was afraid.

The raven man had said I could see him like that was a surprise. Now that I was facing him, I wished there was some way to unsee him. A way to unsee, undo all of this. A way to get out of here, with its strange worlds and its balloons that didn't act like balloons and people who spoke in ciphers. If they weren't going to give me the key, I wanted to go home.

The raven man seemed nonplussed. "Keep your voice down if you insist on speaking in English. What happened to the balloon, Kai?"

Kai scowled, crossing his arms over his chest. He looked taller, broader, stronger than he had a moment ago. I glanced quickly back and forth between Kai and the raven man. They wouldn't fight, would they? "Not here, Ashasher. Good god, what is happening this morning?"

The raven man's eyes shifted to the balloon clutched against my chest. Puzzlement and then confusion crossed over his face, and he tilted his head. "How is she holding it?"

"She was just stopped by the Volkspolizei, so maybe we can move this somewhere more private before it happens again." It wasn't a question, but it wasn't an order either. Kai shifted on his feet, his eyes darting around the street, his lips pressed together in a thin line. I was starting to recognize his anxiety. His gaze fell on me. "You weren't supposed to leave the house."

"I didn't mean to," was my first automatic response, and I managed it in German. Then I shook my head. I couldn't find all the words so I switched back into English. "I followed Mitzi, but then she disappeared."

"She's good at that," said Kai stiffly. "She knows how to use a crowd to her advantage. But why did you follow her? You were supposed to stay safe."

"I mean, I thought maybe if I went back to the same park? Maybe the balloon would take me home." It sounded silly when I said it aloud.

"That's not how this works." Kai's gaze shifted past me as if he'd dismissed me because I didn't understand how balloons worked.

I jutted out my chin. "I don't need your help. And I didn't ask you."

"Help for what? Why would she think that works?" asked the raven man. "Who are you, dear?"

"Ellie," I said, blinking in surprise. No one had asked me yet. No one had said my name in hours and hours. A day, maybe. I hadn't realized until now how strange that had felt.

"Not here." Kai shook his head. "Walk. Farther into the park."

The raven man studied Kai for a long minute, then peered at the balloon again. I got the impression that he was disinclined to take commands from Kai, who couldn't be that much older than me. Curiosity won out though. I could see on the man's face that he wanted to know who I was, why Kai wanted to keep me a secret, and what the balloon was.

"Walk, then." The raven man fell into step beside me so I was sandwiched between them.

"Try not to do anything that attracts attention," Kai told him, turning slightly to shield me from the curious gaze of a policeman. I stiffened, waiting for the policeman to notice the raven man and call out to us, but his gaze slid over us and moved down the park. When I peered up, the raven man's smile was small and assured. *Then how can I see him?*

I wrapped both arms around the balloon. "Someone has a lot of explaining to do."

"He can explain most of what you need to know." Kai glanced down at me. His eyes were sharp and golden this close, flecked with green, like I'd see if I were spinning on a swing in summertime and letting the world turn into a kaleidoscope.

I frowned at him. "And what I *want* to know."

Kai's eyes flashed with worry and he looked away, starting to cross the street as the lights changed. "Maybe."

The raven man stayed quiet, the type of quiet that only grew more unnerving as we walked. Kai led us across the street and down a tree-lined avenue to a park. He glanced around surreptitiously and then took a seat on a bench. He frowned at his shoes. I watched him for a moment, then sat down beside him. Only the raven man did not sit. He stood there, cloaked in black—half Grim Reaper, half a raven out of mythology—and I nearly asked him if he was Thought or Memory. His eyes met mine and twinkled, and I stiffened out of an immediate fear that he could read my thoughts.

Kai watched me out of the corner of his eye, and I watched him back less sneakily. For a long time, we just stared at each other, measuring the heft of our disbelief in each other's existence. In the daylight, he didn't seem nearly as threatening as I'd thought he was the night before. He looked younger and more tired.

He wasn't particularly cute, but I couldn't tear my eyes away from him. Something about the way he moved, his assurance. At home, I'd steer clear of someone like Kai. But there was a certain magnetism to him, something honest and open for someone who gave so little away.

There was wonder in his eyes when he said, "I didn't think you were real."

I made myself ask him, "What'd you tell the police?"

"That you had slipped and hit your head. You weren't supposed to be out of the house."

"Thank you," I said again.

He turned away, toward the rest of the park, and I watched his chest rise and fall in several deep breaths. He kept talking in English, his accent on the rougher side, the kind that would have made Amanda swoon. I was sure he was using English for my benefit, and that kindness was invaluable. I was lost enough in this place without having to translate too.

"Garrick's dead. We found his body this morning. I'm supposed to identify it this afternoon, but it sounded like they were sure."

I gritted my teeth against the pendulum in my chest swinging toward guilt. Garrick. That was the name of the guy Kai thought was supposed to have my balloon. I looked up at the balloon. *What happened to your first person, balloon? Why didn't you keep him safe?*

The raven man remained silent. The feathers briefly swung low around his neck, then spun high and fast. When I looked at them, I felt dizzy and unsure, like the rest of the world was fading away around him and there was only him against a bright-white background.

Kai's fingers pressed into the top of my knee, hard and painful. I flinched and gasped as air flooded into my lungs, and the rest of the world swooped back in around the raven man, filling in the empty pieces of the landscape. My head rattled like pennies in a can.

Kai's brow knit together. "Don't," he said, "look at the feathers."

The raven man did not apologize. I didn't really expect him to, but there was no acknowledgment at all. He spoke to Kai and Kai only. "Where?"

"By the wall. He came down in the death zone. Two Runners—Christian and Nicki—found him. Paid a bribe for his body. Fucking Volkspolizei."

The raven man rubbed his palm over his short dark beard. "They'll be reimbursed. You did not inform *Wundertätigluftballonschöpfer* that you had found his balloon, or that someone else had it."

I recognized *luftballon* as meaning a balloon like the one in my arms, and *Schöpfer* I had heard in class before as maker or creator, but I couldn't figure out the first word. I didn't have the time or guts to ask.

Kai tensed, a ball of nerves and muscle next to me, like he would spring and tackle the raven man. I mirrored his tension, my eyes darting back and forth between them. I didn't understand the relationship so I didn't understand my loyalties. Who was I supposed to save if it came to blows? I touched the knife in the waistband of my skirt. At least the Volkspolizei hadn't found that on me.

Kai shook his head. "Runner problems are Runner problems."

The raven man's mouth thinned into a line of disapproval. "This is beyond a Runner problem, Kai. Where is she from?"

They spoke of me as if I wasn't sitting right there. I started to answer the question myself, but Kai's hand grabbed my knee again. The raven man glanced at the motion and then at me. I trusted Kai more than I trusted the raven man, so I pressed my mouth shut. I glared at the raven man though, and this seemed to amuse him.

Kai's voice was cool. "I have twenty-four hours to inform the Council."

The raven man tilted his head. The feathers slowed. "Consider the Council informed."

The look on Kai's face was miserable. The facade he kept around the Volkspolizei crumbled in the face of the raven man. "Understood."

"What Council?" I asked.

"You and I have spoken of this," said the raven man, ignoring me. "You come from a society that prefers to treat the outside as undeserving of truthfulness. Here, you must be on the inside, Kai. You cannot—"

"You know nothing about me, or my people." Kai's voice was colder than the ice on the streets. For a long moment, he and the raven man stared at each other, light eyes piercing dark eyes, and then finally, the raven man looked away.

I exhaled. My turn. They could have their showdown some other time. I still needed my answers. "How can I see you?"

"Perhaps it is the balloon," said the raven man. It wasn't an answer, but I was starting to get the feeling that it was all the answer he'd give me.

"Garrick's balloon," I clarified, glancing at Kai. "You think I have Garrick's balloon."

"I know you have his balloon." The misery in Kai's voice sank into me the way the snow had seeped into my shoes. "That's his balloon. I'd know it anywhere. Just like I know he's dead without needing to see his body."

The raven man stepped in one fluid motion toward Kai and grabbed his shoulder. I gripped the knife at my waistband, but I didn't have anything to fear. The raven man's voice steadied me as it steadied Kai. "Garrick's death isn't your fault. Remember that. That blame always lies at the feet of the oppressors, Kai."

When Kai didn't raise his head, just sat there limp with the raven man gripping his shoulder until the man's knuckles turned white, my stomach turned over and heaved. I had to close my eyes and grip the knife tightly to keep from throwing up my bread and butter. A man was dead because of me, and it was someone they both liked.

"Have other Runners reported this?" the raven man asked Kai. "Other missing balloons? Missing Passengers?"

"No."

"You're sure?"

"I am sure." The heaviness in Kai's voice carried the same edge as the heaviness on my chest, the knife at my hip, the churning of my stomach. Everything that had happened—the tug, the place around me so unlike the Berlin I'd seen, the balloon, the wall…It was like seeing an accident about to happen. I flinched and looked away.

But my heart was a betrayer. "So it's real," I found myself saying. Kai and the raven man turned toward me, curious and confused. I clarified. "Balloons. Magic."

Kai looked at the raven man, who lifted his face to the sky. His nod was tentative and tenuous. "Yes."

I nodded slowly because I didn't know what else to do. All those stories Saba had told…and where I was now. My ribs felt like they had closed with a cold, hard grip around my lungs. I couldn't breathe. I let the balloon escape from my arms. I wrapped my bare hand around the string and whispered, "Then why won't it take me home?"

"Balloons are not—" the raven man said in German, the last word unknown to me. I frowned at him, and he repeated in English, "Balloons are not omnidirectional."

I pressed my lips together and forced myself to keep my tone even. "Obviously."

The corner of Kai's mouth twitched, and his gaze shot to his shoes again. I thought that was the closest he'd ever get to a smile, and it felt like a victory. The raven man said calmly, unaffected by my rancor, "What would you like the balloon to do? It brought you here. It did its duty as far as it is concerned."

"You speak like it is sentient."

He shook his head, the feathers spinning so fast I could no longer see his eyes. Kai clarified, translating my sentence from English into German. The feathers slowed, and the raven man's eyes were dark but clear. "The magic may as well make it as such. It knew you somehow. You are meant to be here."

Kai scowled. "She isn't. She can't be." He sighed and added in German, "She is from a different time."

I blinked. Exhaled. Inhaled. My vision tunneled down on a stray feather on the path. It was strange, wasn't it, that no one walked by us. *From a different time.* In my mind, I saw the old-fashioned cars on the street. I thought about the wall and the people with me. I'd known. I just hadn't wanted it to be true. I had seen without believing. *It's impossible. Balloons just go over walls.* But here I was.

Ashasher said, "*Zeitreisende.*"

"What?" I asked. "What did you call me?"

"Time traveler," Kai said, his voice soaked with regret. "He called you a time traveler."

Chapter Five

THE GIRL ON THE OTHER SIDE OF THE FENCE

Łódź Ghetto, Poland, 1941

Benno

The Łódź ghetto was in Poland, and when we arrived, it was already busting at the seams with people. The fence and wall around the ghetto were high and backed up to the forest, a road disappearing between trees. I eyed the forest as soon as we began to walk toward our assigned housing unit. The forest, deep and dark, could hide a family for years. We could stay there, I thought. If we hunted and found a cabin, or built one, then we could live this out. The walls and the guards of the ghetto made my stomach turn. Even in the open air, everything felt as if it was closing in around me.

Papa, he wasn't oblivious. He put a hand on my shoulder and said, "Son. Think of your mother. Think of Ruth."

It was cruel, but I knew why he said it. I looked over my shoulder at Mama, walking hand in hand with Ruthie through the mud and the gray sadness of the ghetto. They were singing that damned alphabet song again. Mama would die if she lost another son, and then…What happened to Ruthie if something happened to Mama or Papa? I couldn't just leave them behind to try the forest.

So I stayed. Papa went back and swung Ruth up onto his shoulders. He said, "Ruth, you have to be a big girl now."

They led the way into our apartment on the second floor, Ruth shrieking with laughter as she bent over, barely fitting into the doorway, wrapped around Papa's head. Mama and I, we tried to smile as we watched them, but I think we knew what was coming before we even admitted it to ourselves.

When we arrived at Łódź, the sun beat down on us, and though we were walking through snow and mud, we were hopeful. They showed us a small room where we would live as a family. The people who showed us around were Jews. They told us we would have jobs and work. They told us if we worked hard, we would have enough food. They said to us, "We are a community. We will survive this, b'ezrat HaShem."

G-d willing.

G-d will.

G-d willed.

Łódź worked under the thumb of Chaim Rumkowski, the head of the Council of Elders in the ghetto. He told us that the only way for us to survive was for us to be irreplaceable. To prove our worth. So under his leadership, Łódź supplied the German army with uniforms, metal replacement parts, and electrical equipment as Hitler marched across Europe. We fed the hand that bit us. Rumkowski said he was saving us, but it wasn't hard to doubt that. Around us, people starved.

When we arrived, we were still well fed. We were fat. We were soft. The people in the ghetto, they were thin. The ones who were emaciated, we skirted on the streets. They had tuberculosis or some other disease, and by the time they were that thin, they were days away from succumbing to their bed and the disease, if not deportation.

We got a loaf of bread for the family to share for the entire week, as long as we all went to work. Ruth was too young for work, and the day cares, we were told, had been outlawed. Schools had been shut down a month prior to our arrival. Still, there was a covert, underground system for watching kids as young as Ruth. Soon, I saw boys and girls as young as seven sewing buttons onto coats.

I wished that Ruth wouldn't have to be one of those kids.

They said, *Be careful what you wish for.*

There were few other children in the ghetto. They had been taken, they said, to a children's camp. There were whispers from the new Polish residents and from a few of the Germans though. No one who left on a train came back.

Rumkowski said, *Give me your children.*

And they whispered to us, *You are new. Hide your little girl.*

We could hide her, but not from the cough. It came only a few weeks after we arrived at Łódź. I woke in the middle of the night, listening to the deep chest cough from her tiny body. Mama woke too, and I heard her whispering with Papa. They begged others on the street for medicine and for hot rags, anything. Some people shook their heads slowly, tears in their eyes, and closed their doors in my parents' faces. Others shoved into our hands what they had—and then closed their doors. We were a family with the sickness.

"Go to the fence by the cemetery," whispered a girl down the street to me. "That's where we leave notes for people who help us from the outside. Someone will find your note. You must be careful. The police will shoot you if they see you."

The fence was well patrolled, and the police shot without asking questions. But the gravestones and the trees in the ghetto cemetery made it easier to stay in the shadows, to look as if I were going to pray and not creeping to the corner where the fence was low and the barbed wire loose. And out of the gray and the wild, free world beyond the fence, I saw a flash of color. A girl about my age with glossy curls and a purple dress that must have cost a small fortune was throwing sticks for her dog down the long, empty street alongside the ghetto.

I whispered to her, "Miss. Please."

She turned around and backed away from the fence, staring at me like she hadn't expected someone from inside the fence to speak to her on the outside of the fence. "You can see me? It didn't work then."

I didn't have much time so I didn't dwell on the oddness of her question. I knew the risks when I said, "Are you from the resistance? My sister. She needs medicine."

The girl turned away from me. "You are a *Jude*."

"My sister…" I began haltingly. "She's five. She didn't get to bring her favorite doll here." The girl on the other side of the fence didn't walk away. I kept talking. "She loves toffee and her favorite holiday is Purim, when we dress up. She was the only girl who smiled on the train here. Do you know why? She saw a balloon. Just a red balloon outside a gap in the door. She's just a child, but if she doesn't get medicine, she'll die. She has a cough."

The girl turned back to me, her face stitched into a frown. "I don't have medicine. I have magic."

"Medicine can be magic too," I said, desperate and angry. I'd wasted my chance on a rich girl who didn't have a clue what I was talking about, who wouldn't help me, a Jew. I couldn't see her through my tears. I said, half hoping someone else from the resistance was out of sight, listening. "Please."

Then, to my surprise, she turned away from me and threw another stick for her dog. "Come back tomorrow."

Chapter Six

ANOMALIES

East Berlin, German Democratic Republic, March 1988

Kai

Leaving England with my little sister to accept an offer to work for the Schöpfers here in Berlin, to leave the free world and step into a Communist state, hadn't been the easiest choice by any means. But our people, the Romanichal, couldn't keep Sabina safe. I wasn't even sure if they wanted to keep her safe anymore. There'd been talk of institutions. Her magic was wild and barely controlled at home. She was smart—too smart, maybe—for her age, and she lashed out at the children who teased her. They'd ended up on roofs and in trees.

Sabina's magic wasn't something our neighbors and family could understand. It wasn't something even I understood, but when outsiders started coming around, asking for Sabina, talking about her talents and how they could "use" them, I knew I had to get her out. We'd tried London, but they'd shown up there, demanding to see her.

Going behind the Iron Curtain kept Sabina safe from those who were looking for her, and I liked what I did here—color me surprised. Shuttling people from a state of fear to a state of opportunity felt like doing something *good* for once. And god only knew that I needed to feel like that after leaving home.

My family had roots in the Kalderaš Romani, but we'd lived in England for long enough that we were Romanichal now. We spoke what some called Angloromani, but mostly it was a mix of English and Romani. It was still the language Sabina liked to use with me, but speaking it made my heart ache. Sabina and I had moved into the *gadjikano* world, the non-Romani world. We'd left without permission. We could never go home, even if we wanted to. We were *mahrime*. Contaminated from the outside. I had left everything, all to protect my sister.

But for all the things I've done in my life, I never thought one of the hardest would be the walk back from a Council meeting with Mitzi to the safe house where Ellie had been for three days now. Mitzi kept pausing to wipe tears off her face. Her bright hair was all neat and tidy, tied back and proper for the Council, her lower lip trapped under her top teeth to keep it from trembling. We'd both had to testify about Garrick's balloon, but that wasn't the part that was gutting us. We'd both expected more answers than we'd received. But as soon as the Council heard that Ellie said the wall had fallen more than twenty-five years before she visited Germany, they'd stopped talking to us and started shouting at each other. It'd been the end of anything useful and the beginning of everything terrible.

"What are you going to tell her?" Mitzi asked, her voice trembling. Mitzi didn't tremble, as a general rule, and I'd never seen her like this. She was always one thing or another, all or nothing, but never afraid or sad. Not like this.

I shot her a look as I fished the key out of the depths of my coat pocket and fumbled until the key slid into the lock. She couldn't honestly be suggesting I lie to Ellie. "The truth, Mitz."

"Kai," Mitzi said, and she put a hand on my arm. I stopped and slumped against the door. She pressed close to me and leaned her head against my shoulder. I could barely hear her through the roar of trying to keep the sadness inside me. "Be gentle with her."

Normally, I'd give Mitzi a lot of crap for being this teary. But I couldn't blame her. Not now. I nodded, put my arm around Mitzi, and pushed the door wide open so we could walk in together. There were a lot of people in this cursed-for-nothing world I wouldn't do a damn thing for. Mitzi was among the minority of people for whom I'd give up my life and not even blink an eye. I had nightmares about someone making me choose between Mitz and my sister.

We knocked the snow off our feet and shut the door loudly. The house hummed as the door locked behind us, the key warm in my pocket. Undoubtedly, the Stasi had wanted to bug this house more than once. They'd bugged our neighbors instead. Sometimes I felt guilty about that, but our neighbors didn't seem to know or mind, and it'd be far more dangerous for our Passengers and the girl upstairs if we were bugged by the Stasi, East Germany's secret police.

Above us in the bedroom, feet hit the floor. Mitzi turned away from the stairs, taking a whole bunch of really fast and deep breaths, like she was about to jump off a cliff when all she was trying to do was pretend she wasn't crying about a girl who would be in tears within a few minutes.

Ellie ducked her head and stared at us from the top of the stairs. She'd pulled her hair back into a ponytail, and even from the bottom of the stairs, I could see how blue her eyes were. I had to swallow and look away as I hung up my coat. She'd been so ferociously brave the other day in the park. It'd been hard to keep my eyes off her. Then again, she'd been staring right back at me.

"You're back," she said, her German a little more comfortable the more she used it. She'd been practicing with Mitzi last night, and I thought her problem was more confidence than anything else. It was strange, hearing her talk in German. I liked her voice in English. There was a certain softness to it.

"You cannot speak of the future to anyone," Ashasher had told Mitzi and me, standing alone in the room waiting for the rest of the Council. "And you shouldn't ask her about it. To know the future is to change the future, and that is playing a game we cannot win." Then he looked away from both of us and said, "I would not want either of you to put Sabina's safety here at risk."

The threat was implicit. I understood. And from the determined, angry set of Mitzi's mouth, she did too. I was losing track of the places in East Germany where I could speak freely about everything on my mind.

Clearing my throat, I tore my gaze from Mitzi to Ellie. "We should talk."

Ellie's first foot hit the second stair, and then she just sat down at the top of the stairs, like yelling up the staircase was exactly how I wanted to explain this completely ass-over-heels situation to her. I raised my eyebrows and jerked my thumb toward the living room in invitation, but Ellie just curled her fingers around edge of the step. I wasn't going to pull her off the stairs, if that's what she was worried about. I just didn't want her throwing herself down them.

"The Council had a meeting," I said, sinking to a step at the bottom. I figured this would be best in English. I couldn't risk her not understanding me. But I could barely look at her. I stared at a spot on the stairs where the paint had chipped away instead. "They're the Wundertätigluftballonschöpfers. Magical balloon makers. Mostly we call them Schöpfers. You met one of them, Ashasher. He and Aurora, the other Schöpfer who made the balloon, examined the evidence and had a couple of us testify. No one tampered with your balloon. Garrick's balloon. It was a rare, unfortunate chronological anomaly."

"A chronological anomaly," she repeated, her voice faint at the top of the stairs. In the kitchen, Mitzi banged around and then hiccupped loudly.

"The problem is…" I picked at a splinter on the stairs. "No one knows what happened to that balloon, so no one really knows how to get it to do the magic again. To get you home."

She blinked at me, her eyes wide and luminous from the top of the stairs. She was startlingly pretty, even when she appeared vulnerable. I added hurriedly, "Ashasher and Aurora, they're working on it. And they're the best of the best. They practically invented balloon magic. Hell, Ashasher started it all. We just… We just don't know *when* they'll get you home."

"If it'll ever happen," Mitzi said in the kitchen.

I shot her a scowl, but Ellie didn't seem to have heard her. Ellie's face had gone completely empty, totally blank. My heart sank. Passengers cried all the time, but mostly about leaving their family. This was different. I couldn't tell her if she'd ever see her family again, and it hadn't even been her choice. I climbed the stairs two at a time.

How could I tell her that I hadn't expected that answer from the Council either? I'd assumed that Ashasher or Aurora knew how to do the magic and, though it was illegal, would do it to rectify a mistake. I'd thought we'd be able to fulfill our promise to her. But all I could give her was the truth, and it wasn't enough.

"Hey," I said. "You there?"

Ellie rose slowly, turned around, and walked back down the hall to the bedroom. I saw her face just as she shut the door behind her. Completely pale. Radio static. Nothing but white noise. Shit.

I trudged back down the stairs into the kitchen. Mitzi looked at me over her shoulder as she took the kettle off the stove. "That went well."

"Thanks for the help." I sat down hard in a chair. The thump of my ass hitting the wood echoed inside me, and I crushed my fist against my sternum. My heart hammered. Some days I woke up knowing I wouldn't win. Some days, I took my pulse to remind myself that was the most important thing. If my heart still beat, I could still go on.

My heart beat, and the man who had made me laugh, read me passages of books, and shared his knowledge, his fears, and his dreams with me over the last week was dead. Garrick lay on a slab in a back room of the Council's offices deep underground. They had no morgue in their compound. Schöpfers did not age like most people, and we so rarely lost Passengers and recovered their bodies.

Instead, Garrick was packed with ice, gray-skinned and in his bloodied clothes, among the piles of papers on balloon theory. A fierce academic, he would have killed to see that office when he was alive. And now he had died for no good reason. He had died because of a "chronological anomaly," the same reason a girl from the twenty-first century was here, audibly sobbing in the room above me.

The world was an absurd place, and it kept on spinning, getting more absurd with every rotation. Why did we even try?

"Kai," Mitzi said, sinking into a chair across from me. She nudged a mug across the table with her knuckles. "You should take a few days off."

"Allergic to boredom," I said, tapping my throat. "Closes up my throat. Can't breathe."

"You're allergic to your own thoughts," she said, correcting me in her no-bullshit way. "Kai, we just lost a Passenger you liked a lot. Under crap circumstances. Take three days off. We're not getting assigned a new Passenger until next week anyway. Even you can't fight probation."

"Should I take up knitting?" I scowled at her. "I don't slow down. It'd be much easier to just get a new Passenger tonight."

"Go knit with your sister," Mitzi said, her mouth and eyes knotting into a deep frown. At the edges, I could feel the admonishment. She'd left under the guise of not putting her family at risk because of her work as a Runner, but her family knew Mitzi was gay. She couldn't have gone home if she wanted to. She hadn't seen her sister in three, maybe even four years now. Since before Sabina and I came to Germany. If my sister would let her, Mitzi would adopt her. I almost told her not to tell me what to do, and then Mitzi added, "Remind yourself why you're here."

I didn't want to give in, but god, when Mitzi was right, she was really right. I opened and shut my mouth, then sighed. "Think that'll work?"

"It's got to be better than whatever long, dark tunnel your mind was entering," she said. She took the mug of tea back. "We all cope in different ways, Kai. If you need to be busy, go see your sister."

I pushed my chair back. It scraped noisily along the floor, and I pressed my palms into my knees. "And you, Mitzi?"

"What about me?" She knew exactly what I meant. Some girls could pull off coy. Mitzi couldn't, and she knew it. Her eyes stayed lowered to the tea and the steam.

"Garrick was your Passenger too." The reminder was unnecessary, but easier than asking her how she planned on coping. I was her family. Me, and the other Runners, and Aurora and Ashasher. We were all Mitzi had now.

"I have tea. And I want to be alone. And someone's got to make sure she"—Mitzi gestured with her hand toward the ceiling— "doesn't kill herself."

"Mitz."

"I'll be here when you get back, Kai. I want to be alone for a little bit." Her voice sobered up. Enough for me to trust her.

"Done. Enjoy your tea, Mitzi."

"I always do."

I didn't linger any longer than I had to in the hallway. Mitzi wanted to be alone. I wanted to move. The girl upstairs wanted to go home. Two of the three of us could get what we wanted.

I stomped through puddles on my way back to the Council workshops. The Council took fewer than five students a year here in East Germany. Almost all their students studied in Paris and London before being sent on assignment around the world. But the danger of East Germany was exactly why the Council had agreed to take Sabina here. It'd be much harder for the others who knew about magic—the Zerberus, who wouldn't say why they wanted my sister but only that she was useful—to find her here.

The Schöpfer workshop was underground through the subway tunnels. There were two entrances, but one was only for the Schöpfers who could use magic to hide themselves and bypass the guards. The only time we Runners used that entrance was to replace the helium tanks for the balloons, a magic written on our arms in our own blood to hide our comings and goings. The rest of the time, we went into the tunnels by one of the ghost stations beneath the death zone by the wall. The ghost stations used to work, I guess, before the wall and after the War, but now they were closed. The trains came by from West Berlin but didn't stop. Couldn't risk anyone wanting to leave.

As an outsider, it was sometimes bizarre to look at the East German government's thought process. The government and its party members truly believed they were building a better society. Okay, maybe once they thought that, but over the last couple of years, it had become clear that mostly they were clinging to power with the ends of their gross, old-person, yellow-fungus-covered fingernails. And in order to keep power, they locked everyone in. There was this apartment complex I walked by all the time. The wall cut right through the neighborhood, down the middle of a street. Mitzi said when the wall first went up, people would try to jump from their apartment windows over the wall and onto the Western part of the street. The government barred the windows and evicted all the residents to prevent anyone from getting to the West.

They didn't even *pretend* they were keeping the West out for the East's own good. No. They were just flat-out, pull-no-punches keeping the East from getting out. I guessed that was the least of the lies that government told its people though.

There were days here where I could almost forget I lived in a place with such rigid rules and expectations. There were concerts in the park and the theater, with tickets cheap enough that I'd brought Sabina with me. If I had business on the other side of the city, I took the tram past a university and the sidewalks there were packed with people. But there was always an undercurrent of suspicion and hesitation. There were private conversations for the home, and public conversations. There were the television shows everyone discussed—the ones on state-owned channels— and the Western television shows that Mitzi and I only talked about inside the safe house.

I couldn't be too mad. I'd given up everything two years ago to keep my kid sister safe, and if I had to do it again, I would. Most people didn't get it, but the way I saw it was that if I couldn't rely on my family, I could make a family to rely on. Now Sabina and I were here, behind the Iron Curtain, in the makeshift family of Ashasher, Aurora, and Mitzi.

If people who wanted to institutionalize her came for her again, I'd move her. If the people who wanted to take her talents for their own use came again, I'd take her somewhere else. I'd do what it took. Go anywhere. Somewhere deeper inside the USSR. Into the woods of Poland or the mountains of Yugoslavia. Sabina would never need to defend herself. That was why she had me. I was Sabina's Berlin Wall. I kept the outside out for her. I kept her safe.

In the Schöpfer workshop below the Council meeting rooms, chaos reigned, per usual. The room was large—a former mechanical workroom off the subway line for trains before the wall went up—and entirely made of gray stone with thickly painted yellow railings so the rust didn't creep through. The Schöpfers were not exactly big fans of imperfections. Take it from someone who had been asked a dozen different ways that morning if he was sure, absolutely positive, that no one had interrupted or tampered with Garrick's balloon.

The room smelled like paper and ink and blood caught in the stale underground air. My tongue stuck to the roof of my mouth. On the second level, along the metal-staired walkway leading to the loft where the Schöpfers stored their books in a haphazard library, a couple of younger Schöpfers sat, legs dangling over the sides of the walkway and kicking in the air as they debated—loudly, might I add—the rate of heat transference in blah-blah-blah.

I tuned out. Math and science weren't my thing. I liked to be moving. An itch had already started crawling up my neck from being underground here. From the ceiling floated red balloons, some decorative and some floating lower, heavy with magic, waiting for their Runners. Between them, chains of paper doves—the first things the Schöpfers practiced magic on before they were allowed to write equations in blood—rose and fell, as steady as breathing.

"Heard you had an accident," someone said next to me and I jumped, surprised to be caught off guard.

Trina Peters, another Runner, leaned on the wall, turning over a cigarette in her fingers. I'd never seen her smoke them, just carry them. We all carried a few to bribe any guards or local citizens who got too curious. Like Mitzi, Trina rebelled in her own quiet ways. Most of her head was shaved except a long lock of hair that hung over one of her eyes. Her more straight-laced partner, Norm, was watching a Schöpfer at the next table build a balloon. I didn't usually watch my Schöpfer—Aurora—build my balloons, but some Runners did. And I bet after news of my balloon mishap spread, there'd be more and more Runners in here. It seemed fruitless. It wasn't like we'd know if an equation was wrong.

Trina flicked a floating dove out of her face, and it nearly collided with me. I scowled at it, and it rose back up to the ceiling while I considered Trina's suggestion that *I* had an *accident*. It wasn't quite an accident, but it wasn't not an accident either. There wasn't much I could say—the Council had forbidden Mitzi and me from speaking of what had happened.

Trina gave nothing away beneath her lock of hair and heavy brow. She studied the floor, avoiding my eyes. So finally I said, "Shit happens."

"Why are you here?" she asked, keeping her voice low. I bet no one was supposed to know about Garrick and Ellie's balloon. "If I got questioned by these clowns this morning—."

We both stilled as one of the Schöpfers swiveled toward us, fixed us with a stern eye, and then returned to her work. I said quietly, "My sister. Came to see her."

Sabina wasn't a secret here. We had stirred enough controversy and interest when we arrived with our English accents and dark skin that the Schöpfers never saw the point of hiding her here. Trina nodded a bit, lifting her head to scan the room.

"How's she doing?" Trina asked in a tone that told me she knew exactly how my sister was doing. We both watched her Schöpfer dip a pen in the ink mixed with the Passenger's blood sample and begin to write the equation onto the red balloon held in front of her by two curved metal clamps. The blood ink disappeared every few marks, absorbed into the integrity of the balloon. This Schöpfer wrote with a steady hand, and I was grateful. I'd been here before when a Schöpfer with a less steady hand had accidentally popped a balloon with the metal nib. Blood and balloon had splattered everywhere.

"She's fine," I said, because *fine* covered just about everything I didn't want to talk about.

I knew where Sabina was in the room. I had known from the moment I walked in. Try being not white in a room full of white people. You find the nonwhite people in the room real fast. Try being Romani in a room full of *gadje*. You find the other Romani, even if they aren't your people. My sister was the only other one, standing at a chalkboard under the walkway's overhang. She rocked back and forth on her feet, heel to toe and back to heel, like she always did when she was thinking really hard. And even with her back to me, I knew that she was chewing on a long, dark curl.

My sister was a genius, which I knew, but seeing her at the chalkboard was proof. She had one of those minds that took to mathematics like a fish to water. Plus, she was born a Schöpfer, born with magic in her blood. Some people are, some people aren't. Even if I understood the equations, anything I wrote in blood ink onto balloons would be useless. My sister, on the other hand, pushed the boundaries of what Ashasher said they thought balloons could do. She was working on an equation to increase flying distance of the balloons now. Last month, she and Aurora had worked together on an equation that expanded upon the DNA in Passengers' blood samples so that one family member's blood sample could be used to write equations for anyone in their family.

Genius. Someone in the family had to get all the brains. Sabina would turn thirteen in a few weeks, but she still seemed young to me. Her concept of evil was the Schöpfers' consistently tight hold over her independence.

I remember Garrick asking me about my accent, and I told him that I emigrated from England. He had laughed at me, until he heard I came here for my sister. He said that he was an only child, but he often thought that if he had any siblings, he'd do just about anything in the world for them.

I wished now that Sabina had met Garrick. Pea, meet pod.

Garrick was always writing in his little notebooks, jotting away, mouthing the words as he wrote in a shorthand nearly unintelligible to anyone. It was like his own private little code. The first time I met him, he was wearing a blue button-down shirt buttoned right up to the throat and tucked into poorly fitted jeans. He kept brushing his dirty hair out of his face while he wrote.

I had asked him, like I ask every Passenger, why he had to leave East Berlin. He had glanced up, squinting at me over his nub of a pencil, and deadpanned, "Too punk for them, I guess."

I would have adopted him into our little family for that alone, if we hadn't been sending him over the wall.

"Kai," Sabina said, standing in front of me, her dark eyes wide and her long, wavy hair tied back in a braid so she looked like a miniature of our mother. She held out a paper dove, its wings beating slowly. I cleared my mind and smiled at her. As soon as my fingers touched the paper bird, its wings stilled. Not enough magic, Sabina once told me. In me, she meant. It felt a bit like the little paper bird had died when I touched it, and I hated that, but she loved to make the chains and she loved to give them to me. So I took the dove, as always, and tucked it into my pocket.

She pressed her mouth into a line. It was a move she'd learned from Aurora, without a doubt. She slipped her hand into mine. "They said we could go out. For a walk."

I glanced over her head at Aurora, her teacher and my Schöpfer. Aurora's dark hair stood out in the sea of blond-haired Schöpfers around us. Ashasher said she wasn't born Aurora, and she wasn't born here. I had figured that out on my own. No one knew how old she was, but I'd been here two years and she hadn't seemed to age a day. To me, Ashasher looked older by the minute, but one of the older Schöpfers here told me that Ashasher hadn't seemed to age since he'd recruited him in 1961, when the wall went up. Maybe that Schöpfer was looking for gray hair, while I was listening to Ashasher's voice.

Aurora, like Ashasher, was one of the founders of the original Council, with the idea that magic and science had an intertwined connection that could save lives in places of unimaginable oppression. Now there were Councils in every city where people were oppressed or lived without certain freedoms, all overseen by a shadowy organization that simply made sure that the rules for magic were obeyed in each of those Councils and cities. Sometimes, on a good day, when our Passengers made it over the wall and I felt like I'd truly saved a life, I was proud to work for the founders of balloon magic. I tried not to think that too often, but some days, even most days, I was proud of the work I did.

Aurora met my eyes and inclined her head slightly. Lessons over for the day. Maybe she realized I needed this much more than Sabina did.

"A walk," I agreed. I'd have to take care not to walk her by the wall. My sister didn't filter very well. The last thing I needed was to be questioned by those guards after being questioned by Schöpfers this morning.

"You think so hard," Sabina said, swinging our hands between us, "that your eyes go cross."

"They do not." I scowled at her.

"I hear the Zeitreisende is very pretty," she added, smiling at me. I guessed Ellie didn't need a name here among the Schöpfers. Easier to call her by what she was than who she was. Time traveler. Sabina's language moved languidly from English to Angloromani to German. A new language forming from her mouth, even as her hands wrote out an equally strange one and made magic of it.

I shook my head at her, trying not to smile. "Sabina."

Next to me, Trina failed to cover her laugh. Sabina kept smiling, all innocent. "She's not pretty?"

"She's very pretty," I said without thinking. Ellie *was* really pretty. But there was just no way anything was happening there. "And she's from the twenty-first century. And she's going home."

"Maybe," Sabina said. "Maybe not. Let's walk."

Mitzi was right. Getting teased about a girl by my little sister was exactly what I needed.

Chapter Seven

TWO FLAMES

East Berlin, German Democratic Republic, April 1988

Ellie

Days came and went, marked only by the punctuation of doors opening and shutting below me, the low hum of Kai and Mitzi switching shifts. There was always someone in the house. I was never alone, except that I was always alone. Mitzi knocked and left trays of food outside my door, but never came in, never forced the issue. Part of me wanted her to. I wanted someone to stomp up and down and tell me they cared if I lived or died. But there it was: they didn't care.

Why should they? I was a girl who shouldn't be there. I was an accident. A mishap. An anomaly. I'd never been part of the popular crowd at home, but here, this was an entirely different feeling of being an outsider. I wasn't just an outsider, I was an outlier. I didn't belong here. I couldn't keep up in conversations, even the ones I eavesdropped on while trying to practice German in my head.

I thought about sneaking out, but then I remembered the police who had stopped me the first time. I made myself promise that I wouldn't sneak out until my German was good enough to get me out of trouble if I got into it.

I didn't know where I'd go. But I couldn't stay here forever. I knew that, and still I couldn't make myself get up. Stop wallowing, I told myself. Get up. When I heard Mitzi's footsteps, I'd coach myself to interact with her. To ask her questions. To smile. To say thank you. But when she brought me food, the paper, and clean clothes, I couldn't find the courage. I stayed quiet. I tried bribing myself and bullying myself, but nothing worked.

I had a list of things I missed. My phone, Amanda, getting silly photos of our cat from my mom, the internet, showers with hot water that lasted more than three minutes, my own shampoo, Friday night services at synagogue. Simple things and big things, and they started to sound the same to me in my head. I tried to make a song out of what I missed, but even that was hard.

Mitzi left the paper, and I tore out the date she kept circling. I collected the tiny pieces of paper in a small pile. Sometimes when I woke up, I still thought it was a dream. The tiny pile of dates was the only proof that I was in a different time. I couldn't make myself say the word. I couldn't. If this was a scam, it was the best stupid kidnapping ever. But it wasn't a scam. It wasn't a kidnapping. A week passed after the mysterious Council's determination. Since I had arrived in 1988. Time passed. Time I shouldn't have been in. Time I couldn't escape.

I hadn't missed a Shabbat service since my Bat Mitzvah, so it felt strange to hold the newspaper in my hand and read the word *Freitag*, the German word for Friday. I should be at synagogue with my parents, lighting candles at home with Mom, telling them about my week at school and Amanda's ridiculous antics.

If I thought about what I was missing too much, I'd cry, and I'd done a very good job of not crying so far. I curled back up in bed, trying to make the stack of dates as perfect as possible, when below me, the front door opened and shut with a bang. Kai called out, "Hello, darling."

I stopped to listen. It'd been a few days since he'd been by the house. Mitzi below me said something back in German that made Kai laugh. I listened to them, their words curling up through the thin floors. Nothing was private in this house. Or between houses. I could hear the neighbors' nightly fights in their bedroom, their hushed whispers over a son who had gone missing, over a daughter who wouldn't quit her political organization. They whispered, but Mitzi and Kai never did. They never sounded afraid.

"I'm going to talk to her," Mitzi said. "Did you read my note last night?"

"I did." The oven door opened and shut, and Kai said something about whatever Mitzi was cooking. "We'll have a new Passenger next week, by the way. They're unsuspending us."

"Then *you* talk to her, Kai. She can't just mope around. *Unsuspending* isn't a word in any language."

"She's not moping." Kai's voice chilled the entire house. "She's grieving. Christ, you Germans. Just because you have no emotions—"

"Shut it, Kai," Mitzi's voice pitched and shook the floor. I gritted my teeth and closed my eyes. "You do not get to derail this conversation."

"You heard Ashasher. We lose our jobs if we ask her questions."

The quilt tickled my nose, but I didn't dare sneeze or move. The questions filtered through the fog of my mind slowly. *What questions? What do they want to ask me?*

"God, why do you think I don't understand that? I said I'd talk to her, not interrogate her."

"You don't want to know? It's the future, Mitz." Kai's voice switched abruptly, smooth and coaxing. He was baiting her. Mentally I willed Mitzi not to rise to it.

I didn't have to worry. Mitzi's voice steadied. "Wanting to and doing so are completely different. Maybe that's your problem. You talk to her or I talk to her, but we can't babysit any longer. It's not good for her, and it's not good for us."

"She's grieving."

"We're all grieving," Mitzi said, and then their voices turned instantly too loud as the pipes in the walls trickled and fell mute. She must have turned the water off. "We're in charge of thirteen more Passengers this month that we need to successfully send over the wall. I don't feel obliged to the girl upstairs, but I do care."

"I know, I know. I'm not going to ask her about the future, and I won't let anyone else ask her either. Like Ashasher said, to know the future is to change the future. I am going to go get her out of bed though. I have something for her. Maybe it'll cheer her up," Kai said, just barely loud enough for me to hear.

I frowned against the edge of the quilt, curious. What did he have for me? I couldn't hear what happened next but Mitzi laughed, loudly, and Kai joined her. Their voices dropped to a murmur, and then I heard footsteps on the stairs. I knew Mitzi's by this point. Kai left me alone in the nights he spent downstairs, and these steps had to be his steps. Steady like a metronome, nearly ominous, the start of every horror movie I hadn't successfully watched. When the bedroom door opened, I held my breath.

His footsteps echoed in the room. He sat on the edge of the bed. His fingers touched my hair. And for some reason I didn't understand, the touch sent a shiver through me, snapping the fragile dam holding back my sobs.

"Hello, saddest girl in the saddest city," Kai said in English, his voice gentle and low. I couldn't see through the tears filling my eyes, but I stuffed my fist wrapped in the quilt into my mouth to suffocate my crying. Kai tugged the quilt away from my face. "There's that pretty face."

That got me to snort, unprettily, and glare at him. He was all blurry through my tears, but I saw the part where his smile pulled up one side of his face. In the evening light of the room, he seemed neither as intimidating nor as angry as he had the last few times I'd seen him.

He amended his statement with a half shrug. "Crying doesn't make anyone feel pretty."

My voice was hoarse from disuse. There was snot on my lips. "You really know how to talk to girls."

"If you venture out of bed, you'll find out I'm surrounded by them. C'mon. Sit up."

I shook my head, courage shriveling within me. He poked me in the shoulder. Hard. "Ouch."

"Get up."

"Where I come from," I said grumpily, "guys don't just come into strange girls' bedrooms and sit on their beds."

"I don't think you're that strange."

I closed my eyes. "Where are you from?"

"Ah, that old question. If I had a mark for every time I'd heard it, I wouldn't be here, would I? I am Romanichal, which is the word we use for Romani who've been in England for a long time. I was born near High Wycombe, outside London. I live here. You?"

"Pittsburgh," I said. "My grandfather was German. What's Romani?"

"Some still call us Gypsies, but many of us prefer Roma or Romani. You should get out of bed."

"Why?" The breath I took smelled like the fresh air still clinging to him.

"It's Friday night, isn't it?" he said, pointing at my stack of dates. "I have something for you downstairs."

"What?"

"You have to come downstairs," he insisted. "You'll like it.

I think. We're breaking at least thirteen rules I know of." He slapped the bed. "Up you go."

With bravery I didn't know I had, I shook my head. "You don't care about that. Rules don't matter to you."

The corner of his mouth turned up and his eyes narrowed as he stood, backing toward the door. "Rules don't matter much to me, but I need the job, so if I broke rules, I promise it was for a reason that'll keep you happy and alive until we can get you home."

Home. He was lying.

"If you let me die," I said without thinking, "then you can stop pretending I'll get home one day."

He stopped by the doorway, and I watched his shoulders rise and fall in a single deep breath. He said, his voice so low I almost missed it, "Death is one way of going home, Ellie. But you're not going to die. Berlin has enough ghosts. Germany has enough ghosts. Europe has more than enough ghosts. Choosing to be a ghost is disrespectful to all the real ghosts."

He might as well have slapped me across the face. I swung my feet out of bed. "What do you know of ghosts?"

"As much as you, I imagine," he said and left the room.

I'd gone to a different time and still managed to find the opposite sex as cryptic and difficult as I'd always found them. I huffed and flopped back on the bed, rolling his words over in my mind. Then I took a deep breath and sat up, wiping at my face with the heel of my palms.

"No ghosts," I said to myself, and silently added a few bad words aimed at Kai as I got out of bed.

Reluctantly, I found a purple shirt and jeans that fit well enough to be decent. *Decent for who, Ellie?* And then I thought of Kai. Furiously, I shoved him out of my mind and glared at myself in the mirror. I didn't have time for that. *Time. Ha.* I pulled a sweater over my head, and then brushed my hair and found my shoes. In retrospect, if I had known I'd be time traveling, I would have picked more comfortable shoes.

Down in the kitchen, Kai stood behind Mitzi, who was filling a kettle with water at the sink. He said in German, "You're jealous."

"I'm not jealous." Her voice cracked a little bit. I paused in the doorway, unsure whether I should say something now or not. Then Mitzi leaned on the counter. "I'm just used to the two of us being the outsiders."

Kai poked her in the side, making Mitzi laugh. "Stop. Jealousy isn't cute on you. You and me, Mitz, we're the unstoppable duo. Other Runners are jealous of us. Broken balloons and time travelers can't change that."

"You're sure?"

"Positive. Right, Ellie?"

I flushed hot at being caught eavesdropping in the doorway. Mitzi shot me a look that I couldn't read, and I made myself return the stare. I looked around, unsure of what surprise he had for me and what I'd be looking for. Something that broke the rules. Him and Mitzi? But for some reason I didn't think that was it.

"Here," he said, gesturing to the kitchen table. On the table were two little candles in silver candlestick holders. A box of matches sat next to them. For a long beat, I stared at them and couldn't place them. They were out of context, out of time, but then I sucked in my breath. He'd brought me Shabbat candles. He brought me, somehow, a piece of home, even though I was so, so far from home. Distances I couldn't even imagine.

"Ellie?" asked Mitzi hesitantly. "Are you all right?"

I swiped at the tears running down my cheeks. "Yes. Sorry. Thank you. Both of you."

They nodded, and Mitzi turned back to the stove. I rocked on the balls of my feet for a moment, unsure if I should light the candles in front of them, or whether this was for another time.

But Kai gestured to the table again, and I stepped forward. With trembling hands, I struck one of the matches. Habit or maybe even tradition steadied my hand, and I lit both candles. I shook my wrist, extinguishing the match, and held my hands over the candles, whispering the prayers. My mind cleared slowly, the words bringing me out of myself and back into the present—whatever that was.

I sank into a chair, hands clasped to my mouth, and watched the flames dancing at the end of the wicks. "You know what's weird?"

"What?" Kai asked, easing into a chair next to me and propping his feet up on the empty chair so Mitzi couldn't sit down. She smacked him with a spatula and then set a plate of cookies in front of him.

"A world where it's illegal to practice my faith, but where magic exists," I said quietly. "That's not the world I knew. It's like the *reverse* of everything I knew."

"There's magic in your time too," Mitzi said. "You just didn't know about it."

Except, I did. My grandfather had told stories about magic my entire life, and I just hadn't been listening. I'd loved the act of storytelling without giving particular weight to the stories, and now when I tried to remember them, I could only remember the one about the red balloon. The flames danced in front of me, shielded from the view of the front windows by the half wall dividing the kitchen and the living room. I'd said words that my parents and grandparents and great-grandparents and everyone before them had said over twin flames.

"How long?" I asked. "How long has there been magic and magical balloons?"

Kai slid his feet off the chair, and Mitzi sat down across from me. They exchanged a look, and then Mitzi sighed. Her English was careful. "I don't know the answer to the magic part.

I imagine it's always been around, showing itself in different ways. But the balloons, they started in the nineteen thirties as Hitler rose to power."

"So they came out of a specific need," I clarified.

Kai said something to Mitzi in German that I didn't catch and then said to me, "This was one need, and one solution. I don't know details—"

"Because you haven't asked," I interjected.

"—but I assume there've always been uses for magic," he said, his gaze sharpening. "Why?"

I shrugged, not knowing how to explain all of the tangled feelings inside my chest. How much it felt like home to light Shabbat candles here, very far from home in every possible way, and how strange it felt for magic to be real, to be everywhere I'd been without me experiencing it before the red balloon. That reaching for the balloon that day in the park and striking a match to light these candles had felt the same.

"I don't know," I said honestly into the silence.

"Best thing to do for a muddy mind?" He stood up, brushing cookie crumbs from his pants. "A walk. Fresh air is good for people, no matter what decade they're from."

I raised an eyebrow at Mitzi, and she rolled her eyes at Kai. "She really shouldn't be going outside. This isn't what I meant by cheering her up, Kai."

"We can't keep her a prisoner. And you're the one who wanted to do something to get her out of bed. Can't have it both ways, Mitzi."

"I didn't really imagine you'd be parading her in front of the Volkspolizei. She's already been stopped once. How are you going to sweet-talk your way out of this one?" snapped Mitzi, uncrossing her arms. "You understand we can't send her back where she belongs if she's rotting in a Stasi prison!"

Kai's eyes flickered to me, like he remembered our conversation upstairs about not needing to go home if I were dead. He leaned over to Mitzi and kissed her forehead. "We're going to Sebastianstrasse. We promise not to attract unnecessary attention, girl with the very blue hair."

Mitzi scowled at him. "You only call me that when you want to piss me off. It's condescending."

"When did I last call you that?" Kai demanded.

"When you broke up with Marie and I started dating her," Mitzi said.

I blinked, but Kai continued on as if this wasn't a revelation. "I just think it's weird to date someone with the same first name as you."

"Who's jealous now? Besides, I don't use my full name," Mitzi said, her voice drier than the toast she often made me. "I have a name, Kai. Use it. I'm not some random girl at some club."

"And upstairs, you called me the saddest girl in the saddest city. You called me the girl with the terrible German accent when I arrived," I pointed out to Kai.

Mitzi tossed me a smug smile and crossed her arms. Maybe I was forgiven for distracting Kai from her and their work. "See? It's a pattern."

"I promise to use your names almost always." He pouted dramatically at Mitzi, who turned away, but I thought only to hide the smile on her face. He turned to me, stuffing a cookie into his mouth and saying around it, "Ready?"

Boys of any time period were all the same. I rolled my eyes. "Where are we going?"

"Adventure," he said, cookie crumbles on his lips. I tried not to stare, but I failed miserably. When I thought of what Amanda would say, I blushed, and Kai grinned. Mitzi stared at both of us with raised eyebrows.

Tearing my eyes off his mouth, I made a face. "I've had my share of adventure this month, thanks. Hit my quota. I have no more adventures. Can I go back to bed now?"

He shook his head, a dark lock of hair slipping loose from the ponytail holder. "Nope. You're up. You have momentum. Come on. The sun's setting. You have to promise me something though," Kai said, washing his hands. "Only speak German out there. Too dangerous. *Allons-y!*"

"That's French," I said without thinking.

"Is it?" Kai asked with wide eyes. "Oh no. I can't believe all these years I've been speaking French in Germany. That explains how no one ever understood me."

I flushed again from being teased, but behind Kai's back, Mitzi gave me a thumbs-up and a wink. Maybe I had misjudged her when I first arrived. I slid on a coat and took a scarf from the hooks by the door. Kai gave me his almost-smile. "Come on. Fresh air. Adventure. I swear we won't get arrested."

"Inspiring," I said, but followed him out the door anyway.

Chapter Eight

OUT AMONG GHOSTS

East Berlin, German Democratic Republic, April 1988

Ellie

Outside, Kai said to me, "Tell me what you miss. Maybe we can find an equivalent here."

The answer came quickly, my days upstairs in bed finally paying off. "My phone. My bed. My friends. Shabbat. My mom taking silly pictures of our cat."

He ticked them off. "We have a phone, bed, and new friends. We did the candles, so we covered that…" He didn't say Shabbat in public. I winced, realizing I probably shouldn't have either. He continued, "I can't help with your mom, but I'm sure we could find you a cat. There. Homesickness solved."

"Not quite. But thank you. For the candles. That meant a lot to me," I said, breathing in the fresh air deeply. "I miss the internet. Wherever you are, if you have an internet connection, it's like being home."

"I don't know what that is. I don't think we have that yet," he said cheerfully.

I frowned, trying to keep with his long strides. "Should I not mention things that don't exist? I don't even know when the internet was invented."

"My point is that as long as you're here, I'm sure we can find things that will help," he said quietly. "But you must try not to turn into a ghost. Understand?"

I'd thought I wasn't nearly that transparent, and now I fought to keep the telltale guilty blush off my face at being so easily read. I kept my hands in my pockets, avoiding eye contact with everyone around me. My heart pounded in my palms. "*Ja*."

"Home is a *fantasie*," he said after another block. "We make up our homes and our ideas of home. Some days, I can't even bear all the guilt I feel at finding my home in a city that nearly everyone wants to leave."

I almost asked him what he meant, but when I glanced up at him, his face was closed and tight. Was that what he meant in knowing as much about ghosts as I did?

As we walked through streets, he would occasionally pause and casually name whatever we were standing next to or looking at. He never pointed, and I guess he didn't want to draw attention to us, though no one gave us a second glance. The clothes Mitzi loaned me let passersby's eyes glide right over me, so they didn't even notice that Kai was teaching me German. Some of the words I knew and others I didn't. The language lesson made no sense, unless he believed I'd need to know these words because I'd be staying long enough, and I dismissed that thought immediately. The chances of me walking around alone were about as low as my chances of learning to spell *freundschaftsbezeigungen*.

"What's the point?" I finally asked him, stopping in the street. "Of going on. If it was an accident that I'm here, and you don't know how to send me back, then what's the point?"

He gestured with his hand. "Come on."

We turned a corner and stopped immediately, my heart clutching my throat with clawed fingers. The wall. The Berlin Wall. Thin and concrete, razor wire in big lazy loops on the top of it.

"This isn't…" I managed to say before I swallowed and tried again. "This isn't how I thought it'd look."

Kai spoke right against my ear, the words for me and me alone. "There's this wall, then bare land for meters until the Berlin Wall. We call the middle land the death zone. There are few ways to leave here, but the balloons offer a chance to the most at-risk people."

Guards everywhere, and cars waiting in a long line to pass through the checkpoint. Police patrolled the area, their olive-green uniforms making me shake a little bit. *Don't get caught. Can't get caught.* Kai's hand settled on my back and I jumped, nearly bursting into tears from adrenaline that couldn't spike any higher in my body.

His lips nearly brushed my ear, and his breath was warmer than the wool around my throat. I closed my eyes. "We live in a prison. We help people escape to the West, to freedom. We are helpers. And, Ellie, so help me, we're going to get you home."

Home is a fantasy, he'd said, but he kept promising to get me home. I didn't know which words to trust, where to place my faith, and it took me a few minutes to compose myself. I made myself look at the wall, the same way I made myself look at memorials. *Bear witness*, we always said, and here I bore witness not to the memorial but to the wall in real life.

All the facts in history books couldn't prepare someone for standing in a place where history was present tense. I knew about the wall from reading for the trip. I knew that the wall came down in 1989 after the German Democratic Republic, the official name for East Germany, was forced to follow the rest of the Eastern Bloc's liberalization. They had been resistant to the

Soviet Union's new policies of glasnost and perestroika, or openness and transparency, combined with economic and governmental reforms.

Openness and transparency didn't fit so well with Communism, it turned out.

There was no gum on this Wall. Just a quiet sort of despair, dusty gray and sharp. It reminded me of the apartment buildings hanging around the Karl-Marx-Allee. I had never seen this side of the wall. Every picture I had seen showed graffiti.

"I've always seen it with art," I said, keeping my voice low.

Kai turned to me slightly. "Art?"

I didn't know the German word for graffiti. "Street art."

His eyes brightened, and my heart skipped a beat. "On the West side?"

"It must be," I said, shaking my head. "You can't even get to the wall here, can you?"

"Not for lack of people trying." Kai's eyes were cool, the gold in them dimming as they watched the guards move back and forth up the line of cars.

"If they're going to die, why do they try?"

"You have not found something you wanted so badly that you'd die for it?" he asked, his eyes never leaving the wall.

It took me a moment, but the only way I could answer was admitting the truth. "No."

Kai's shoulders went up and down in a shrug. "Everyone calculates their own risks."

Walking out the front door this afternoon had felt like a calculated risk. I didn't tell him that though. I just stood there for a long time, watching him watch the wall until I could figure out what I wanted to ask him. "What if we were caught?"

His head snapped on a swivel, even though we were on an empty street, and I bit my lip, looking down shamefaced. I should have known that was a risky question to ask, even in German.

The last thing we needed was to attract the attention of a police officer. Kai shook his head slightly.

"There are things you can't say out here. But I promise you, we won't be."

"If we were?" I asked again.

"It wouldn't be good," he said finally.

I knew that much, but he'd dodged the question twice so I decided to let it drop. Two police officers wandered toward us, their gait too deliberately casual, so Kai touched my elbow and we began to walk again, parallel to the wall. The sun was beginning to dip behind the rooflines, sending warm light over the glittering, wet streets and up the sides of the buildings. The neighborhood we entered had narrower streets with overbearing rectangular, concrete postwar apartment buildings, like they'd been built using the same footprint as the rubble of the destroyed ones.

Someone once told me that the Allied forces had dropped more tonnage of bombs on Germany in World War II than the total tonnage of bombs dropped anywhere else by anyone else in the war. I could believe it. I tried to imagine the city without the new buildings, as ugly as they were. It must have looked as if the streets were gap-toothed, as if Europe's twentieth-century troubles had been nothing but a state-level bar fight.

As the streetlamps flickered on, we wove through crowds of people, past historic old buildings with repaired facades, past Soviet-style gray administration buildings, past dozens of apartment buildings. Though my legs ached from all the walking, I didn't want to stop and Kai seemed to understand. We wandered, our shadows absorbed into the low light of night. A steady drizzle started up, but we just pulled up our hoods and kept walking. I thought about what he'd said about finding safety and pleasure in a place that was nothing but pain for so many other people. He felt the same way about escaping to East Berlin that I felt about coming to Germany at all. Guilt.

"So how do you bear it?" I asked him when we weren't near people who could hear my accent. His brow furrowed in confusion, though he didn't look at me. I clarified. "You seem to love what you do, despite where you are, but everything you do is a secret. No one will ever know how many lives you save."

"The people never mentioned in history books still made history," he replied, his voice calm and even. "Whenever I doubt myself, I remind myself of that."

I wanted to tell him that people would write books about boys like him one day, boys who lived in fairy tales and changed the course of human history and human imagination. But then I realized he was right. They wouldn't write about magic balloons or Kai or Mitzi or anyone else here. No one would ever know what I already knew and had to accept as fact. What happened to all the people the Schöpfers and the Runners helped? How did they tell their story? Did they keep a secret until they began to lose their mind to dementia, the story coming out in fantastical memories that couldn't be real?

Part of me was angry for those people, those hundreds or thousands of people living in my day who knew that magic exists but were forced to remain silent. Like my grandfather remembering a girl with a red balloon who saved him from a death camp.

"My grandfather," I said haltingly. "He kept it a secret. No one knew how he escaped Chełmno. My mother looked it up. The records show he was on the train out of Łódź, and then he disappeared. When people asked him, he said he was lucky. That G-d had chosen him for saving. But he told me stories. One of those stories was of a girl with a red balloon who saved him."

Kai looked sideways at me as he led me to an apartment building. His gaze was partly obscured by his hood, and it reminded me of the night I met him. "No one believed him."

I inhaled, breathing in the cool night air, the sound of rain splattering on wet pavement. "I did. When I was little. But when his stories started getting mixed up, I started to wonder if any of his stories had been true."

"I miss believing," Kai said, his voice dropping so low I nearly missed his words. Then suddenly, he reached for my hand, yanking me into the shadows beneath a fire escape. *Police.* I twisted against Kai and looked for the telltale gleaming boots and distinct uniforms, but the streets seemed empty. Then, on the other side of the street, three dark silhouettes turned the corner and walked with a red balloon west toward the wall. The balloon looked exactly like mine, waving around in the light rain as if it understood its mission.

"Let go," I whispered. It wasn't the police. So why was Kai still keeping us in the dark?

He shook his head and held a finger up to his lips. His grip on my hand remained tight and painful, and his arm trembled a bit. The tallest of the three figures handed over the red balloon, and the second person wrapped their hand around the string. In a blink, the second person was gone, invisible.

Through the drizzle, we watched the remaining two turn toward the wall, and when I glanced at Kai, his gaze followed theirs. He breathed a sigh of relief.

I squinted into the dark. "Can you see it? The balloon, I mean."

He shook his head, raindrops flying. "No. When the Passenger takes the balloon, it becomes invisible to the naked eye. Only the Schöpfer who made it can see it now because their blood is in the magic too. We know that they make it to the other side when a light in that church goes on."

"How do they know when to let go?" I asked.

Kai's eyes watched the other two people left on the street. "Passengers can see everything, and here, the Schöpfers only write the balloons to be higher than the guard towers. So they know when they reach the church. The magic is specific enough to control all of that."

But he stopped talking as the other two people began to walk back down the street. If Kai and Mitzi were balloon Runners, then the pair accompanying this balloon must have been too. They were both dressed in dark colors, and the taller one wore a lighter colored scarf, maybe purple or light blue. She clearly led the way, and the smaller person trailed behind as they turned away from the wall. Their footsteps slapped against the wet sidewalk as they walked down the street right by us. I kept waiting for Kai to call out to them, but he stayed silent, gripping my hand so tightly I nearly cried out. I couldn't help but wonder if he was protecting or hiding me. They weren't the same thing. Not at all.

Instead, his frown deepened. "Shouldn't be any balloons going over the wall tonight. But it went over safely, so it can't have been broken. Your balloon…I've never had that happen before."

"Magic and balloons," I whispered, shivering from the cold and the dark. "And Walls and time."

Kai's voice was low and sad. "The things that get us out and the things that keep us in."

Chapter Nine

THERE ARE NO MACCABEES HERE

Łódź Ghetto, Poland, 1941

Benno

The day after I went to the fence and whispered to the girl on the outside, a man was shot for walking too close to the fence on his way to synagogue. At home, only Papa, Ernst, and I went to Shabbat services, and we were not very religious. But here, we clung to the synagogue like it was keeping us alive, and maybe it was. Papa knew the man who was shot. We spent Shabbat services reciting the Mourner's Kaddish, over and over. *Yitgadal v'yitkadash…*

His name was Benjamin Ginsburg. *May his memory be a blessing*, we said that day. What we really meant was *May his death be a warning, may his memory not be in vain.* I did not go to the fence that day.

Ruth was thin, but wavered on. I brought her home my soup. Mama cried and scolded me, but took it from my hands anyway to feed to my sister. Ruth's hands shook too hard when she coughed. She would waste the soup.

Our days were marked by the time before and the time after we received our daily soup. Our weeks were marked by the loaves of bread we received. We were supposed to receive three loaves of bread because Papa, Mama, and I were all working. But instead, we would get one, or two. Almost never three. Sunsets and sunrises meant nothing to us anymore. Even Shabbat became the day before we got more bread. We said prayers on empty stomachs to a G-d who didn't seem to be listening to us.

A few days after Benjamin died, I made it to the fence without getting shot. The search lights pooled past me and I crouched, counting the seconds before I could run to the corner. It was a crapshoot, a wishful guess, and an impossible hope. And yet, by the fence, in the grass, there was a small brown bottle of liquid. Penned on the label: *For the sad boy's sister. Administer two drops two to three times a day.*

I ran as fast as I could. Up the stairs into the tiny apartment, one room with a curtain dividing it, like this was a place I could call home. But my parents were there, and my sister was there, and that was enough. Home, without running water, without hot water, with broken windows and thin walls so we could hear the neighbors roll over in their sleep. Home, where my sister lay, a bag of bones beneath a blanket, shivering and coughing.

When I handed over the medicine, my only thought was: If this doesn't work...

She couldn't die. Not Ruth. She was bright and vivid, and when she smiled in my memories, the sun slipped free of the clouds.

Mama and Papa fought over the medicine. Mama didn't want to trust it. She said it could be arsenic. She said no one outside the fence wanted Jewish children to survive. Papa said Ruth was going to die if it was arsenic, and die if it wasn't, and on the off chance it wasn't arsenic, it was her only chance to live. They fought and shouted for hours, until I thought either I'd kill myself to escape that noise, or someone would come to take the medicine that everyone must have known we had by then.

We gave Ruthie the medicine. And day by day, she grew stronger. I remembered the girl at the fence, throwing sticks for the dog. She'd said she didn't have medicine, but that she had magic. Maybe she had a little bit of both.

Ruthie recovering was a sigh of relief for us, and slowly, we adjusted to life at Łódź. Adjusted did not mean giving up. We adjusted. We worked twelve hours a day and grew used to being hungry. But then there was music, and art—quietly, of course, because we were forbidden to meet in groups—and then Rebekah arrived.

The last of the Berliner Jews arrived by train in November, and on the train was Rebekah. Inga from our old neighborhood who had once kissed my brother Ernst behind the schoolyard came running down the street to tell me. I could have kissed her, but I wanted too much to see Rebekah.

She was tired and sad, but she smiled wider than the ocean when she saw me. I hugged her, even though her father glared in disapproval at us, and whispered to her that life wasn't so bad now that she was there. She whispered back that she was afraid, so afraid. Her mother wasn't with them. She had been sick, so the Gestapo held her in a different camp to recover before she came here. I didn't tell Rebekah what I feared. The sickness was already here. Her mother wasn't coming.

Rebekah and I joined a youth group where we sang Yiddish songs and dreamed of Palestine, a Jewish homeland, and quietly, where others couldn't see us, we walked home hand in hand. It was a relief, this small sense of normalcy. We might live in an overcrowded miniature city, but we were still teenagers. We had friends at work and people we avoided.

Our neighborhoods became our homes. I resisted, but slowly, the memory of our house in Berlin faded and was replaced by our apartment in Łódź, the mud, the stench, the ache in my stomach.

Rebekah's family was assigned to the other side of the ghetto, closer to the Gypsies, because that was where there had been room for newcomers. That was where the last people sent away on trains had lived. When I realized that, I couldn't sleep for a few nights. Our homes were made of ghosts.

The walk back from Rebekah's place was long, quiet, and dangerous. When I came home late at night, only hours before work started again, Mama and Papa were already in bed. But Ruthie sometimes woke when I came home.

"Is she pretty?" Ruthie asked me.

"You don't remember Rebekah?" I whispered back. I didn't know why I asked her this. I was beginning to forget what life had been like before too. "I'd say she was the prettiest girl in the whole world, but the prettiest girl is right here. The prettiest girl needs to go back to sleep."

"What if you marry her? Will she move here? Where will we go?" Ruth wanted to know.

I didn't have any of the answers. And when I kissed Rebekah one night, just before Hanukkah started, she asked me the same questions. I didn't have any better answers then, but the answers came to us.

They, the Nazis and Chaim Rumkowski, began deportations that December. Hundreds of people at once, herded back onto trains, disappearing into the ether. First were the Gypsies. Groups of quiet-eyed people with long shawls wrapped around them, marching proud and silent to the trains. The Nazis instituted a curfew and searched the apartments one by one when people did not report. Their names were on lists, and they were brought by gunpoint to the trains. They were shot if they tried to flee.

Ruth's name was on the list, but our neighbor's grandfather substituted his for hers by giving Rumkowski a handful of notes and his ration card. He said that Ruth was better. She ought to get a chance to survive the war with her family.

Rebekah's name was on the list too. I didn't get a chance to say good-bye. I saw her look over her shoulder one last time at me, her eyes full of tears and her round cheeks hollowed out with hunger and grief. She gave me a little smile, and then stepped up onto the train and into the darkness.

I wanted to be shot that night. I went looking for trouble. When they lifted the curfew, I went to the fence. But they didn't patrol that corner as well as before. The girl with the magical medicine was there, wearing a black coat over a purple dress, like there wasn't a war going on all around her. She stood there in the snow as if she had known I was coming. Her raven-colored hair fell in soft waves around her face, and her eyes were dark and solemn.

She said, "I saw the trains."

I said, "I don't want to talk about the trains."

She nodded, as if she understood—and how could she possibly understand? She was a girl on the other side of the fence. But I wasn't ready to go back. Not yet. So I swallowed and said, "It's Hanukkah."

She sat down in the snow, tucking her feet beneath her skirt. "Tell me."

So even though I was freezing and the snow must have soaked her straight through, I told her the story of Hanukkah. Once, in a land far away, the Romans ruled the Jewish homeland. They came into the land and seized it by force. They told the Jews they could not practice Judaism. They burned the temple and destroyed it, wrecked it with their idols and their hatred. And so Judah and the Maccabees went into the mountains and planned a war.

It took them years, but they were insurgents in the night, fighting back against the oppressive force, until slowly, the small but mighty army pushed back the evil one. When they won, they found they only had a tiny amount of oil left for the Eternal

Light. They lit it, and though it should have only lasted a day, it lasted eight, and that was why Hanukkah was celebrated for eight days. The temple was rededicated.

The girl in the snow lifted her pale face to me and said, "If I were a Maccabee, I'd free you."

"You're just a girl," I said. "Not a Maccabee." And then I added quietly, "And I'm just a boy. I'm not a hero either. I wish I was."

For a long moment, we were silent, but it wasn't uncomfortable. For the first time in a long time, I let myself feel hopeless and young and afraid out there in the corner of the cemetery. I'd almost forgotten the girl was sitting there when she said, "If all of you die, what will happen to your story?"

I tilted my chin to the sky, into the snow. It drifted down slowly on my face, which was numb from the cold. Whenever I closed my eyes, I saw Ruthie's hand in my mother's hand and Rebekah's face, sad and alone, as she boarded that train for the last time.

"I don't know," I admitted. "I guess stories die with people."

"I hope not," she whispered back in the night. "If you die, I will celebrate Hanukkah. I'll tell that story."

She wanted to be kind, but I hated her right then. Because she had the possibility of hope. She was on the other side of the fence. Simple borders and demarcations made such a difference in someone's future, hopes, and dreams, and the promises they could make. How pointless the world could be.

Chapter Ten

DOVES AND MAYBES

East Berlin, German Democratic Republic, April 1988

Ellie

When Mitzi and Kai didn't have a Passenger, they liked to watch the other balloons go over the wall. I knew Kai was looking for more balloons that acted as mine had. They took me with them sometimes to a rooftop near where Kai and I had seen the rogue balloon. Each time, I looked for more balloons along the wall, bobbing in the dark alongside a Runner and a passenger. The first few times I tagged along, Mitzi kept telling Kai that this was too big of a risk with me. I didn't have papers, and if I was caught, the consequences would be unthinkable. He kept telling her that they couldn't treat me like a prisoner.

Up here on the roof, we could see to the other side of the wall. The lights in West Berlin turned off and on, twinkling and mesmerizing, as if there were a secret Morse code hidden in their patterns. I couldn't stop thinking about what would happen if there were more broken balloons. More dead Passengers, maybe. More people pulled through time. More dots that didn't connect on a timeline.

I had ventured, timid, into a world of magic and secrets, a world so gray and regimented that even those who knew nothing of magic balloons sought out brightness. The skateboarders breaking rules, Mitzi's friends who came around and made her hair look dull against the rainbow of their heads and the metal in their faces, the balloon seller in the park.

"You can ask me, you know," Kai said one night up on the roof. His sister was with us, so Kai was pretending not to watch for Passengers and Runners going to the wall with balloons. It'd been his first night off all week. "Or Mitzi. Anything. Whatever we can answer, we will."

Mitzi was teaching Sabina how to do a fishtail braid in her hair. Sabina didn't seem to be listening. She sat, her fingers working quickly over a paper square, folding it into a little white dove. When she let it go, it began to float up into the air, joining the others she'd folded. I couldn't stop watching. My heart felt tight inside my chest.

Kai didn't have the answers to the questions I wanted to ask, but I didn't tell him that. Instead, I said, "What's she doing?"

He glanced sideways. "Making doves. It's one of the ways the Schöpfers practice. She's well past that stage, but I think it soothes her."

I sank down next to Sabina and said softly, "Can I try?"

Sabina's head jerked up, nearly hitting Mitzi in the face. She studied me with her dark eyes, not as shifting as Kai's but deeper, somehow, the way Ashasher seemed like he could look straight through me. She nodded and handed me a square of paper. I watched her fingers as she folded slowly, showing me the way.

I folded the paper in half, and half again, my mind tripping ahead of me. I'd loved to make origami once, when I was young, but I'd stopped. I didn't remember why. But the draw I felt to the balloon in the park was the same as the draw here. Something tugging at me in the center of my chest.

I sat my dove on my palm, and its wings began to move up and down. I looked up, startled, to see Sabina frowning at me. Mitzi tilted her head and started to say something, but stopped. My dove didn't fly, not like Sabina's, but it moved of its own volition, and my eyes filled with tears.

The look on Kai's face was full of wonder and fear. No one had ever looked at me like that before. I started to ask him what was wrong, why he looked at me like this, but he clapped his hand over my mouth. His skin was warm against mine. His palm smelled like fresh air. His eyes were wide and serious. "Don't ask questions we don't want answers to, Ellie."

He wasn't magical and he couldn't read minds, but I'd always been an open book. This time, he was wrong. I wanted answers. I just didn't want answers that came with more questions.

He looked at Sabina and Mitzi. "Not a word. Do you understand?"

Sabina and Mitzi both nodded, and we didn't talk about it up on the roof. But the next day, Mitzi brought me a stack of paper from the workshop, and I folded doves until my room was full of them. Each time, my fingers were a little faster. I remembered making an origami crane move when I was little and a friend accusing me of tricking her, of putting strings on the wings. It'd hurt, and I hadn't understood it then.

Kai was wrong. I didn't ask questions because this time I knew the answer.

Sabina never came back to the roof with us. Kai said it was because she was working, not because of the doves. I wasn't sure if I believed him. Kai suggested one night that they could get me over the wall easy enough, and at least then I'd be safe. I'd be whisked back to America. Right place, wrong time, instead of wrong place, wrong time. Half was better than none, he said. I didn't know what to say because he was wrong—it wouldn't be better—but I hadn't turned him down yet.

Kai and Mitzi passed a cigarette between them as they quizzed me on my German. Mitzi teased Kai, and the few times I joined in, she seemed delighted to have a coconspirator. She hooked her pinkie around mine and declared me *klasse*.

"That'd be your Stasi code name," she said, her pinkie tight around mine.

"No," Kai argued. "It'd be *Reh*. A doe. With those eyes."

He didn't look at me, so he couldn't have seen the flush rising on my cheeks. But Mitzi snorted. I pushed it back at her, even though my voice shook a little bit. "What's your name?"

"Oh, we know what my name is," Mitzi said, lighting a new cigarette. "I'm *Farbe*. Kai is—"

"Enough, Mitzi," Kai said, his voice low. "She doesn't have to worry about the Stasi."

"Liar," Mitzi said softly, and neither Kai nor I had any reply to this. I knew they were trying to keep the police from noticing me. But if the police were monitoring Mitzi and Kai already, then they knew about me. I was strangely unalarmed by this revelation. I'd time-traveled. What were the Stasi after that?

Some nights, Kai and Mitzi let slip gossip from the balloon workshop. Balloons unaccounted for in the stockrooms. A Runner who had disappeared. Maybe the Stasi, said Mitzi, and Kai nodded, but neither of them sounded convinced. We all paused when we saw movement along the wall and breathed simultaneous sighs of relief when the person kept walking, alone and dark, throwing shadows from the streetlights.

"Sabina could spy for us," Mitzi said one night.

"No," Kai said without blinking. "We're not asking her to do anything illegal. She's a kid, Mitzi."

"Yes," Mitzi said, moving around him to stand by me instead. She almost always stood between us, as if to remind me that their friendship came first, but tonight she placed me in the middle. "Because the rest of what we all do is so legal."

"You know what I mean," Kai replied darkly.

When Mitzi asked me to tell a story, I couldn't. I didn't know which one to tell. I didn't know which one felt most true. Sometimes, I thought my memory was lying to me. Maybe I remembered things wrong. Maybe I only remembered things the way I wanted to remember them. I built the maybes up inside me like a wall around my heart and hid behind them.

Chapter Eleven

A GIFT OF FREEDOM

East Berlin, German Democratic Republic, April 1988

Ellie

The nighttime was so full of adventure and adrenaline, avoiding the police and looking over the wall into West Berlin, that the daytime dragged in comparison. I couldn't leave the house because I had no papers, and it was, naturally, harder to sneak around in broad daylight. When she caught on to my boredom, Mitzi brought me a radio. I hadn't ever seen one that wasn't in a car, but I didn't tell her that.

She showed me the dial and tuned it to a pirate radio show called *Radio Glasnost*. "We make it here on tapes, but you can't broadcast it here. Too dangerous," she explained, moving the radio closer to the window for better reception. "So it gets smuggled back into West Berlin and broadcast over."

I asked her how she found out about it, and she tossed her head a little bit, giving me a wicked smile. "They need *someone* with good music taste to run the tapes to the West Germans."

The punk music from the show infiltrated my dreams. When I helped Mitzi cook, she translated lyrics for me. I couldn't understand all of the German politics, but I started to catch on to certain stories and she filled in the blanks. Kai hated talking politics, but Mitzi didn't.

When I asked Kai why, he just shrugged. "It's her life. This is her country. It's not mine."

And she gave up everything for it. I asked her once if she had family, and she shrugged. "I do, but they don't know where I am. It's better this way. They can't inform on me, and I can't put them at risk."

I'd stared at her and finally blurted out, "I'm sorry."

It was the first time I'd seen her look a little sad. She had squeezed my arm as she passed me on her way upstairs. "Don't be. It isn't your fault."

Kai, Mitzi, and I were playing cards over lunch (a game of Hearts could keep even a sad mind busy for an hour) and listening to the radio when we heard the front door lock turning. Mitzi snapped off the radio. Kai moved fluidly out of his chair and grabbed my arm. He hauled me upright and shoved me toward the pantry in the kitchen while Mitzi headed for the front hall.

"Ow," I whispered, rubbing my arm.

"Stay quiet." His hand gripped my arm a little tighter as if to prove a point. "Don't come out until you hear me call you. *Verstehen Sie mich?*"

"Ja," I said, and he shut the door in my face. *Never change, Kai. Never change.* Hot and cold. (Literally hot. It was hard not to blush at the thought of his hand on my arm just now. And at the same time, cold. He held his cards close to his chest.)

The pantry closet smelled of stale pretzels and the foul glue they put down to keep out the mice. I'd probably die from inhaling that in a space without ventilation, but maybe whoever was out there would kill me too. I held my breath so as not to die and so I could better eavesdrop. The footsteps in the front hall were heavier than Kai's or Mitzi's, and I heard German exchanged in low voices. The longer it went, when I heard Kai's voice pitch higher but I couldn't make out the words, the more my muscles began to shake with anxiety.

Stasi, or Volkspolizei. That's why Kai was panicking. I sank to the floor, pressing my head against my knees.

The other voice, new, was definitely male. Calm and authoritative. I couldn't make out all of the words—German was still easier for me if I was figuring out context too—but then I heard him say, "*Papers.*" And I really started to panic. I curled my hands into fists, my nails cutting into the soft flesh on my palm.

They had found me. And since I didn't have papers, they'd hand me over to the Stasi and I'd never get home. I would break under torture. They'd be waterboarding me for information I didn't have, and I could never make it stop. I'd die. I'd die. I should eat some of the rat poison. I thought about it for a good long moment, but I was too scared, shaking too hard to stand up and find the box in the back of the pantry. In my mind's eye, I could see it: red with bold black letters warning that it was poison. If I just held a handful of it, I could take it as needed. I unfurled myself and scooted backward, fumbling as quietly as I could. I found the box and its worn-down edges. I scooped a handful of the teal powder into my hand and curled it back into a ball.

When the door opens, I'll just take it. It's like my own cyanide pill.

The heavy, unfamiliar footsteps crossed the foyer and into the kitchen.

I won't feel a thing.

I wished I had a paper dove then. That a Stasi or a Volkspolizei wouldn't be the last thing I saw.

More German. A chair knocked over. The clatter of a cup to the floor.

Mitzi and Kai couldn't keep them from finding me. They were only teenagers like me.

A voice, dark and low, "*Wo ist sie?*"

"*Verstecken*," Mitzi said. Hiding. Not for long.

"I'll get her. Ellie," said Kai, his voice faint behind the door. "Come on out."

I shook my head even though he couldn't see me, rocking back and forth. Tears streaked my cheeks and left damp spots on the knees of my jeans. The door jerked open and I flinched, burying my head against my legs. *Do it, Ellie, do it.* But I couldn't make myself bring my fistful of rat poison to my mouth. I couldn't.

"Ellie?" Kai's voice dropped, filling with worry. He sank to the floor next to me, touching my shoulder. "Ellie. It's Ashasher. Remember? The raven man. He's here for you."

My shoulders shook despite how hard I held myself in so I wouldn't just burst into hysterical laughter or sobs. Ashasher. Not the Volkspolizei.

I hiccupped and Kai sighed, slipping an arm around my shoulders, surprising me. His warm voice next to my ear whispered, "You're safe. Take a deep breath."

I inhaled deeply, trying not to transfer all my anxiety into the skin on the back of my neck where Kai's arm brushed against my bare skin, grazing the soft hairs that had escaped from my ponytail. He took another deep breath and said, "You have to breathe out too, Ellie."

I breathed out in a burst of laughter. I could feel his smile in the small space between us. I hiccupped again. "Ashasher."

"Yeah," Kai said, his thumb running a small circle on my shoulder. I shivered, and he stopped immediately. It wasn't uncomfortable, but it made the space between us feel small and the closet feel very large.

"Not Volkspolizei," I added to convince myself.

"Definitely not Volkspolizei," he reassured me. His hand ran down my arm, and I held my breath. He tugged at my fist. "What's this?"

"Rat poison?" Hard to explain that two minutes ago I'd been planning my suicide to avoid interrogation and torture.

Kai's expression was unreadable in the dark, but his breathing changed, turned ragged at the edges, as if he had just run a long distance. His warm fingers slid between mine, and he unbent my fingers from my palm, letting the cyan powder fall to the ground between us. Without saying anything and without letting go of my hand, he pulled me to my feet. I shook as we walked out of the pantry and to the kitchen sink.

Mitzi and Ashasher's gazes hung on us, heavy and stubborn, as Kai turned on the faucet and ran all four of our hands underneath it, rinsing off the poison. His face remained stoic and thoughtful as he turned over my hands, small and pale, in his larger brown ones.

The water ran teal and the steam rose from the basin, smelling slightly acidic. Kai's eyes lifted to mine, and his mouth tightened. I almost said I was sorry.

But I wasn't sorry. Instead, I whispered, "No ghosts, remember?"

He squeezed my hands, and his Adam's apple bobbed in his throat.

"Ellie," Ashasher said.

I blinked back at Ashasher. Today the feathers swirled slowly, a languid movement, like a finger stirring a small circle in a pond or a pool. "Yes, sir."

Kai snorted and Ashasher smiled, a strange and disconcerting break from his smooth and otherwise calm face. His dark eyes, intermittently visible through the feathers, narrowed slightly. "You don't have to call me, sir, Ellie. You thought I was here to take you home."

Kai dropped my hands and gave me a hand towel. I dried them, thinking of the owl towels in my mother's kitchen. Home. I hadn't thought that was a possible reason for Ashasher's presence, and for a split second, my heart skipped a beat. But he wouldn't have said it like that if it were true. I said, proud of how my voice barely shook, "I thought you were Volkspolizei, actually."

Ashasher's head tipped to the side. His voice sounded gravelly and genuine when he said, "I apologize for any anxiety I may have caused you, dear child."

Maybe a month ago, in my time, with my school classmates, I was a child. But I no longer felt like a child. I was no more a child than Mitzi or Kai who ran around with magic balloons and helped the Stasi's most wanted escape East Berlin. I stayed quiet.

Ashasher reached into his coat and withdrew a small folded piece of paper. "In lieu of successfully returning you to your time period, the Council has decided to provide you with papers so you may travel as freely as any East German citizen. That is to say, not very freely at all, but freely enough to be in broad daylight."

I took the paper with trembling hands. "What?"

"You can go out," Kai explained, his voice quiet and gentle. "In daylight."

"You're not a prisoner," Mitzi added. "No more than the rest of us, anyway."

"You could leave," I said. "On a balloon."

Mitzi shrugged. "Not really. We all have reasons for staying. But at least you don't have to stay in the house during the day anymore."

I looked at Kai, then Ashasher. "Can I go out alone?"

"When your German is good enough," Ashasher said. I deflated a bit. My German was still rough, even with the radio and newspaper practice. "And we are still working on a way home for you, Ellie. It involves some politics and us learning magic we aren't supposed to do, but we *are* working on it."

"Thank you," I whispered. I held the paper to my chest. A brand-new passport. This one could carry me over the threshold in daylight. And the threat of the police had been mitigated, at least a little. I was no longer a vampire by circumstance.

Chapter Twelve

ZERBERUS

East Berlin, German Democratic Republic, April 1988

Kai

Ellie stuck in my head like a burr, and I couldn't shake her loose. I did the night shifts, didn't talk much to her, and definitely didn't take her out again, even though she had papers now. I couldn't forget the look on her face when I found the rat poison clenched in her hands. I couldn't decide if she was the bravest or most foolhardy person I'd ever known. Or the way she'd whispered, *No ghosts, remember?*

I knew avoiding her was a shitty thing to do. But there were only so many times I could put myself in the position of being alone with a girl from the future who I really wanted to kiss. I nearly did then in the kitchen, in front of Ashasher and Mitzi, and I couldn't risk that happening. It probably violated some sort of code of conduct to make out with a Passenger. It definitely violated Romipen, our Romani way of life.

There was just something about her. She was vulnerable without being fragile, and a part of me was jealous of her, and awed by her. Apparently in my head, jealousy and awe made me want to kiss her? It didn't make sense to me either. The way the doves she made moved unnerved me. I kept waiting for Sabina to say something to Ashasher or Aurora, but she didn't. And I certainly didn't mention it to anyone, lest they want her to stay and become one of them instead of finding her a way home.

Mostly, I didn't want her to become a Schöpfer. One of them. Anyway, work kept me busy and all. I had a new Stasi tail. The Volkspolizei passed by the house too many times for me to be comfortable, and a bald man in a tan coat kept showing up whenever I went out for food or tried to go to the workshop. Whoever he worked for, he made me work to slip away from him. On top of that, we had two musicians in a row, and honest to god, I have nothing against music, but neither of them got the *be quiet* command. They both sat in those houses playing the music that got them in trouble in the first place. What part of *Lie low and keep your head down* did they not understand? Every Passenger petitioned the Council to get over the wall. Their spots were valuable.

The Council was one of those rumors, the same way conspiracy theorists were pretty sure that the West had infiltrated the Communist parties around the world. Like that explained Gorbachev. When would people learn that no leader of any state, free or Communist, gave a shit about us people? We were all out here, flotsam and jetsam, floundering. We only had each other. That's all.

I collected cigarette butts on the rooftop and looked for balloons at the wall. But whoever had sent that one off when I took Ellie out was being careful. All the balloons stayed on schedule, and no one else died like Garrick. Mitzi began to relax, but I couldn't. Something about the whole thing just rubbed me the wrong way.

I thought about it as I leaned against a tree and I scouted out a potential Passenger for the Schöpfers. A good portion of the petitions were from the secret police, the Stasi. They knew people were leaving. They kept eyes and ears on all of us Runners. We knew that much because they kept tabs on just about everyone who hit their radar. Our movements were unpredictable; we were young; we weren't infrequently caught after dark and arrested for breaking curfew.

Truth be told, we didn't mind so much if it kept them off the Schöpfers. If the Schöpfers were arrested, we'd be shit out of luck. If I got arrested, I'd be shit out of luck, but I wasn't the whole program. Sometimes we Runners asked what would happen if we got arrested, and the Schöpfers were always vague enough for us to know they wouldn't risk the whole mission to bail us out.

This potential Passenger was a former Politburo official. He had copied documents. He was on house arrest, making it hard to move him, but interestingly, his house arrest didn't seem to stop him from chatting with the police officers outside the door. Rather amiably. I flicked my lighter on and off while watching him. I was trying to figure out if I trusted him or whether he was just a very good plant when a knife blade caressed my throat.

Not good.

"Drop the lighter, Runner," said an absurdly pleasant voice. Male. Melodic. The kind you expect from someone about to drop you to the floor with a red smile.

The inside of his wrist had an infinity symbol tattooed, and I smiled.

"Zerberus," I said, naming the organization that oversaw all Councils. They were our watchdogs, things of fairy tales and legends. They rarely interfered where Councils worked though. This was new. I'd definitely never heard of Zerberus holding any of us Runners at knifepoint.

I focused on what I knew. The angle of the knife told me he was taller than me. My elbows were probably at kidney level.

Convenient. "I love the way you say good morning. It's so pleasant. Upbeat. Refreshing in this day and age."

He was quiet for two beats, then the knife tapped my neck. I flinched despite myself. "You have a mouth, Kai Holwell."

"That's what all the girls say," I quipped, but my pulse jumped in my neck, colliding with the knife. He knew my name, which meant he knew more about me than I knew about him.

"Ah. Come along then. That Passenger is a Stasi informer. He did in fact copy documents, but they will pardon him if he can turn in one or two of you. Not even all of you. Let's have *kaffee und kuchen*, shall we?"

Yes. Because coffee and cake was exactly what I liked to do with strangers who held knives to my throat. I swallowed back a number of witty replies. The knife lifted from my neck and I turned, carefully and slowly in case he'd rather I die facing him. The guy wasn't much older than me, in his early twenties, with a shaved head and tattoos up the side of his neck. His left arm had a python going down it, ending with the head on his palm, and his right arm was bare except for the infinity symbol. He stood maybe six inches taller than me, but was easily twice as broad.

Long story short, the guy was a beast. And in a world that was far more hierarchical than it cared to admit, this beast was my boss's boss's boss. He pointed at a café down the street, and I willingly followed. I wasn't inept. The best way to do my job well and save lives was to stay alive.

We sat down over coffee, and the Zerberus representative— who attracted a lot of attention in the café, and not the kind of attention I wanted to attract—held up his finger to his mouth. He took a ring off his left hand and placed it on the table. It began to hum, low enough not to vibrate on the table but just enough that I could hear it, and the curious looks in our direction turned away.

"That's a neat trick," I said coolly. "Willing to trade for it?"

"Perhaps." He leaned back in his chair and gestured to me. "Tell me, Kai. How is your sister?"

I flinched, pulling my eyes away from the ring on the table. "Better here than she'd be with you."

Almost three years ago, Zerberus came for my sister. At the same time, my family wanted to put her in an institution. Leave her behind. Someone said she was a genius. Someone said she was insane. It didn't matter if they wanted to use her, or my family wanted to forget her for what her magic had done when it ran over her edges. She was still my sister. I brought her here, accepting Ashasher's offer, because the Zerberus rarely cared what individual Councils did. They didn't know names. They didn't care to know names. The Zerberus needed the Council here, where life was terrible, more than they wanted the Council to hand over my sister. At least, so I thought. Until now. I should have known they'd come for her eventually.

"She is well, then." The man poured a little milk into his coffee. "My name is Felix Kohn, and you know who I work for. I am not here for Sabina."

My chest deflated in relief, but my words still came out with more bite than I intended. "She is not yours to take."

"Nor is she yours," Felix said, raising an eyebrow. "She is thirteen, yes? She makes her own decisions."

"If you're not here for her…" I said, trying to keep my voice even. Not that easy when the person you'd give up just about everything for had been threatened in previous conversations. "Then why do you care about me?"

"Because you are protecting the Zeitreisende," he said. "We confiscated the balloon in question before the Council destroyed it."

"The broken balloon? The Council…Ashasher and Aurora said that they had to destroy it," I managed to croak. *Ellie. They're coming for Ellie.*

"That decision was made without consulting us. We were able to confiscate it prior to destruction." Felix offered me a cigarette, and I shook my head. I needed to focus. "We do not believe that magic was accidental, Kai."

I blinked. "What?"

"What happened was not an accident. They said it was an accident, but it was not a 'chronological anomaly.' It might not have been the intended effect, but the equations on that balloon were altered subtly and the ink is profoundly different." He sipped at his coffee. "We're concerned the Council has been compromised."

I looked around at the crowds of people around us. "By Stasi?"

Out of the corner of my eye, I saw Felix shake his head. His pale-blue eyes unnerved me when they fixed back on my face. "No. Tell me what you know about Ashasher and Aurora."

Frustration welled inside me. Made the inside of my skin itch. I pressed my lips together and then said carefully, "I don't know much. Honest. Aurora's Polish, I think. And Ashasher... I've never asked."

"Why not?" Felix asked calmly.

I lifted an eyebrow. "What, you haven't noticed the feathers? I don't know what they are or how he controls them, but I was raised to respect magic where it exists. And I'm not messing with that."

"Aurora and Ashasher are at the heart of all of this," Felix said. This I knew. He looked around the café at the others dining around us. "You and I...Would we be who we are without the work we do?"

I didn't like where this train of thought was going. "Then why come to me? What if I'm one of them?"

"You're not," he said.

The dots connected in my head. "You've been tailing me."

He shrugged. "We have reason to believe that you would not betray the work you're doing here. You have gone to extreme measures to keep your sister safe, even from elements of Zerberus, and so we believe you'd never willingly or knowingly put her in danger."

I shoved the coffee toward the middle of the table and stood up before I even registered his words. "Willingly or knowingly. Is she in danger?"

"We don't know, but we do not think that the Council is targeting its own people. Sit down, Kai. You're attracting attention." Felix's voice remained mild. I wanted to punch him in the face as I obeyed. He surveyed me with his heavy brow and those scary eyes. Like he knew me. I pushed back my chair again, and he frowned. "Kai, we came to you for information and for assistance. I want you to tell me if you see anything suspicious or know of anything."

I thought about the balloon going over the wall on the wrong night and the missing balloons from the storeroom. The Runner who had disappeared. "Why me?"

"Because you have Eleanor Ruth Baum," he said simply. "And I believe you will protect her as fiercely as you protect your sister."

"How do you know this?" I asked him. The other part of my brain said, *Ellie's full name is Eleanor? As pretty as she is.* Like a damn burr in my brain, that girl.

"You think we'd let a girl like Sabina, with all her talent and all of her incredible intellect, disappear with just anyone? When you moved her here, we thought about taking her against your will and hers. We worried about her safety. But you proved to be as good a guardian as we could have hoped."

Nothing like being told that someone had *let* you protect your sister to really kick off the day right.

I said, "What makes you think I'd give you my loyalty?"

Felix's smile was small and cruel. "I don't need it. I just need you to know that I need the information to protect Mitzi, Sabina, and Ellie. Otherwise..." He spread his hands wide, letting his voice trail off. Just like Ashasher had done after the Council meeting.

Blackmailed. Or close enough. I scowled at him. "And how do I find you?"

"Here. I like to have coffee here in the afternoons," Felix said. "Take care, Kai."

"Fuck off," I said as pleasantly as I could. "And thanks for the coffee."

I took the coffee cup when I left. I needed another cup at home anyway.

Chapter Thirteen

GOD AND THE GHETTO

Łódź Ghetto, Poland, December 1941

Benno

I came home from work one day and found my father sitting shirtless in our freezing home, staring at nothing in particular. I clapped my hands together and exhaled. My breath puffed out slowly, a gray ghost wisp in front of my face. I watched him out of the corner of my eye as I checked the hiding spot for our bread. There was none left. We'd all go hungry until the next day's soup. No surprise. Mama said she had a few marks and would try to buy a few beets off a lady in the hatmaking factory.

"Papa," I said. "Why are you shirtless?"

He said, "I traded it for a cigarette."

"Are you a fool?" I cried in shock. I went over and shook him by his shoulders. "What did you do that for?"

All his bones stuck out of his chest. His stomach was wrinkled and rolled over the tops of his trousers. He smelled, but then, we all did. He stared past me at the door and said, "We don't even have a mezuzah."

We didn't have a mezuzah on our doorway, not a single one,

back in Berlin. I didn't tell him that though. I said, "I'll try to find one."

He nodded and said, "Without it, how can God see us here?"

"Perhaps God doesn't care," I said.

"You are weak," he said, "if your faith in God can be shaken by a few evil people."

"It's not a few, Papa," I said. "It's a continent. They will not stop until we're all gone."

He shook his head and then made his most rational statement of the night. "You get those words out of your mouth before your mother and Ruth get home. You must not let them hear you despairing."

I was not despairing. I was beyond despair. I was flat. I went about each day the same as the day before and the same as the day before that. I had no doubts that tomorrow and the day after that would be more of the same. We could not break bread at Shabbat because there was no bread. We could not say the Kaddish because there was no wine, no water, just dingy snow. Maybe my father said prayers still, in hopes that someone, somewhere, could hear them. But I didn't. Not anymore.

I just wanted to do the best job I could as often as I could. Food, and sleep, in the shared bed with my sister, the rats, and the lice, with the sound of Ruth's remaining cough. This was what I lived for. I lived for trading a few marks next week to the boy who chased after the potato truck with a fork on the end of a stick. He gathered enough potatoes to charge four marks a spud. Ghetto economy.

I hoped the Judenrat, the Jewish council that ran the ghetto, froze to death. I hoped my father did not. Though I was younger and thinner than him, Mama and I found one of my old shirts that fit him. We dressed him where he sat, and Mama only made noises of agreement when he expressed his concerns about the lack of a mezuzah. We cling to strange things when we no longer believe we'll see the sun.

Chapter Fourteen

A BODY IN THE STREET

East Berlin, German Democratic Republic, April 1988

Ellie

I felt parts of me waking up that I hadn't known existed. Recklessness, when I should have been afraid. Courage, when I should have been wary. Once, I'd considered myself even and balanced. Now the only feelings that surged through me like pulses of electricity were extremes. My mood rose and fell, but it was highest when I was out of the house.

I wanted that high more than anything. Maybe even sometimes more than I wanted to go home. Home had never felt like this. I didn't tell Mitzi or Kai this though, because I didn't want the balloon makers to stop looking for a way home for me. And because the guilt gnawed away at my courage, at my recklessness. I was reckless in a place where they couldn't risk being anything less than cautious.

When I decided to sneak out of the apartment, it felt like a betrayal. My German is strong, I told myself, as I borrowed one of the warm keys off the hook in the front hallway. *I won't get caught.* But the Volkspolizei and the Stasi were not the only ones I worried about catching me. I heard Kai asking Mitzi about whether she had been approached by a man with a python tattoo on his arm and an infinity symbol on his right wrist.

Mitzi had said, "Don't be a fool, Kai. He's an informant. He couldn't be real. I've been doing this longer than you. I've never heard of Zerberus approaching a Runner."

"I didn't tell him about the balloon Ellie and I saw."

"Probably for the best," Mitzi said after a pause. "He really thinks the balloons are being tampered with?"

When I asked Kai, he told me eavesdropping was rude. It was easier to bribe Mitzi into spilling the beans. While I French-braided her hair, she caught me up on all the gossip. I didn't understand why Kai didn't tell the Zerberus what he knew, but I didn't like the idea of someone who scared Mitzi and Kai. I hadn't even known that was possible. They flaunted their Stasi code names, the police who lingered outside the windows, the suspicion of their neighbors. But here, suddenly, their wariness had me on high alert.

My desperation to feel and move won over my desire to remain within the bolded lines of the rules in this world. One evening, I found myself putting on my coat, hat, scarf, and mittens before walking out the front door after Kai. I didn't see any soldiers or policemen around the street, and definitely no scary guys with python tattoos, so I said a quick prayer of thanks to cover my bases and set off in the damp spring night to follow him wherever he was going.

For me alone, East Berlin was as frightening, aloof, and wary as it appeared from the window—with an added dose of foreboding. I thought I was breathing too noisily, so I rewrapped my scarf around my mouth, trying to muffle the sound. I crossed under streetlights and my shadow split into two figures. My heart leaped and jumped around like I'd gone for a run. I turned, looking over my shoulder frequently.

When Kai stopped, I took advantage of the opportunity to catch my breath. I had no clue where I was. We'd moved into an area far from the house and the entrance to the workshop, my two reference points. I knew we were moving away from the wall, which didn't make sense to me since the rooftop was literally against the wall. I chewed on my lower lip beneath the scarf, wondering if I was going to be able to get home. *Home.* Kai knocked on a plain dark door. It opened and as he stepped inside, Mitzi's teal hair caught in the light of the hall.

At that point, I realized how insane this idea was. I'd followed someone I'd known two months across a city I didn't know at all for no reason other than to do something that didn't involve sitting still. The strangest thing was how lonely standing four blocks away from your only friends could be. My desire to be closer was a dark ache that lurched in my stomach.

"Ellie Baum," said a soft voice behind me.

I spun around, stepping away from the wall and into the light of the streetlights. A woman dressed in a long black cloak and with her dark hair swept back in a tight ponytail followed me into the light. "My name is Aurora. You don't need to be afraid. I'm one of the balloon makers."

I'd heard her name enough that I relaxed, but only a fraction. She was a Schöpfer. She had made the balloon that Garrick used. *My* balloon. The broken one. I whispered, "I know I'm not supposed to be out. But—"

"I imagine you're tired of being dragged around like a small child." She tilted her head a little bit. In the night, the only way she stood out from the shadows was her purple scarf tucked into a black coat long enough to brush the streets. She looked past me. "I've been worried about the balloons."

"Because of the people who died," I guessed.

She inclined her head just enough that I read it as a yes. "I want to make sure that their Passenger goes safely tonight. I am rather attached to him, you see."

Just then, Kai and Mitzi emerged with an old man between them. Mitzi handed the man a cane, and they exchanged a few words. My heart clenched as he turned, looked upward at the house, and blew it a kiss. He slipped and staggered on the wet streets. Mitzi held him up by an elbow. Kai reached inside the house and took hold of a red balloon. He shut the door behind him forcefully, glanced up and down the street, and then the three of them turned and headed back up the street in the direction of the wall. Another Passenger then. This one frail. I wondered how they picked the Passengers. I thought about asking Aurora, but she gestured for me to follow her so I tucked the question away in my mind.

We wove our way through the city, spilling through archways and narrow wandering streets and wide boulevards. The houses around us changed from older homes with small gardens to large apartment complexes built by the GDR government.

At the apartment complex by the wall, Kai unlocked the door and pulled the red balloon into the stairwell I knew well. They were sending the Passenger from the same rooftop where we stood so many nights. Mitzi helped the Passenger through the doorway. He looked older than my grandfather. I wondered if he had fought for or against the Nazis, and then I tried to crush that thought from my mind.

"You should go," Aurora said gently. "Before Kai and Mitzi see you on their return."

"Can you see the balloon?" I asked curiously.

She nodded. "But sometimes, I still like to see the light on the other side of the wall. Sometimes, even I do not trust my own eyes and my own magic."

"Do you think I was foolish to take a risk like this?"

Aurora paused and looked at me. "We take the risks we need to take, Ellie Baum. We all need to feel free. I'll keep your secret."

I whispered my thanks and then turned around, orienting myself. The guard tower was around the corner, and though my papers were a comforting presence in my coat, I didn't really want to run into that sort of trouble. I began to walk back on the street, largely ignored by the people around me, and I liked that anonymity. Sneaking out and passing as an East German on the street sent a powerful thrill through my veins. I shivered again. I wished I'd stayed and walked home with the others. Or at least asked Aurora to walk me home.

The streets were unnaturally still by the wall, and I held my breath as I cut across the street and down an alley toward the street where I lived. I could hear the tram in the distance and the rumble of cars idling at the light on our corner. Feel my heartbeat in my palms. *Almost home. Almost safe.*

I tripped and stumbled, hitting the ground. I rolled over, grimacing and rubbing my knees, and stared at the boot that I'd tripped over. A boot. Attached to a leg. Attached to a body. I clapped my hand over my mouth, trying not to scream, as I scrambled to my feet. My hands shook violently, vibrating against my face as I wiped at sudden tears in my eyes. My breath rattled in my chest. The alley remained empty, but I tried calling for help anyway.

"*Hallo? Hilf mir!*" My voice echoed off the damp buildings. Not a single light turned on. No one appeared at the ends of the street. I stepped closer to the body, masked in shadows. I nudged the foot with my foot. Probably some drunk—but the foot felt stiff, and the body didn't stir.

"Oh my G-d, oh my G-d, oh my G-d," I whispered to myself. I dropped my hands to my sides and shook them out hard. "You can do this, Ellie. Okay, just check for a pulse."

I crouched by the body, by a limp, pale hand sticking out of a dark jacket sleeve. Sobbing, I turned over the cold, stiff hand with my thumb and forefinger, my other hand clapped over my mouth. The hand opened slightly as I turned it, and I barely stopped the scream from escaping my mouth when a cell phone tumbled out of the person's hand.

A *cell phone*. Another time traveler. Someone from *my time*. I covered my face and took a deep breath. *Ellie. Focus. Breathe.* I inhaled slowly, and let the breath out slowly. My legs shook, so I rocked onto my knees. I turned over the phone. The screen still lit up, but it didn't find any service. Duh. No satellites. I swallowed and checked the text messages, looking at the date. Not the same year as me. Three years before I even came to Berlin and saw the red balloon. But another time traveler for sure. And for some reason, this one didn't survive.

"I have to get Kai. I'll be back," I promised the corpse. I stood up, feeling dizzy, and slipped the phone into my pocket. I turned to walk up the alley, and stopped dead in my tracks.

A tall, broad-shouldered man walked toward me, shrouded in shadow, but I could see his shaved head and the tattoos going up his neck and down his arms. The python tattoo. The infinity tattoo. *The Zer-whatever-that-word-was guy. The one Kai and Mitzi were talking about.* I opened my mouth to scream, but the man held up a finger and said quickly in perfect English, "Don't scream, please, Ellie. I am here to help."

He made no move to hurt me, frozen as I was, just beelined for the body. He pressed his fingers into the dark, I supposed by the throat, and waited. He sighed deeply. "Dead."

"I just found him like that," I squeaked in German.

"You're not in trouble," he murmured, standing up and looking around the alley. "Go home, Ellie. I'll take care of this. You shouldn't be here if the police come by. Go home."

"He died," I said softly. "But I lived."

He sighed. "You did. Go home, Ellie. Tell Kai what happened when he gets home. He knows how to find me."

"But he's from the future," I said, looking at the body. "So he just dies here? He is just a missing person that'll never be found?"

"How would you like me to inform your police?" His cool tone chilled me straight to my bones.

I flinched. "Who are you?"

"My name is Felix Kohn," he said, crouching by the body again. "I work for the Zerberus, but I expect you knew that. We're the watchdog group for the Councils who use magic balloons to help people escape from places where human rights violations are occurring. Normally, I take care of people like Kai's sister who are considered very valuable because of their talents. But I've been assigned here because of your balloon."

"Where's his balloon?" I asked, looking around the alley.

Felix's eyebrows raised, and his eyes flickered up to me. "That is a very good question. But that is my job, Ellie, not yours. Go home. Stay safe. Tell Kai and Mitzi what happened."

I nodded, backed up a few steps, then spun, running home as fast as I could. I didn't care if I attracted any attention. I shut the door hard behind me and sank to the floor, shaking like mad. Only then did I realize I still had the second time traveler's cell phone in my pocket. I hung up my jacket and curled up on the couch, pulling a blanket around my shoulders. Tucking my knees up to my chin, I waited for Kai and Mitzi to come home.

I tried to make paper doves, but I failed. We were short on paper, so I smoothed out my attempts again and again until there were no creases on the page.

Mostly, I waited and tried not to cry.

Kai and Mitzi stomped into the house a few hours later, laughing and joking in German that I couldn't translate. They both stopped in the doorway of the living room, staring at me. Mitzi murmured something to Kai and disappeared into the kitchen. I heard her filling a kettle for tea. Kai slowly pulled off his coat and scarf, watching me with unsure eyes. He sank down onto the couch next to me, leaning his elbow on the back.

"You look like you've seen a ghost," he said, and his eyes

flickered around the room. Like there'd be a visible ghost to explain my condition.

"I…" I swallowed and closed my eyes against the tears swelling up in them. My fists came up to my face again.

"Ellie," Kai whispered and scooted closer to me. His hands closed over mine, and he tried to tug my fists off my cheeks. "Ellie, *was ist los*? What's wrong? Please."

"There was a body," I finally managed to say. My voice sounded weird in my ears. "In the streets. I followed you. There was a body. Then Felix came."

"Breathe," Kai ordered me. "Ellie, you have to breathe." I took a deep breath, and he relaxed a bit. "Start again, Ellie. You followed us tonight. Okay. Where was the body? What body? Why was Felix there?"

"There was another time traveler," I said, lifting my chin to look at his eyes through the space between my shaking arms. "This one was dead."

Chapter Fifteen

ZEITREISENDER

East Berlin, German Democratic Republic, April 1988

Kai

Another time traveler. Ellie's words sank into my gut, a heavy stone dropping into the ocean. I stared at her, at her light-brown hair pulled back into a messy knot, at her tear-swollen blue eyes. Her hands in mine were ice-cold, the kind of clammy cold that came from adrenaline kicks, and her bottom lip trembled. I tried not to think about her sneaking out…That was a whole different conversation. I might be an idiot sometimes, but I wasn't the type of idiot who'd scold her for leaving the house alone when she just tripped over a body in the alley. I shuddered at the thought. I wouldn't have wanted to trip over a body, and I'd seen dead people before. What were the chances she had?

"El," I said, my voice cracking like a fault line. I pulled at her wrists until she scooted forward, and we wrapped our arms around each other. The sobs snapped from her, and I closed my eyes against the force of her. I whispered something nonsensical, an old Romani rhyme that meant as little to me as it did to Ellie, and ran a hand down her back.

Mitzi came back into the living room and set down a tray with tea on the coffee table. She sat on the other side of the couch and rubbed Ellie's back. Mitzi usually couldn't stand crying people. People crying made her want to cry. She leaned over Ellie's back so we were sandwiching her between us. I don't know if we thought we were going to protect her from her sadness or what, but it seemed to help—the lullabies and our pile of sadness on the couch.

I raised an eyebrow at Mitzi, who nodded her head a little at me. I ran a hand down Ellie's back to her waist and pressed her backward a bit. She didn't let go of me. "Ellie, I have to go find Felix and Ashasher."

"Please don't leave," she whispered into my chest.

God, I really didn't want to leave. I didn't want to leave anyone, honestly, and I didn't want anyone to leave.

I pressed my lips against the side of her head. Not exactly a kiss. Definitely not nothing. "I have to go. I'll be back."

I forced myself not to look at her when I slid off the couch and headed for the door again. If I turned around, I might not leave. And if I didn't leave, too many others wouldn't leave. If there was a dead time traveler, I had more than one dead body. It meant that Felix, damn him, was right. Ellie's balloon wasn't a mistake. Someone was tampering with balloons. It might mean that Peter, the old man we sent over today after he was denied permission to join his family in West Berlin, was the Passenger who died for the balloon to cross time. The light had gone on at the church, but I needed to find a way to verify he had survived.

First, Felix. I checked the café, but there was only a feather sitting on a table. I rubbed my face and stared at it before pocketing it, in case it was one of Ashasher's feathers. I didn't know if it was a signal to Felix or to Ashasher, but either way, I didn't think it should sit there in public. And maybe I wanted it. Ashasher never specifically said that his feathers had magical properties, but they flew around his head and his mood determined their speed. Better to be safe than sorry. So the feather went into my pocket.

I waited for a few minutes in the cold, but my mind kept spinning back to Peter disappearing with the balloon and Ellie crying on the couch. If I stood at the café any longer at this time of night, I'd attract the wrong type of attention anyway. I bounced on the balls of my feet, trying to think. Ashasher, I thought, he'll know what to do about a dead time traveler and a Zerberus here making things difficult. Maybe he left the feather for me on purpose. I headed off for the workshop.

The whole way, I was sure that I was being followed. I tried not to look suspicious by glancing around, but I doubled back on my tracks a few times. No one seemed to notice me, but I couldn't shake the feeling of being watched. If it was Felix, I didn't get why he wasn't stepping up to find me. And if it wasn't Felix, I didn't like my chances. After a few laps, I finally went into the tunnels. I couldn't delay any longer.

The workshop was quiet. Still. No doves. No balloons. The space felt bigger, emptier, lonelier without the steady buzz of activity. I waited for the walls to fall down around my ears, for people to come crawling out of the ventilation system or whatever else they did when they were hiding. The Schöpfers stayed in rooms attached to the workshop, while we Runners bounced between whatever safe houses weren't being used. We were disposable. They made sure we knew it. Sabina stayed with them, thank god. She'd do something as irresponsible as Ellie, walking out of the house in the middle of the night for no reason other than feeling bored or wanting to seem exciting. God only knew what went through their heads sometimes.

I took a deep breath. "Ashasher?"

"Kai?" Sabina said, stepping out from behind a column where I hadn't seen her and Aurora standing. She frowned. "What are you doing here?"

"Why are you awake?" I asked, frowning at Aurora. Aurora's hair was loose for once, a wild halo around her face, and she seemed distracted, her eyes following lines on a chalkboard. She didn't acknowledge me in the least.

"We're troubled by equations," Sabina said, turning back to Aurora. "We're trying to solve everything that's gone wrong in the world ever."

This was the version of my sister that couldn't be trusted to make responsible life decisions. This was the version of my sister that I knew very well, the one who would jump from moving trains just to find out what it sounded like when she landed, the one who cut herself to see if she could see her blood change colors. The Schöpfers weren't supposed to be encouraging this type of thought process though.

Three o'clock in the morning, and my sister was talking about solving the world's problems in a mathematical equation. I walked over to the blackboard and said, "What? You found the world's problematique is solvable with a balloon and some pixie dust?"

Sabina tilted her head and frowned at me, her eyes unfocused. "Problematique sounds like it's from French."

"It is," Aurora murmured and then tapped her chalk against the board. "I'm concerned about the distance of dissonance between two balloons with the same magical properties."

She might as well have spoken Latin to me. I rolled my eyes and said, "Aurora. I'm looking for Ashasher."

"We're all looking for someone," came her vague reply. She erased something on the chalkboard with the heel of her hand. She didn't turn to me at all, but Sabina hadn't stopped staring at me.

I pressed my fingers to my forehead. "Are you two high? Did you get my sister high?"

"I don't need altering substances," Sabina said. "My brain is wired alternatively already."

"True," I agreed. I gestured for Sabina to nudge Aurora, but she didn't move. "I need Ashasher."

"He isn't here," Aurora said, still not turning around. "No one who's supposed to be here is here. Everyone who isn't supposed to be here is here."

Whatever the hell she was smoking, I did not want it. I scribbled a note on a piece of paper:

Ashasher,

2nd Zeitreisender. Please find me immediately.

KH

"What do you need from him?" Sabina asked, watching me tape the note beneath Garrick's photo.

I brushed two fingers against his photo and then put the fingers to my lips. "There's a second Zeitreisender."

Sabina and Aurora both turned to stare at me. "A second time traveler," repeated Aurora like her words were made of glass.

"Yeah. But this one was dead on arrival. I can't figure out if our Passenger tonight is still alive."

"Did the light come on?" Aurora asked a little sharply, like she was coming down off her buzz. Sabina anxiously glanced back and forth between us, shifting her weight and wringing her hands. God, whatever they were on was a bad trip. I shrugged and nodded. Aurora turned away with a huff. "Then he is alive."

"Then another balloon went out tonight. This is our night. No one else is scheduled. Where is Ashasher?"

"Undoubtedly working, as you should be. We will look into it. You may go home, Runner." Aurora dismissed me by my title, right in front of my sister.

I took a deep breath. *They're higher than kites right now. You can't fix this now. Let it go, Kai.* "Try not to let my sister wander off while you're smoking whatever shit dope you found, Aurora. Good night."

"Temper, temper," she murmured, but her voice carried all the way into the tunnels.

When I returned home, the lights were off downstairs. I carefully unlaced my boots and took off my coat in the front hall.

"Kai?" whispered Ellie, sitting up on the couch and startling me. I jumped and stumbled, hitting the wall and nearly falling over. She exhaled hard and said, "I'm sorry."

"Hey," I said, resisting the strange and immediate urge to go to her. "You just startled me."

"Did you find Ashasher?" she asked, stumbling over his name sleepily. God. This girl. She'll be the death of me.

"No," I said, scared to leave the hallway. I didn't even want to turn on the light. If I saw her, I'd want to hold her, or kiss her, or I didn't even know what. "I left him a note."

"I'm sorry I left the house. But when I was following you—" she began to say.

"Now that I'm back," I said sharply. "Ellie. If we were ever picked up by the Stasi…"

"I knew what I was doing," she replied. She brushed her hair behind her ear, and my eyes followed the motion. I swallowed and nearly missed her next words. "Aurora was out there. She said she was worried about the balloons. She wanted to make sure your Passenger got off safely. He did, didn't he?"

I paused and then dismissed the brief thought. "Yes, he made it safely."

"Good." Ellie's hands twined in her lap. "Do you think it's painful?"

For a moment, I had no idea what she was talking about. Then it hit me. I whispered, "Dying?"

"Do you think it hurt? For Garrick? For Dylan?"

I didn't ask how she knew the second guy's name. She walked across the room until I could just see a glint of light across her face from the hall light at the top of the stairs. She looked older than sixteen for the first time since she'd come here.

I said, "I think they died right away. They wouldn't have felt anything."

Her lips twitched a little. "Are you saying that to make me feel better?"

"Yes," I said.

"Thank you," she said, and rose on her tiptoes. She kissed me gently, her mouth soft and sure, just like her. I stood speechless in the hallway while she walked up the stairs. The door to her room clicked shut, and I heard the bed above me creak.

I closed my eyes. *Scheiße.*

Chapter Sixteen

IF, THEN

East Berlin, German Democratic Republic, April 1988

Ellie

Kai tried to slip out early in the morning, but I'd thought he might. I was in the kitchen making breakfast when I heard his feet on the stairs, the sound of his jacket sliding on, and the jingle of keys. I took a piece of toast with me as I headed toward the door, holding it in my mouth as I slid my arms into my coat in the front hallway. I wasn't going to mention the kiss, but I also wasn't going to let him pretend last night didn't happen. His eyes weighed heavily on me, and for a moment, I thought he might not say anything at all. But it was Kai, and he couldn't not say anything.

"Ellie," Kai said, his voice clear and steady despite the worry crisscrossing his face. "Please stay here. I have to go to work. I can't…"

He didn't finish his sentence, and I didn't ask him to elaborate. I buttoned up my coat and took the toast out of my mouth. Because I was *not* a teenage boy. "I'm not asking for permission anymore. I went out last night and returned home safe, didn't I?"

"Ellie, you found a body," he pointed out, his hazel eyes more brown and green, wide and wary.

"The body would have been there whether I had left the house or not," I said and stepped toward the door. "It's not Schrödinger's body."

"El," he said, and his hand wrapped around mine. I stilled as he stepped closer to me. His kind lie to me last night, my lips against his, everything distracting me from my purpose. I couldn't get home if I didn't figure out who was tampering with balloons. "Don't be ridiculous."

"Ellie is already a nickname," I said, my tongue thick in my mouth.

I stared stubbornly at the door. He lowered his head so his face was dangerously close to mine. "What?"

"El is not my name. Eleanor or Ellie. Ellie's already a nickname. It doesn't need to be nicknamed any more." I closed my mouth to prevent further babbling. It had sounded stronger in my head.

"Okay," he agreed, and brushed my hair behind my ear. He's going to kiss me, I thought, but he didn't. "You're not going to look at me."

"No. Probably for the best. I'm trying to remember I'm mad at you for trying to make choices for me."

His laughter swam through my blood. "I have to go scout out a Passenger and then go to the workshop. I'm absolutely not taking you with me, but if we were leaving the house at the same time, and you just happened to come along, I can't…wouldn't… say no."

Relief brought the house, the closeness of him, and the rest of the world back into focus. I wanted to smile or laugh. Or look up and kiss him. Saba used to read me a book called *If You Give a Mouse a Cookie*. Apparently my future—ha!—biography would be titled *If You Give a Girl a Magic Balloon*. On page six, I'd kiss that tall, scowling guy who my parents would definitely disapprove of, but it'd be understandable because that's what happened if you gave a girl a magic balloon.

To be fair, Kai was rather kissable.

But now was not the time for kissing. Instead, I lifted my chin and kept my eyes trained on the door. "Okay. On one condition."

"All right."

I stole a glance at him. "I have questions. You'll answer them. No roundabout poetics or metaphors or anything that sidesteps the real answers."

He laughed, low and sweet, his breath warm and smelling like toast against my cheek. "You're something else, Eleanor Baum. All right, I'll answer your questions."

If you give a girl a magic balloon, she'll become something else.

He disappeared, and I waited by the door until he reappeared with a second piece of toast for me, his jacket on, and keys in hand. He opened the door, and we both stopped short at the police officer standing at the bottom of the steps.

I'd forgotten about all of the risks in this world while I was busy flirting with Kai. But here, fear looked me right back in the eyes. The officer glanced at me, then Kai. "Good morning."

"Good morning," Kai and I said back in unison, our voices stiff.

He nodded to us and stepped out of the way. Kai locked the door behind us, and we walked past the officer. Kai's hand slipped into mine, and our sweaty palms trembled between us. When we stepped around the corner, I almost doubled over with relief. Kai pulled me to the side, wrapping his arms around me. He kissed the side of my head. "You're fine. We're fine. Let's just go."

I nodded against him. It was a reminder that the only people I could trust were him and Mitzi. Felix and the Schöpfers and the Volkspolizei and the Stasi…There were too many unknowns, and every doorway, every corner, every shadow held a threat.

"Have you known people who were picked up by the Stasi?" I asked him.

He hesitated and then said, "Is it going to make it worse to know?"

"I don't know," I said honestly. "Maybe."

His shoulder bumped mine lightly. "I know people. The ones who get out don't like talking about it. They're shadows of themselves. But we're not going to let that happen to you, Ellie."

"I read that some spies in the Cold War carried cyanide pills with them," I said. "We should do that."

"Or we can just be careful." I heard the pause in his voice though. We both knew that caution might not be enough.

It took a few minutes, but eventually, I relaxed until I finally came to a halt in the middle of the sidewalk. I lifted my face to the sky and opened my mouth, trying to pull as much of the warm spring air as possible into my lungs at once. The sunlight felt glorious and rejuvenating. When I opened my eyes and tried to watch where I was going, I could see Kai smiling out of the corner of my eyes. I lowered my face instantly. "What?"

"Nothing." He cleared the smile from his face. "Nothing."

We crossed the street and slipped south across the city. Every few blocks, I could see the wall to my right in the bareness of the area around it. Kai knew exactly where he was going.

"How do you do it?" I finally asked. He gave me a sideways look with a raised eyebrow so I clarified. "All the unanswered questions. All of the unanswerable questions."

"You want answers. Go to the wall," he said after a few beats of silence. I wasn't sure he was ever going to answer me, and then the nonanswer frustrated me.

"You said you'd answer straightforwardly."

"I'm not?"

"You speak like the wall is a person." I swung our hands in frustration. "Or like it's a sage or a church or something."

"This city," Kai said, "is allergic to trust. And desperate for it. Even cities want what they can't have. The best we can do is trust the people around us and hope for the best."

I thought about that for a long moment. Here, it was hard not to look at everyone. It was hard not to want to touch everyone. Maybe that was why I didn't mind Kai holding my hand. Maybe that was why Kai held my hand at all. In a city where most lived in miserable conditions, void of common courteous interactions, things began to feel false, like everything existed through panes of glass. I thought it was the way we—they—protected themselves from getting close to people who could inform on them.

What oppression like this did was inhibit personal, individual connections. Personal connections created a community, and community wasn't the opposite of individualism. We were collectively a whole made of millions and millions of moving parts, each of us our own gear interlocking with another gear and turning the world a little farther in the right direction.

I wanted to stop everyone on the street, hug them, and whisper, *The wall will come down*, but the wall would come down and things wouldn't get better, not right away. They'd built these walls within themselves, survival instinct embodied, and it would take more than a magical red balloon to carry these people onto the other side, no matter how resilient they were.

I understood suddenly why Kai was so reticent and cautious, hot and cold, giving and taking, two steps forward and three steps backward. Fear was the foundation of all types of Walls, including the one to my right. I understood now. I understood him.

We verified the identity of Kai's next Passenger at the restaurant. She was six months pregnant out of wedlock. When she had begun to show, she'd lost her job as a teacher. When she couldn't get another job, she became unemployed, which was illegal. She was arrested on charges that she was demonstrating and propagating antisocial behavior.

I barely contained my anger, and anger was not my favorite feeling to carry.

If you give a girl a magic balloon, she'll rage against the machine.

Kai laughed softly as we left the restaurant and headed north again. "Your mind is working so fast I can barely keep up, and it's playing out on your face like a television screen."

"It's stupid," I spat out, grabbing for the only German word I knew to explain the absurdity of the woman's predicament. A passerby glanced at me and stepped out of my way, his eyes following me. Kai grunted and pulled me down a side street, less crowded than the main road.

"It's East Germany," he said.

"Right now," I started to say, about to tell him it would change, that the Monday protests started in a year, and in eighteen months, the wall would fall. The government would begin to dissolve into particles that, one day, I would again read about in history books. I closed my mouth around the words. I wasn't supposed to talk about the future with them. That alone could change it.

I growled in frustration. "Don't you want to know?"

He shrugged. "Sure I do."

"Things change, Kai," I managed to say. I couldn't give specifics. I didn't want the guilt of changing history like that on my chest. "They change for the better. But it's too late for a lot of people."

"It wouldn't change if it wasn't for those people, Ellie." Kai flicked his fingers in the air. "Domino effect."

I chewed on my lip. "I guess."

But it didn't feel like enough for me. That people had to suffer so that the wheels of history could turn. It didn't feel fair. There had to be a way to help the people around me *now*, before the protests and the wall came down and reunification happened.

Kai slipped his hand around mine again and pulled me toward a metal gate closing off a subway entrance. The German signs on the gates were faded, the paint peeling off, but I could read the words: *Achtung! Betreten Verboten!* Kai withdrew a key from his pocket and fit it into a lock.

I blinked as the gate hummed, high-pitched and in tune, something I almost knew, and then there was a soft click. Kai pushed the iron gate open. I was about to refuse to walk into the dark with him when he said quietly, "*Geisterbahnhof.*"

I stared at him in the dimly lit stairs. "What?"

He slipped the key back into his pocket. "Ghost stations. The trains from West Berlin go through, but they do not stop here. Come."

At the base of the flight of stairs were a poorly lit hallway, columns, and walls of thin, crumbling tiles that had been white at one point. A sign on the wall warned passengers to stand back from the tracks, and a large, faded sign said, Potsdamer Platz.

I stopped in my tracks. "I've been in this station."

We stood next to each other, staring at the sign, dripping snow onto the floor, trembling from adrenaline and the cold, hand in hand. The sign was bent and broken around the edges, black with white lettering, and the subway station was not at all what I remembered. The one I had passed through was clean and bright, the floors and walls and ceiling in good repair, and the sign was large and proud. The announcements for trains came regularly, and the platform had been packed with people from all over the world. Moment by moment, I swung between believing that I came here by some stroke of magic and time mix-up, and believing I was in a dream.

This felt implausibly real. I hadn't known about the ghost stations or that the Potsdamer Platz station had been one of them, but this was the old, run-down version of the one I'd seen. The one I'd seen had people from Sweden and people from China and people from the United States standing next to Germans, not just East and West Berliners. The one I saw had friendly people handing out maps and giant maps on the wall where everyone tried to figure out how to get wherever they wanted to go.

This station was empty and the walls stripped. This station didn't want people inside it. It had no intention of helping us get anywhere, and our presence felt unwanted next to the decaying tiles and tired sign.

"It looks different then, doesn't it?" he asked and then blew out a hard breath. "No, stop. I'm not supposed to ask. I just said I wouldn't."

"You already know the wall comes down. What's a little more information?" We stood there in silence for a moment and then I added more softly, "It's used. It's the shiny, busy platform I told you about when I first came here."

Kai's arm brushed against mine. "One day, I'll stand there too. But there's the chime. We need to move. The guard will be by soon."

I didn't argue this time when he began to walk, and I had to keep up as he headed down a long platform into darkness. Then he dropped my hand abruptly and jumped onto the tracks, followed by a rush of silence and then the loud, echoing clap of his feet slapping, wet and determined, against the base of the tracks. I couldn't turn back now, so I gritted my teeth and slid down from the platform onto the wet, dark tracks.

We walked a few steps before a thought occurred to me. "Why don't you use the tunnels to escape? They go into West Berlin, don't they?"

He turned his head slightly but I couldn't read his expression in the dark. "The trains run too frequently. You can't run the tracks fast enough between places of safety for how often and how fast they run the trains."

I hesitated, but could not avoid the next question. "You've tried."

"Not me," he said, turning back toward the darkness. "Others. Many others. No one's made it."

Calculated risk, I thought again to myself. Everyone thought they were invincible enough until they were not. Everyone thought they were desperate enough until they were not. I stared down the tunnel. I was trapped in a land and time of magic and intrigue, a place where balloons helped people escape terrible regimes. *Would I run?* I stared into the dark and tried to think about how long we had been down there. How fast could I run, and how far apart were the stations? Then, abruptly, I realized that I wouldn't try it. I couldn't try it. I didn't know if that was my cowardice or risk assessment. Maybe both.

After a few minutes of walking in complete darkness, the kind where you forgot whether you were walking straight or forward or uphill or downhill, Kai explained the ghost stations to me. The previous stations were still used by West German trains to pass through on their way to other stations.

"Why did you leave England?" It seemed safer to ask questions in the dark.

I heard his footsteps hesitate at first, and I thought he might not answer me. Then he did. "My sister. She's…She's a little different. And she has magic. Some wanted to institutionalize her. Some wanted to use her magic for evil. I brought her here to protect her."

"She's lucky to have you," I said softly, because I didn't know what to say. People fled Germany just a generation before Kai because it wasn't safe to be different here. And he had to come here to find sanctuary. A few years made such a difference. Time seemed increasingly illogical the longer I was in 1988.

"Yes," was his reply, but it wasn't proud or egotistical. It was simple. She was lucky to have him.

"What's up with you and Mitzi?" I asked, braver in the dark. His steps paused. "What do you mean?"

I considered my words for a moment, because I couldn't figure out how to ask whether she thought I was a threat and decided to say instead, "I can't tell if she likes me or not. She's hot and cold."

And the more often you and I touch, hold hands, and banter, the harder she is to read. But I didn't say this. Not even in the dark of the tunnels.

"I think she's tired," Kai said softly. "You're just another friend who isn't German. Another reminder that she's had a hard time with her own people."

"Why?"

"Dangerous to be gay in East Germany," Kai said. "She's a liability."

"They said that? Kai, that's terrible."

"It is. It's not you, Ellie. And it's not really her either. It's..." I couldn't see his hands, but I could imagine the gesture. "All of this."

I let go of my other questions to concentrate on walking in the dark. Nothing could have prepared me for the stench of dampness that never found air, for the crystallizations that formed on the walls and felt like grit on my palms. The air was sour, thick, clinging to my hair and skin like fingers ghosting over me. We reached the iron door at the end of the tunnel with the rusted bar that groaned and creaked when Kai wrestled it to the side.

Kai opened the door. "Come in."

The room took up several stories, the ceiling rising far above our heads with thick beams of exposed steel crisscrossing at several levels. All the railings were painted a gross yellow, like the kind they used on roads. *Caution! Do not fall over this very obvious railing!* The walls were gray stone where they weren't covered with maps, fluttering yellowed papers, and bookcases. On the main level were three rows of huge, long wooden worktables with green-and-gold desk lamps, all glowing warmly. Stacks of books and papers covered the tables. Wooden chairs with low backs and arms were pushed out and in, and dragged all over the room. The worn carpet by the chalkboard had several purple, red, and green floor cushions, and the couches were a dull brown with piles of blankets in all colors. A poster commemorating the 1980 Olympics was taped to the wall nearest to me.

"What is this place?"

"The workshop. This is where they write the magic for the balloons." Kai picked up a piece of paper and handed it to me. "Too deep in the tunnels. Stasi never find us back here. It's the safest place to work."

The equations on the page didn't make sense to me—math wasn't exactly my forte—but I recognized them: the variables, the square roots and imaginary numbers. How magic could come out of math was another mystery. The list of unknowns in this world was increasing steadily. I put the paper down on the table and ran my fingers over the damp mark left behind on the wood from a cup not too long ago. No one was there now, but they had been here recently. I glanced up at the upper levels, at the ladders connecting steel beams that served, I think, as walkways from bulletin boards to bookcases to bulletin boards.

A chalkboard had a list of names, one of whom was Kai's next Passenger, the one we just saw. I tapped my finger on the board. "What happens next for her?"

"We'll take her to a safe house, draw her blood, write the balloon, bring her and the balloon as close to the wall as we can, and send her over," he said. "We're using a safe house in another sector since you're in our normal one."

I flinched, a little guilty. "Am I taking up space? Can you save fewer people because of me?"

He startled, dropping the piece of chalk he was using to check off the woman's name on the board. "What? No. Ellie, no."

I wasn't sure if I believed him, not after everything I'd seen. I nodded and walked away from the chalkboard to a bulletin board with a map tacked to it. Flag pins stuck out all over it, and a tiny cursive font detailed names, but not addresses. Adiela in Cape Town. Peter in Northern Ireland. Rashaad in Iraq. Ebrahim in Iran. Meriem in Algeria.

"Who are they?" I asked.

Kai glanced up from the equations he was reading. "Where Schöpfers and Runners are helping people in places of crisis. We don't put down the addresses in case we're compromised."

I blinked. "So it's not just here."

Kai shook his head and walked up to the map, tapping it with a finger. "Not just here. Wherever we're needed. We don't play sides. We don't work for governments. We help people get out of places if they're at risk."

I smiled a little bit. "You said *we*. You usually talk like it's the Council and the balloon makers, and they're a separate mission and entity from you."

His gaze slid over to me, and his almost-smile twitched in the corners of his mouth. "You're too sharp for your own good, you know that? Here. I want to show you something."

He stepped back so I could move over to the chalkboard where, at the edge, someone had taped an old-fashioned color photograph with a name and dates written underneath. I stepped close to it and stared at the dark-haired guy with a careful smile and deep-set almond eyes. I touched Garrick's name beneath it. *4 August, 1954–21 March, 1988.*

Swallowing, I turned away and wandered through the workshop, looking at all the papers. My name was on a large sheet of paper marked up by a dozen different hands. Over my shoulder, Kai translated it: "Ways to Return Ellie Baum to Her Time Period." He showed me a note from a head organization allowing the Council to investigate uses for illicit magic to return me home.

I felt like I was in a museum, or a fairy tale, or a movie set.

"This is incredible," I said. "Ashasher and Aurora wouldn't mind me being here?"

"Oh, they'd mind very much," Kai said, and he sent me a sly smile, like we were coconspirators in a crime. I thought about the broken balloon, the missing Runner, the flags all over the world, and all of the dangerous puzzle pieces, but Kai stepped closer, distracting me. My mouth went dry. His kaleidoscope eyes tipped toward golden. "Calculated risk, sponge."

"What did you call me?" I stepped away from him, away from the blackboard with its uncertain and indecipherable equations. "What does that mean?"

"Sponge," Kai said and frowned. "It's not a German word. You soak up everything around you, don't you? You're quiet because you're always absorbing everything. Everything's personal to you. Everything is." He paused and turned away from me. "It's very real."

He shrugged and added after a beat, "But I don't know you yet."

I imagined storing all the too-much things about me in my heart, with little valves letting them out slowly or not at all. I thought about my full-to-bursting heart sponge so much that I almost missed the word *yet*. The word wrung out my heart with its promise to fill it up again.

On our way out of the workshop, I stumbled over one of the rails and let out an embarrassing squeak. He caught me by my arm, and I spun toward him before I realized it, my free hand on his chest. I could feel his heartbeat all the way through my palm, up my wrist, sliding through my veins to my heart. Our breath shared a ragged pulse.

His hand came up to touch my cheek, warm, dry, and smooth. His fingers curled against my temple, his thumb running across my cheek. I imagined his eyes turning to molten gold in the dark of the subway tunnel. His hand on my arm tightened only slightly before our lips met. The last time I'd kissed him, after the second time traveler, he'd stood still as a statue, just letting my mouth brush against his. The shocking ambivalence of that reaction was only a shadow now, his mouth capturing mine with extraordinary determination.

We kissed as if this were the solution to everything that lay ahead of us, as if a girl from the twenty-first century and a boy from the twentieth century kissing in an abandoned subway station beneath a divided city could untangle the terrible ways in which time looped and history replayed itself.

Chapter Seventeen

TIES THAT BIND

East Berlin, German Democratic Republic, April 1988

Kai

Ellie was playing solitaire in the front room, a paper dove opening and closing its wings next to her mug, when I came to get her. I must not have done a good job of hiding my emotions because her smile dropped off her face pretty damn fast.

"What's wrong?" she asked, scrambling to her feet. She slipped the dove into her pocket. The rest of the cards tumbled off her lap and scattered on the floor. I shook my head, still trying to catch my breath, and grabbed her coat off the hooks. She took it from me and slid her arms through the sleeves. "Kai, you're freaking me out."

I was freaking myself out, to be honest. I really didn't want Ellie around the Schöpfers. They had a tendency to see us normal people like we were little experiments, things to be studied and examined and discarded at the snap of their fingers. And it'd only be worse because she *time-traveled*. But they wanted to see her because they thought they'd figured out why and how the balloon worked for her. And if they figured that out, maybe they'd be able to get her a way home.

"Ashasher and Aurora," I said at last, opening the door for her and then switching into German. "They want to see you. At the workshop."

She glanced over her shoulder at me while I locked the door. "You look scared."

I tried to smile. I had practice faking emotions for Sabina, but for some reason, I couldn't with Ellie. I said hoarsely, "I'll be with you the whole time."

She blinked and then nodded while she brushed her mane of brown waves back over her shoulder. She didn't look as afraid as I felt, or as I expected her to look. "Okay."

I didn't get why I felt her trust was so misplaced. I wanted to earn it, but I didn't know how. I just knew that I'd never seen Ashasher and Aurora so worked up and animated like they were this morning. I slipped my hand into hers, and we set off for the workshop.

Dropping into the train tunnels brought back a slew of memories from the other day that didn't help to slow my heart or make it easier to breathe. Every time we bumped into each other in the tunnels, I thought about stopping and kissing her again. All my life, I'd never understood how people could get distracted so easily. I went eighteen years before understanding: distractions were five foot six with a mane of perpetually tangled brown curls and blue eyes that could bring a man to his knees. Everyone has their own definition of distraction, I guess.

As I closed the door to the workshop behind us, Ellie's eyes nearly popped out of her skull. She hadn't seen it so busy. Schöpfers were examining a red balloon lit up by stage lights and held delicately in the metal clamps in the middle of a table. I could barely see the equations on the thin skin of the balloon, but I wasn't here for a balloon. Not today. Ashasher sat in the corner with Aurora, the feathers moving at slow speed while Aurora's eye makeup seemed to drip down her face a little more than usual today. My sister was noticeably absent.

Eyes followed Ellie, and I expected her to be shy, but she walked behind me, her bottom lip trembling but her feet steady. The girl was way more incredible than she'd ever give herself credit for being. We crossed the workshop to the place under the overhang where Ashasher and Aurora had ceased talking just to watch us walk.

I realized too late that Ellie and I were still holding hands. Ashasher raised his eyebrows, a hidden motion behind the crown of feathers, but I knew him well enough that he gave himself away. Aurora blatantly stared at our hands. It was too late to drop Ellie's hand now. Not if I ever wanted to kiss this girl again (and yes, I did).

She must have figured out that everyone was staring at us, at her holding my hand, not at her. Her fingers tried to untwist, but I just held her hand tighter. We weren't giving in to that nonsense. I'd already become mahrime, outcast from my people. Here, in this world, they could not judge me for this.

"Ellie," Ashasher said in greeting, the feathers picking up speed. "Kai. Thank you for coming."

"Aurora," I said, and gestured a bit with our hands. "This is Ellie. You met the other night."

For the first time in good light, Ellie and Aurora appraised each other. Then, in careful, absurdly careful German, Ellie said, "I forgot to say thank you. For working to find me a balloon that will take me home."

Aurora shook her hand slowly, tilting her head to the side. "It took me a few days to sort it out, but I think I know why the balloon picked you, Ellie Baum," she said. "You look like him. It's even clearer now in the light."

Aurora turned, dropping Ellie's hand and crossing to the chalkboard. She tugged Garrick's photo off the slate and brought it back, handing it to Ellie. Ellie had seen it before, but of course Aurora didn't know that. Ellie studied the photo, a frown curling up the softness of her face. I studied Garrick's dark curls, his slim face, his long, delicate fingers always with a pen between them. At first, I didn't see it, but then... Their eyes were the same shape. They had the same crooked smile. The same ears. Ellie turned the photo over and read the name off the back of it.

"Garrick Aaron Hirsch," Ellie said aloud slowly, and then her eyes widened. She jerked and looked up at me. "Hirsch. He has the same last name as my grandfather. And his middle name... That was my grandfather's father who died at Łódź."

"We pulled Garrick's file," Ashasher said, looking around. "Where'd it go? Christian, find Garrick Hirsch's file."

"I heard you both met our Zerberus friend," Aurora said in the lull as some young Schöpfer behind us scrambled to do Ashasher's bidding.

"He's a real piece of work," I said, trying to take a deep breath. Ellie said nothing, just stared at the photo. "Did you talk to him?"

Ashasher's smile thinned his mouth. "The Zerberus will not speak to us. By coming to you, they have made it clear whom they are investigating in the case of Ellie and Garrick's balloon. And now there's a second balloon. Even we cannot ignore the facts. It is unlikely, Ellie, that your balloon was accidental."

I instinctively tightened my hand around Ellie's as she said, "I figured."

Ellie's shoulder bumped into mine, but my mind was still on a delay. "But why? What's someone trying to accomplish?"

"I think it's fair to say that their goal isn't to kill people in the future one balloon at a time. Beyond that, I cannot say at this time. We don't know enough," Ashasher confirmed, gesturing with a limp hand to himself and then Aurora. "The Zerberus are holding us responsible for the magic that caused the balloon to cut the fabric of time. Even if the magic to do that is experimental at best and by far illegal. It was banned before the wall was even erected."

He shook his head while Aurora's eyes shifted away from us, her mouth tight. I couldn't imagine that it was a particularly pleasant experience to be investigated by the Zerberus. Couldn't be much more pleasant than knowing the Stasi were investigating you. That thought made me shiver. Aurora wasn't nearly as off-the-handle high as a kite as she had been the other night though, if she appeared this uncomfortable. Maybe she understood how serious it was. No more flippant comments from her today.

"If magic can go through time," Ellie asked, her voice cautious enough that I turned back toward her and the way she frowned her worry, "then why is it illegal? Why not use magic to do good?"

Aurora cleared her throat. "The illicit nature of time travel through magical means comes from the complications arising in the brittle nature of history."

Alright. So maybe she was high. Sometimes I wanted whatever they smoked here on the weekends. Other times, like now and the other night, I didn't think it sounded so awesome.

Ellie stared at her and then, with a single raised eyebrow, turned to me. I said, in English, "She said that time travel is illegal because history is so easily altered."

"She couldn't have just said that?" Ellie asked. Fair enough question. I shrugged, trying to hide my smile. Aurora and Ashasher were my employers, and Sabina's safety relied on their generosity. I could tell her more later, but not then.

"Time is like fabric. You can fold it and bend it and unravel it and twist it however you wish. The consequences are always extremely dangerous and frequently, as you've seen, fatal," Ashasher said. He probably thought that his explanation would make more sense to Ellie. I grew up watching Sabina discover that the things she wrote down on paper turned into magic. I was used to hearing complicated and usually nonsensical descriptions to explain illogical events.

"So was Garrick trying to go to the future and only the balloon made it?" Ellie asked as a Schöpfer finally arrived with Garrick's file. I reached for it, but Ashasher interfered, taking it between his long, delicate fingers.

We all fell silent as Ashasher flipped slowly through page after page, the feathers rising and falling around his head like hurricane tides. I had seen storm clouds swirl like this. Inevitably, he was going to look up and report impending doom: that Garrick was actually Ellie or some sort of shit like that, because I honestly wouldn't have been that shocked at this point.

"Here," Ashasher asked, pushing the file into Aurora's hands and tapping at something on the page. He gestured to Aurora with a small wave. "It should be your right to say this."

"Benno Hirsch," said Aurora quietly.

"My grandfather." Ellie lifted her chin.

"When we interviewed him about his family history, Garrick said his father's brother, Benno, died in the Holocaust at Chełmno, along with his mother. Garrick's grandfather and aunt, Aaron and Ruth, died at the Łódź ghetto." Aurora closed the file. "But we know Benno survived."

Ellie stared at Aurora, her mouth dropping open. I held my breath, glancing at Ashasher, who met my eyes and shook his head just a tad. He didn't know what was going on either. Then Ellie whispered, "You."

Aurora tipped her head a little to the side. "Yes."

"What?" I glanced at Aurora and then back at Ellie's washed-out face. "Ellie?"

"You saved my grandfather," Ellie said, her eyes never leaving Aurora's face. "You saved Benno Hirsch from Chełmno."

We all knew that Aurora had been the first person to write a balloon used in the field, and we'd known it was in her native home of Poland. But I never thought that the world would spin like this, bringing a girl from the future to the past, that time would be a twisted, knotted bastard like this. Now I could only hope that finding this knot could help me keep my promise to Ellie to get her home.

"I did," Aurora agreed, her voice soft. She sank into a chair and said, "I never thought I'd meet his granddaughter. I didn't see that line in Garrick's file when we first interviewed him. But it makes sense. We tie the magic to the Passenger's blood. You grabbed the balloon because of Benno, and because of Benno, you, and Garrick sharing genetic material, the balloon recognized you. That is why you survived when the other time-traveler did not. And maybe, with this information, Ellie, we can get you a balloon home."

Ellie reached out, and Aurora took her hand, two pale and shivering people reaching across space and time. Aurora's eyes glittered with tears, but Ellie was the one who said softly, "Thank you."

Chapter Eighteen

FREEDOM IS ANOTHER WORD FOR HOPE

Łódź Ghetto, Poland, March 1942

Benno

When Papa died, I didn't cry. He simply fell asleep and didn't wake up. Mama, who woke next to her cold, dead husband, didn't cry either. He had disappeared from us sometime after the new year, as the calendar turned from 1941 to 1942.

Somewhere beyond here, the war raged on. We only knew its progress from the work we did. Because of my nimble fingers and sewing skills, taught to me by my mother years ago, I sewed with some younger boys and the women. Day after day, I stitched the same six buttons onto the same cut of coats, made at the station before me. Beyond us, bombs dropped. Men and women lived and died, just like here, but the ghetto's war was fought with disease and hunger. The ghetto's war was fought in lost minds. Papa stopped going to work. They were going to give him a wedding invitation, as we called the notices for relocation. Relocation, deportation. We began to mix our words. Words lost meaning here in the ghetto. They meant everything and nothing in the same breath.

Papa never got relocated. He simply gave up. His heart stopped when he went to sleep. Over his body, Mama and I whispered the Mourner's Kaddish (*yitgadal v'yitkadash s'hmei raba*) because he believed in God and an afterlife, and he would have wanted us to say those words over him. We hugged each other, and then we did not have time to grieve. We went to work, because we needed to take care of Ruth, who had never recovered from her illness in the fall.

Life waited for no mourner. Not here in the ghetto.

When Papa died, I didn't cry.

When Ruth died, my heart stopped too. She took some part of me across into the other world, wherever the dead's souls go when they're gone. I didn't know I wanted to believe in an afterlife until Ruth was gone. She died, crying of hunger for days and days, even when Mama and I gave up our bread and soup for her, almost doubled over in pain ourselves. She died painfully and without relief. Her body turned stiff so quickly that I imagined she had been halfway to death for a long time. Mama cried too. I remembered when Ruth was born, the way her pink fingers curled in the air, clinging to my fingers.

Those pink fingers in my memory were the brightest bit of color in my life. Everything was cold and gray in the ghetto these days. The cemetery didn't have room and we didn't have a headstone, but they found room for Ruth to share with the other children that died that week in the ghetto. I had forgotten, until I was standing there by the fresh dirt, how many people were dying this winter. In Berlin, we had not been comfortable for years. But this—one day, there would be a boy to my left. And the next, he'd be gone. Dead. A girl with bloodshot eyes replacing him. Our eyes were always weary from the work. My eyes were weary of crying, weary of sewing. Weary of seeing everything I saw.

For months, in the dead of winter, I hadn't seen the girl at the fence. I had to be careful about visiting the fence when snow was on the ground because our tracks showed so clearly. Snowstorms were ideal, but my coat was thin, and the girl was not there in the storms. I cursed myself for not thinking of this.

But in March, I heard someone whistle softly by the fence, and when I looked for the culprit, I found her, without her dog, on the other side. She wore the same purple coat over a green dress. She appeared thinner and more tired, but she was on the other side. She was free.

She said, "I lit candles for Hanukkah."

I said, "That does not make you Jewish. If you wanted to be Jewish, you and I could trade places."

She made a face at me. "I don't want to be Jewish. I wanted you to know that in case you died, I wanted to keep that story alive for you."

I didn't tell her that we didn't tell stories for ourselves. We told stories for others. We told stories because our bones were full of ghosts whispering, *Tell the story*. I said, "I didn't die. But my sister did."

The girl's face fell, to my surprise. She sucked in a deep breath. "I'm sorry."

I nodded and said thank you. We stood there for a few minutes, and then the girl on the other side of the fence said softly, "Will you tell me another story?"

Passover was coming up. So as quickly as possible, I told her the story of Exodus, of Pharaoh and his cruelty to his slaves, of Moses who came back from the desert with the word of God behind him, of the ten plagues, and then of the freedom of the Israelites. As I told her of the Red Sea parting for Moses, I imagined the fence breaking apart and letting us free into an untroubled world.

At the end of the story, the girl said, "Don't you Jews have any happy stories? You've told me two sad stories. Tell me a happy one."

"I've told you two stories that end in freedom," I protested. "How much happier could you ask for?"

"But all of the story that comes before that tiny little bit of freedom is sad," she said.

"If the story was happy, you'd care less about that tiny little bit of freedom," I explained to her. "We wouldn't like the daylight if it wasn't for the night. We wouldn't notice the stars if not for the endless dark of night. All the story, like you said? That's the important part. The sad parts are all about surviving. We are a people who survive. We endure. We will endure this too."

She thought about that for a moment and said, "Do you think you were put on earth to endure?"

I shook my head and said, "I don't think I was put on earth for a specific reason. Do you?"

She shook her head, paused, and then met my eyes warily. She nodded a little bit. "Maybe. You didn't believe me then, and you won't now."

"Try me," I said. "I've come to believe in the unbelievable."

She said, "I have magic. I believe I was put on this earth to help people. To use my magic to counteract all the evil here in this world."

I said, "What kind of magic? Like Houdini?"

She shook her head, her raven hair flying wildly. "No. What I write becomes powerful. I have magic in my words and numbers."

"Write me out of here," I said without thinking.

Her smile back made my heart restart in my chest. It had been still for days since Ruth's death, but now it thumped again. The girl said, "That's exactly what I'm hoping to do."

I held my breath as she waved good-bye and set off away from the ghetto. I didn't believe in magic, but I could try to believe in the kind of magic that might set me free.

Chapter Nineteen

MAPS AND THREE-HEADED DOGS

East Berlin, German Democratic Republic, May 1988

Ellie

It was Mitzi's idea to let Aurora and I work together. Aurora needed help sorting maps and other things the Zerberus kept in Berlin, and apparently the younger Schöpfers were more interested in writing magic than organizing dusty old papers.

To be fair, if I could write magic, I'd only want to do that too. When I saw all the paper doves and the young Schöpfers practicing writing bloody equations onto the wings of the doves, I thought about the doves I made back at the safe house.

But I couldn't get myself to say anything to Aurora or Ashasher about how the doves flew for me. I remembered the fear and worry in Kai's face when he told me not to ask questions to which I didn't want answers. If they knew I could make doves, would they insist I make balloons? Would they make me stay instead of finding me a way home?

Maybe knowing that my doves could fly—I couldn't make myself say what this meant—was why Kai hadn't been happy about this arrangement. I promised to walk with him or Mitzi and not go out by myself again, so he grudgingly admitted that it'd be nice for me to know the person who saved my grandfather. "And," he added, "seeing you every day might keep her on the track of finding you a way home."

So I didn't mention my doves, and neither did he, but I came to the workshop as often as I could.

The first time that Mitzi and I walked there together, she stopped and bought us pastries from a shop. We almost never splurged on anything, so I was surprised when she slipped the cookies into my pocket. She winked at me and swept her bright hair out of her eyes.

She said if I promised not to sneak out again, she'd buy me pastries every day. I asked her if she was bribing me, and she pretended to look offended and then reminded me that I was in East Germany. Of course she was bribing me. That was the currency.

I wrapped my hand around the cookies in my pocket for the whole walk as we hurried along the damp sidewalk. Mitzi was the opposite of Kai, and part of me loved spending time in her energy. She was so vibrant. I couldn't help but walk with a little more spring in my step, have a little smile on my face, and be a little more excited about things to come. With Mitzi, I could forget, for a moment, that police lurked at every corner. And where we were going, Stasi patrolled.

Jumping down onto the train tracks today reminded me of Kai kissing me in this tunnel.

"You're quiet," Mitzi said. "Which means you're thinking too hard."

"Am I that easy to read?" I walked along one of the rails, trying to keep my balance. "I'm just thinking about how confused Kai is."

"Ah," Mitzi said, and she didn't disagree with me. She sighed and said, "When he and Sabina left the Romanichal in England, they became outcasts. He can never go home to his family."

"He isn't Romani anymore," I whispered. I remembered him saying bitterly, "Home is a fantasie."

"He is, and he isn't. He's...When you think he doesn't know who he is, it's more complicated than you know." Mitzi jumped up on the rail in front of me and then added, "And more than me. Even though I'm an East Berliner, I know that on a fundamental level, I am German and all of Berlin is one city. The wall's a false divide. But he doesn't have a Wall. He doesn't have anything to point fingers at."

The tunnel seemed longer and darker today, like the rails just kept going on forever and ever, and a train didn't even blow by us. Something about the way Mitzi described Kai's identity crisis pressed against me, a weight on my chest, but every time I reached for words, they slipped away. But when I tripped over something that smelled and sounded like a rat carcass bursting apart, I tried to concentrate on where I was walking.

Mitzi climbed up onto the platform and offered me a hand. I let her pull me up, and then she cranked open the door. I breathed in the sight of people bent over red balloons, long reams of paper, and tiny vials of blood. The Ellie who existed in that other time, my true time, would have found this grotesque. But now, blood and magic and math and cool, questioning gazes from the Schöpfers soothed me.

As we stood in the doorway, half silhouetted and half in the light, Mitzi grabbed my elbow. "Hey. Don't tell Kai I told you, okay? He's private."

"I promise," I said immediately.

She stepped through the door completely and slammed it behind us. "One map-sorting time-traveler safely delivered!"

At a nearby table, Aurora tut-tutted softly. "There's no need to speak at such a loud volume."

Mitzi rolled her eyes and gestured to the table full of maps for me. I'd sorted nearly three dozen yesterday, and the pile didn't appear to be getting any smaller. I'd ask if it was magic, but I didn't really want to know the answer. Still, at least I was sitting around other people while Kai and Mitzi worked today. At least it was better than sitting in the house alone. I slid into my seat and opened the first map of a city called Odessa. I labeled it USSR and put it in the pile with all the other Soviet country maps. The next map was for Ankara, and I put that in the Mediterranean pile. Not all the names of cities were easy to find, and some of the maps weren't marked at all. Some were in other languages, and it took me ages to go through research books the old-fashioned way. When I jokingly asked for a phone, the Schöpfers handed me a landline. They had no idea how much easier research would be in another twenty years.

Yesterday, I'd asked Aurora what the reasoning was behind the maps, and she'd said that my help there was conditional on my ability to hold my tongue. She didn't like questions very much. When Ashasher walked by, I had asked him and he had repeated exactly what Aurora had said. But today, at my table, instead of Sabina, two younger Schöpfers sat across from me, practicing equations in regular ink on large sheets of paper.

"So," I said casually.

Both of them looked up at me, confused. Other than the soft murmuring of Aurora's voice in the corner, the workshop was almost always quiet. It was busy but quiet, like a library at peak hours.

"Where are these maps from?"

"Oh," said the young woman, looking relieved. She swept a blond lock behind an ear and glanced at her partner. "The Zerberus put them here for safekeeping. We're their archival site."

"The what?" I frowned, pretending I didn't know the unusual word. "I'm sorry. My German is still improving."

"Your German's pretty good," said the young man, smiling at me. I couldn't make myself return the smile, though he couldn't have been much older than Kai. He was thin, almost sickly looking, with light-brown hair and a sharp nose. "Zerberus. It's our parent organization. They oversee all magic balloon operations around the world. For the most part, they just make sure we're not breaking rules and keep track of all our research. They allow most sites free rein beyond that."

"Decentralized," said the woman. "When everything these days is so centralized, they felt that they needed to be the opposite of that."

That made sense, in a strange sort of way. I look around at all the shelves. "So everything here?"

"Is everything the Zerberus have on how the magic works, how the magic might work—theories and experiments—and laws. Some of the magic's been outlawed." She gestured behind her. "We're not allowed to even look through it unless Ashasher or Aurora gives us permission."

"Other Schöpfers are," the young man corrected her. "We aren't fully certified yet. We're still learning."

"I understand." I labeled and sorted the next map, glancing up at all the shelves. That was decades and decades of history around me, filling this room, and suddenly the quiet didn't feel so quiet. Soft voices, like ghosts, filled the space and air around me, whispering. The Zerberus and all of these people writing magic balloons had risked everything to help people be free. And maybe these maps had something to do with that. Maybe these maps set people free where they weren't free.

"Aren't you afraid?" I asked suddenly. "What if the Stasi found these?"

The two students exchanged looks, and then the woman said, "I hope they don't. There's enough here to convict us. And we couldn't help anyone from prison."

"More balloons went missing," whispered a Schöpfer pausing by our table, oblivious to our discussion. He glanced at me, and I looked away, pretending to study the maps in front of me.

"Why haven't they posted a guard?" hissed the woman.

"They did. He said only Schöpfers came in and out," said the new Schöpfer. "It's got to be one of us."

"Don't be a fool. No one's going to risk that. We all have too much to lose."

I wondered who *didn't* have much to lose. But I didn't know anyone's names, and everyone knew who I was. I couldn't ask any questions. I could only listen. They were careful around me though, and little more was said on the subject. I sorted until my eyes began to close of their own accord. I jerked awake, and then began to fall asleep again. Then a hand touched my shoulder and I sat up straight in my chair. Aurora's mouth twitched in the tiniest of smiles.

"I'll walk you home," she said. Her voice never rose, never pitched, never went above a quiet, soft whisper. I didn't know how she could do it. "You've been here all day."

"Thank you," I said awkwardly, standing up. "I like the work though."

"I can tell," she said as we walked toward the door. "I'm appreciative. The students dislike that busy work, and we're under pressure to teach and place the students as quickly as possible these days. The world's changing rapidly. I don't have the time I'd like."

"My grandfather likes to say that none of us do," I told her as I jumped down onto the tracks. I turned around to see if Aurora needed help, but she was sliding, long dress and all, down onto the tracks. I wondered where she lived. Did the workshop have rooms for her and Ashasher?

I couldn't see her face, but her tone was warm. "He would say that. Benno was never particularly optimistic."

I stiffened a bit and said, "Hard to blame him."

She didn't apologize. Instead she said, "Sometimes I wonder if his cynicism made him more resilient. Maybe that's why he survived."

"He survived because of you," I said softly, still in disbelief. I shook my head. "Did I thank you? I can't remember if I said thank you. Thank you. He still calls beautiful days balloon days."

"Does he?" She sounded truly delighted.

We didn't say anything for the rest of the tunnels, but it didn't feel uncomfortable. At one of the major intersections, a police officer leaning against a wall straightened and started to come toward us. His walk was light and casual, as if he'd been waiting for us. Aurora turned me down another street, her face paler than normal.

"They're always there," she murmured. "They're always waiting. Sometimes, I think they know what we're doing, and they just want to know when we'll write a balloon for them."

"Are you ever afraid?" I asked her.

She walked me all the way to the door of the safe house before she answered. "No, I'm not often afraid. I have too many stories inside me to be afraid."

She waited while I climbed the steps to the door and unlocked it with the key Kai had given me. When I turned around, she waited for me to go in, her dark-purple dress damp at the hem and her hair as dark and glossy as it ever was. She was strange and quiet, but then, I thought I understood her. A lot of people found me strange and quiet at home too. My loud and boisterous family didn't really get why I found the world so tiring. Aurora did. Just looking at her that night, I could tell that she found the world every bit as exhausting as I did on a daily basis.

"Thank you," I told her. I'd said it a thousand times, but how do you thank someone for what she'd done for you? For the people she saved?

"You're welcome, Ellie Baum," she said. "I'll see you tomorrow. Thank you for your help. It's been illuminating and invaluable."

Chapter Twenty

WHERE WE ARE

Łódź Ghetto, Poland, March 1942

Benno

The streets were mud and the sky was gray, one reflected back in the other. The cold faded from the air, but it stayed in our bones. And sometimes it stayed in our eyes. One of the men next to me at the factory elbowed me and told me to look bright. He kept his head down and whispered out of the side of his mouth.

"If you don't look bright, they'll put you on the next train," he said.

I wasn't sure I wanted to stay. They used Łódź as a stopover ghetto. A holding pen for people who came to us emaciated and left us little more than skeletons with hearts beating through thin skin. Everywhere I turned, someone was dropping dead of starvation or tuberculosis. Every time I coughed, I thought to myself, This is the end.

When a few of us met for an illegal Shabbat one Friday night, one of the men said, "I cannot believe that the Sabbath is observed in hell."

Last week, a man collapsed in the factory. We wanted to take him to the hospital, but the man in charge of our shift asked what that would accomplish. The hospital had no medicines. The doctors, as well trained as they were, couldn't cure anything. They prescribed potato peels as medicine. If you were lucky, you might get onion broth. So the man died on the floor of our factory. We covered him with our coats.

So when the man next to me warned me against my dead eyes, I thought about his comment as I stood in line for bread and potatoes. I chewed on it as I ate and walked down our street to Number 18, our rooms. Mama said it was good luck to be in Number 18, but we hadn't had much luck at all. If I left, Mama would be left with no one. She'd lost Ernst and Ruth and my father. If I left, what chance did she have?

I never thought I'd be the anchor of this family, but our luck had left me no options. I trudged through the mud and thought about going down to the fence. But I didn't want to deal with the girl at the fence today. I couldn't take her relentless optimism and questions today. I had too little hope and too many questions of my own. I thought about the way my father had given up and about the way Ruth had died. I didn't want to go that way. If I were to die, I wanted to die in resistance. We heard about resistance movements in other ghettos. We heard sometimes they could take out the Nazis before they died.

If I had to choose, that was how I'd go.

But Łódź didn't have that resistance. We couldn't. They were deporting us with too much regularity to allow such a movement to coalesce. The day the man at the factory warned me about the dead look in my eyes, I came home to Mama sweeping our rooms and humming a song I didn't recognize.

"Benno," she said, and she smiled at me. I couldn't remember the last time she smiled. "Chana gave me a second loaf of bread. I wanted to save it, but I don't think it'll stay good. Let's just have one good night."

One good night. I said, "Teach me that song."

So we sat with our bread and our soup on the beds, our knees touching each other as Mama taught me the song she'd learned at work. "*Ani Ma'amin.*" It meant "I Believe."

"I think," Mama whispered to me after the bread was gone and our stomachs ached from unusual fullness, "I'll keep singing that song. Where would you like to go after we get out of here? I promise you that we'll go."

I didn't have to think very long. "Israel. It's warm there."

Mama laughed. "Think! No more snow!"

"Do you think we could?" I asked her.

She reached over and grasped my hand. "I do."

"What's going to happen, Mama? What if they separate us?" They'd done that with some families.

"They won't," Mama said, her voice firm like her hand gripping mine. "We won't let them. But if we are separated, we'll meet in Israel. We'll go swimming in the Dead Sea. I heard you can float there."

I believed her.

Chapter Twenty-One

SEQUINS FOR A CERTAIN KIND OF FUN

East Berlin, German Democratic Republic, May 1988

Ellie

A week after I started sorting maps, Mitzi and Kai came home, both in bright moods. Kai was whistling, and Mitzi shouted for me as soon as the door slammed behind them. "Eleanor Baum! Are you decent?"

"I'm always decent," I said, putting down the book I was reading and watching her literally bounce into the room, grinning. Behind her, Kai twirled a finger next to his head, but he couldn't keep a smile off his face. "What?"

"Come upstairs and pick out a dress. We're going to a club."

"A club's not really my thing," I said automatically. But I wasn't sure I was telling the truth anymore. That was Ellie in my true time. Ellie here? The idea of going out was more thrilling than I wanted to admit. Out of the house? Not sorting maps? Dancing? A thrill, like sneaking out, but without the danger.

"Did it sound optional? No. Come on."

"And I have to wear one of your dresses?" I asked doubtfully as she grabbed my hand and pulled me off the couch. "Sequins aren't usually my thing."

"Apparently, lots of things aren't usually your thing," Mitzi said huffily.

"I imagine time traveling wasn't either, but you're here now," Kai said from the doorway. He looked indecently good, leaning against the wall with his hands in his pockets. He smiled a little slyly, like he knew I was checking him out. "Come on. It'll be fun that doesn't involve dead people or magic."

"Well, when you put it that way..." I teased him as Mitzi dragged me past him and up the stairs. "How can I resist?"

I probably should have waited until I saw the dresses Mitzi had to offer. She essentially emptied the closet in the other room onto the bed she or Kai used, depending who was there at night. I had stopped asking where else they spent time because Mitzi wouldn't tell me, and I didn't want to know what other bed Kai spent time in. Then she started to match outfits that under no circumstances should ever have gone together. Not that I was a fashion expert, but for the love of all things in the world, a black pleated leather skirt should never go with a red sequined top and pink stockings with deliberate holes in them. Red and pink! And a dress that looked like a peacock had been flattened onto cotton. There were actual feathers on it.

"Mitz," I said. "I don't want to look like your nails and hair combination."

"Lighten up, Ellie. You worry too much. Clearly I've let you spend too much time with Kai," Mitzi said. She looked over her shoulder at me as she tugged her shirt off over her head. "Though, neither of you seem to be minding it that much."

My brain flashed back to the train tunnel, to his hands at my hips and the warmth of his mouth against mine. I flushed and said, "We're friends. I think."

"I think we're friends as in I think we're friends but he might secretly hate me, or I think we're friends but we might secretly be…What's the word Kai uses? Ah. Snogging on the side."

I threw a hanger at her. Maturity. "Shut up."

"So you *have* kissed him!" Mitzi cried, and there was zero, absolutely *zero* way that Kai did not hear that downstairs.

I groaned and flopped onto the bed. Mitzi wiggled her way into the leather skirt and pulled the red top over her head. I grabbed the pink tights so she couldn't add them to the outfit, with the bonus of distracting her from that line of work. She pulled at the tights, laughing, and then reached out, tickling me with her free hand. I squealed and dropped the tights, rolling away from her. The grin on my face stretched my cheeks so hard it hurt.

"I heard he was a good kisser. We dated the same girl once. That was such a terrible idea. I mean, not at the same time, but still…" Mitzi pulled on the pink tights. "When are you going to make a move? You mostly stare at him and blush."

"I'm cautious," I argued.

"You're practically speechless around him."

"I wasn't tonight."

"You said maybe six words," Mitzi pointed out. "Wear the peacock dress!"

"We're from two different time periods," I reminded her, my voice falling from playful to serious. I looked around for any option other than the peacock dress and saw none.

"But you're here now," Mitzi replied easily, reminding me of another conversation Kai and I had had. She shook out the skirt and admired herself in the mirror. "Kai is suffering from what we would call *weltschmerz* but he can't quite shake his *fernweh*."

Before I could ask what those words meant, Kai knocked at the door. "Mitz, we should go soon while Rainer's at the door."

"He's right," Mitzi said to me. "Rainer will let you in. Bert comes on after him. He might not. We should get going."

I donned the peacock dress despite my better judgment and told my reflection it was just my version of Halloween this year. Or a belated Purim. Or something that said there was a reason I was wearing this ridiculous dress that hung off me like a big, sparkly bag. Really sparkly. Did I mention sparkly?

"Turn around," Mitzi ordered me. "Sit down. I need to do your makeup."

"Oh hell no," I said when I saw her eyeliner. "No. I'll do my own."

I bent over the mirror, applying a neutral and natural version of Mitzi's flamboyance while she wrestled on her boots behind me. Kai knocked at the door again and pushed it open without even asking. "Girls, hurry up."

"Boy, calm down." Mitzi replied without missing a beat.

He scowled. "I'm not a boy. That's for little kids."

"I forgot you were a man in the midst of being called a girl," she said. "And the part where you just opened the door without waiting for us…Ellie could have been naked!"

"Mitzi," I said. "Shut up."

Kai grinned, and I finally glanced over at him. I wasn't sure where he'd found the time, or the clothing, or whether maybe he was as magical as the balloons, but he looked practically edible. I barely remembered what Mitzi had said about me just staring at him before I jerked my attention back to the mirror.

"You both look fine," Kai said, stomping his boot in annoyance, not unlike the little boy Mitzi had accused him of being a few minutes ago. "We really can't miss Rainer. Otherwise, Bert's going to give Ellie the Stasi inquisition and check her against all the known informants. My tolerance for that is—"

"Yes, we've noticed your patience, darling," Mitzi said with a surprising drawl. She came over and pat his cheek. "We're ready now. Right, El?"

"Right," I said, and closed the makeup. "If I get arrested tonight, it's your fault, Mitzi."

"No one's getting arrested tonight," Kai said, but his brow furrowed deeply. "Why does she get to call you El?"

"You two *really* need a drink. Or seriously, make out already," Mitzi said. As she breezed by us out the doorway, I sneezed and glitter puffed in front of me. She had doused her hair in silver glitter. And considering it was the 1980s in East Germany, I was pretty sure it was made out of lead or mercury or something that was probably going to poison me slowly, puzzling modern-day doctors when I got back home.

"I can handle one of those," I heard myself saying. Then I stretched up on my toes and kissed Kai, right there in the middle of the doorway. Because I could. Because I wanted to. Because hey, maybe Mitzi was right. Maybe we did worry too much. Kai tasted like cinnamon and stale coffee. I sank back down onto my feet, and Kai shook his head, his hair moving around his face.

"Always surprising me," he said, sliding his hand into mine. "Now we're ready…and thanks, Mitz."

He reached out with his hand and ruffled her hair, making it rain silver glitter all over the stairs. We laughed as we stepped into the night, bright and sparkly and with all the stars in the sky above us.

Chapter Twenty-Two

PHANTASMA AND PHANTOMS

East Berlin, German Democratic Republic, May 1988

We meandered through the back streets, avoiding the heavy police presence on the main streets. Ellie still eyed Mitzi's outfit with misgiving, but I was surprised Mitzi had tamed her inner wild child to only a few incongruous color combinations and a handful of glitter. There were nights when she wrote slogans against East Germany on her skin, and those were the nights that I spent more time glaring at her than enjoying the fun. I figured she really did get that the risk was high tonight and we didn't need to tempt fate.

But we hadn't gone out in almost six months. In January, the protests had resulted in mass arrests and Rainer closing Phantasma, afraid that some of his people who were arrested had been outed by Stasi informants in the club. When he reopened, he did it so quietly that I heard the club was empty the first couple of weeks. He probably lost money trying to keep it stocked.

He was going to lose his shit when he saw us. Mitz and I used to be a couple of his most frequent customers. It was one way to blow off steam. Lately, we had taken to midnight conversations in the kitchen, pushing a bottle of vodka back and forth between us while Ellie slept above us. The girl could sleep through anything.

And then, she could take the edge off me in that quiet way of hers. She had no idea. Mitzi was contagious like the glitter she wore. Wherever she went, she made people sparkle because she sparkled. Ellie calmed people because she was calm.

"What does your shirt say?" Ellie asked, turning her head to try to read my shirt as we walked. I stopped to let her read it under the streetlight. I'd worn it as my own little protest, safer than Mitzi's slogans written on the skin and as daring as I'd get with Ellie here. I watched her mouth form the word *sehnsucht*. Then she peeked up, puzzled.

"Sehnsucht," I said, pronouncing the word slowly for her. "It means…ah, like a deep longing, but for something that can't really be defined."

"That makes sense," Ellie said, her bottom lip jutting out as she thought. I wanted to touch it, kiss it. I looked away from her. She said, her voice hesitant, "Mitzi said you have fernweh and—weltschmerz?"

"Similar ideas." Not exactly. Fernweh, maybe. A longing for a home that didn't exist. Too many outsiders thought of us Romani like that. Like every human needs the solidity of a place. I didn't need a place. I wanted the solidity of my own mind, whether or not that required the solidity of a place. Weltschmerz, or a world weariness, I'd argue with, but Mitzi often called me this to my face. She liked to think that she was the bright to my dark. I guess she was.

Phantasma was lights and bass and a floor that shook hearts in their rib cages. It was too many people trying to be alive at the same time. Half the time, like tonight, you could barely hear the music through the blasted-out speakers shaking dangerously overhead, and god only knew what Rainer paid to have the neighbors and police ignore the noise at nights.

Rainer probably had some shady smuggling deals going on. As long as I didn't know about them, I didn't really care. Phantasma was like coming home. At the door, Rainer—all five foot three of him with his slippery smile and his odd eyes, one brown and one blue—got off the stool and shook my hand, slapping my back. He hugged Mitzi and kissed both her cheeks, repeating the process with Ellie, who blushed. Of course.

"Long time, no see," Rainer said, flashing a gold-toothed smile. "I thought you were going to stay away forever."

"Giving you some space," I said. "Others return?"

I didn't mean the general public, and he knew it. Rainer was one of the only outsiders to know about the balloons. He knew because he'd sent his wife and daughter over to the West on them. He didn't want to leave yet. He said big things were coming, and he wanted to be a witness. If I told one person what Ellie had told me about the wall coming down, I'd tell Rainer. He was one of the good ones.

"Sure," he said. "Christian, Trina, Klaus, Heinz, Jules, Paloma, Bernadette...Just you two holding out."

Mitzi said, "Life got busy."

"You mean your fake boyfriend here got a new girl," Rainer said, jutting his chin at Ellie. "Who are you going to play hetero with now, Mitzi, my love?"

Ellie's hand tightened around mine, and Mitzi smiled wolfishly. "Heinz owes me."

Rainer threw his head back and laughed. "I bet he does. Little ass."

I unfurled a West German note from my pocket and pressed it into Rainer's hand. "We're good?"

He didn't even look at it. He could tell by the feel, rubbing it between two fingers as he slid it into his pocket, that it was genuine. He once tried to teach me to feel the difference between counterfeit and genuine notes. I lacked whatever special senses he contained in his fingertips.

We slipped down the stairs, brushing by people smoking on the steps. I kept a tight grip of Ellie's hand until she whispered that I was hurting her and I quickly released her hand. Her fingers touched the small of my back, and we made our way through the mess, people reaching out to touch us, offer us drugs, drinks, music, sex. Anything. It was fair game inside Rainer's club. It was an escape from aboveground. This was underground. This was subculture. This was what we all dreamed about when we fell asleep at night. Some people practically lived here because it was easier than being up there. For anyone with a work ban, it was also the safest place to be.

The music hit us two floors down into the dark of the club, a throbbing steady bass that cut through my chest, making my heart feel tight. I turned around as the lights passed from red to green to blue to black lights and back to red again. In the changing lights, Ellie looked even younger, a little overwhelmed and a little scared. I stopped her on the bottom step and had to put my mouth next to her ear to be heard. At least, that's what I told myself.

"We don't have to be here," I shouted. "If it's too much."

It smelled like pot and sweat and dampness, like the basement never dried out from night after night of sweaty bodies trying to dance away their own weltschmerz. I couldn't hear her reply, but Ellie stepped off the last stair and past me into the chaos. I followed her and Mitzi through the crowd to the bar. Phantasma had one drink. You got whatever they served you that night, and you didn't ask questions. The bartenders wore bras and miniskirts, their stomachs painted with rainbow stripes and occasionally a flag of united Germany. It was risky. The last thing anyone wanted was something permanently on their body that was against socialist government.

"Brigitte," I said, lifting a hand to greet a dark-haired girl with a bar through her lower lip. She probably didn't hear me say her name, but she definitely saw me. She leaned over the bar and slapped me so fast I didn't have time to deflect it. The sting wrapped around my head like tendrils. I winced, bringing a hand up to my hot cheek that was tingling as feeling returned to it. "Hi."

"You broke Karolina's heart," yelled Brigitte over the noise as she poured us drinks out of a brown pitcher. At my elbow, Ellie's eyes were wider than plates, going from my reddened cheek to the drinks, to Brigitte where they lingered over the piercing. It wasn't even the strangest piercing Brigitte had, but I wasn't going to tell Ellie that right now.

"To be fair," I said, "she broke up with me. And then slept with my best friend."

Mitzi shook her head. "Don't involve me. I didn't even know you guys were a thing until after she broke up with me. This was different than that Marie debacle."

Brigitte poked me in the chest. "Because you wouldn't *commit*. You are lucky I did not spit in your drink."

I smiled. "You have my eternal gratitude."

She shook her head and then glared at Ellie. "Who are you?"

"Ellie Baum," Ellie said promptly and held out her hand.

I hid a smile as Brigitte scowled at her and gingerly took her hand, shaking it slowly. Ellie kept smiling, and Brigitte glared at me as she poured Ellie a drink. "She's too happy. Where's she from?"

"Here. She just doesn't get out much. You'd be happy too if it was your first time at Phantasma," I told her.

Brigitte snorted. "I'd be happy for my first time of anything back."

Ellie sipped the beer and made a face. "Oh, this is some awful beer."

"Socialism tastes like shit, sweetheart," Brigitte said in return, rolling her eyes.

Mitzi leaned over the bar and whispered something to Brigitte that made Brigitte's eyebrows go up. She glanced at Mitzi, her eyes traveling up Mitzi's body. It was really strange sometimes, seeing someone check out your best friend so blatantly. Brigitte nodded and said, "See you after?"

"Looking forward to it," Mitzi sang over her shoulder, taking Ellie by the elbow and steering her toward the floor. I once again trailed after them, realizing quickly that I was the third wheel of the Mitzi and Ellie Show.

The middle of the dance floor felt like the middle of a war zone. Bodies and lights and sound made the room tilt. I steadied myself with a hand on Mitzi's hip, instinctively reaching for her. Ellie turned around and shouted something to Mitzi that I didn't hear, but both girls cracked up, spinning around, their drinks to their mouths, starting to dance and drawing me toward them. If this was a bad trip, it was the best bad trip I'd ever been on. I let the music rock through me, taking over my body, watching the lights play out on everyone's faces, hands touching and reaching out.

Mitzi grabbed Ellie's drink from her, nudging her toward me, and we came together, dancing and laughing, barely able to hear each other, but her fingers ran up my arms and my hands found the curves of her body.

Forget time travel. And whatever way time works. Forget all of that. Forget every reason I shouldn't be falling head over bloody heels for this girl with her summer-sky eyes.

I bent my head and touched our foreheads together, watching her eyes flutter closed. I said, hoping my voice didn't carry much beyond us, "Of all the people to grab a balloon, Ellie Baum, I'm glad it was you."

She smiled and tilted her mouth to my ear. This time, my eyes closed. She said, "I bet you tell that to all the time-traveling girls."

I grinned. "Only the pretty ones. Is it working?"

"I was won over by the train tunnel expeditions." She laughed and said, "That's what she said."

"That's what who said?" I asked, but my question was lost in the changing music, our bodies crowded together as people pushed onto the dance floor. Mitzi reappeared, her hands empty and totally slammed. She made kissy faces at us and then twirled off, dancing with some guy wearing only the top half of a tuxedo and washed-out jeans.

Ellie brushed her hair out of her face and pointed over my shoulder at the bar. I nodded and took her by the hand, sliding back over there for a breather and something to drink. Brigitte rolled her eyes when we asked for water, but she managed to find some. We'd probably be the only ones asking for water the whole night.

Ellie drummed her fingers on the backs of my hands, across the thin white scars on my knuckles. "I hadn't noticed these before. Where'd you get the scar?"

"Getting out of England. I keep thinking I'll get tattoos to cover them up, but I haven't yet." I pulled my hands into fists, turning them toward her to look like I was boxing. "A sun and a moon. Duality. Both give off just enough light. I want to do that too."

She pulled my hands down and kissed me again. I didn't want to be here anymore. I wanted to take her home. That was exactly the worst next step, but she sang my body alive. I wanted to sing her alive too. I tugged her off the chair to stand between my legs, kissing her smiling mouth.

"Want to get out of here?" I asked her, half hopeful, half dreading the answer.

"We just got here," she whispered back, her lips brushing against mine.

"I don't care." I ran my hand down the back of her sweaty neck, across the low back of her dress. She shivered.

"Okay," she said. "I'll go."

I moved impossibly fast out of the chair, and then forcibly slow myself down, leading her through the crowd, my pulse drowning out the beat of the room. I gestured to Mitzi over the heads of everyone. She made a face at me when I pointed to Ellie and myself and then the stairs. That was fine. She had plans afterward anyway, and I was not interested in standing between Mitzi and Brigitte.

We climbed the stairs, surfacing from the stink and the heat and the bass, and pushed open the door into the fresh air. Ellie shook her head and laughed, running a finger down her own arm in the sweat that clung to her skin.

"Gross," she said, giggling. She gave me a shy look. "Where are we going?"

I didn't know, but I didn't think it mattered. The rooftop. The house. Anywhere. Anywhere with her. We waved to Bert, who scowled back at us, and headed down through the alley, back toward home. Ellie told me about the one and only time she'd snuck out of her parents' house to go to a house party, which sounded wildly different than ours. I was laughing at her description of people getting drunk around a pool when we turned the corner and both came to a dead stop.

Red balloons. Bodies. Everywhere. Littering the street. At first, I didn't recognize them. I thought they were blankets, or people sleeping in the streets. Then my eyes and mind focused on the stillness of the body closest to us, the unusual clothing, the balloons, some still tethered to hands, others drifting down the street, floating up or down, bumping into walls aimlessly. I heard Ellie whisper something I couldn't process. The stillness of the street became increasingly loud in my head, filling all the spaces that the club music had created inside me. Everything was too quiet. My training told me to think about danger, but all I could think was, There are so many.

"Kai," she said, squeezing my hand. "Kai, that guy. He has a cell phone in his hand."

I remembered her telling me about cell phones, tiny portable phones. She let go of my hand and approached the first body. She crouched by it, her fingers trembling as they took the body's pulse. She looked over her shoulder at me, lips pressed together, and shook her head. She pulled the cell phone out of his hand and pressed a button on the side.

She shook her head again. Her German stumbled for the first time in weeks as she tried to find words from her time that I'd know. That was a strange realization, and it almost caught me off guard in this moment. "It's got a code on it. I can't see inside it. I can see the date though. Kai, they're from the future. Again."

I swallowed and took a deep breath. "How many of them?"

We began to count, but when we got to nine and saw more bodies down a side alley, Ellie put her hand on my arm, making me jump. "This isn't for us, Kai. We have to find Felix or Ashasher or someone."

"Get Mitzi," I said. "Quick."

She slipped the phone into my pocket and scooted off into the dark, leaving me in a street full of bodies. Full of dead people and their broken magic balloons.

Chapter Twenty-Three

AMEN

East Berlin, German Democratic Republic, May 1988

Ellie

Mitzi wrapped her arms around herself. I was too worked up to feel the sweat drying and cooling on my skin. I'd be cold later, I knew. But right then, I was numb to it. The turning of the corner and bodies scattered everywhere. Everywhere. Like a scene out of a movie after the killer virus went through a mall or something. Not all the bodies looked like they were from the same time period though. Some of them wore clothes I recognized, or had iPods or cell phones. I was half hoping as we turned the corner that Felix would be there, fixing things.

He wasn't. Just Kai, slumped against the wall. He stared at the ground, his eyes shimmering, and said, "Sixteen. Sixteen bodies."

Mitzi swore colorfully, stomping down the alley. She stopped at each body, feeling for a pulse. I followed her, unsure of how to help. She didn't look up at me when she said, "You know where to look on these people. Find any ID or anything else that can give them away as time travelers. We're not going to get the bodies off the streets before the Stasi find them."

So behind her, as she checked for a pulse, I stripped the people of their ID, phones, iPods, medical ID tags. My stomach turned when I saw someone was an emergency room resident, another with pictures of her children in her wallet, and another…another from Pittsburgh. Her address on her driver's license was right around the corner from me, but I didn't recognize her. I wondered if there were signs up around the neighborhood with her face. I wondered if there were signs up with my face.

These people would be among those missing people who are never found. They went for runs and disappeared. They stepped outside for a smoke and disappeared. These people…I had read about them in the news. And now I was one of them. How long had balloons been acting out and killing time travelers?

And why had I survived when everyone else was dying?

The whole process took fifteen minutes, especially once we fell into the rhythm. We didn't expect to feel a pulse. I stopped waiting for Mitzi to feel for one before I began to feel for a wallet or purse or anything to take with me. One of the girls from a few years after my year—time was getting complicated in my head—had an enormous bag, so I started stuffing everything in there. By the end, it was biting into my shoulder from the weight of it all.

One woman had fallen at a strange angle, and from a distance, for a moment, I thought it was my mom with her short, curly hairy and her favorite sandals on. My heart stopped in my throat, and I stumbled over the sidewalk toward her, falling to my knees. My hands shook as they brushed her shoulder. Tears filled my eyes as I brushed the woman's hair back against her ear, her skin dry and cold, as cold as the pavement.

It was not my mother. I pressed my hand to my mouth and closed my eyes, trying to breathe. Mitzi squatted next to me and said, "Okay?"

I nodded and took a deep breath. "Yeah. Yeah, fine. I just thought—"

Mitzi said, her voice dropping low, "Don't think. Just hurry. We can't dawdle."

I reached into the woman's purse and picked out her wallet. An appointment card fell out. She must have been on her way to a doctor's appointment when she saw the balloon. My stomach twisted in my gut, and I shoved the wallet and the card into the bag on my shoulder. I couldn't look at the woman anymore. I bit my lip and glanced up at the sky, anywhere to get my eyes off her face. I brushed the hair back over her face. She deserved a little peace and anonymity here.

We headed back to Kai, standing like a sentry at the end. His eyes were less glazed over, a little more focused. He took the bag from me without a word and slung it over his shoulder. His eyes ran over the tears on my cheeks, and I turned away from him, sniffling. I didn't need to be questioned on this right now. To my relief, Kai respected my silent plea for space.

"We shouldn't be here when the Volkspolizei get here," he said, looking at Mitzi. "We need to go to the workshop."

"We need to find Felix," I said, surprising myself. "He helped me when I found that body. He can make them disappear."

"I don't care about making bodies disappear," Kai said, striding ahead of us, Mitzi and I exchanging looks and scrambling to catch up. "I want answers. And I want them now. I don't care what I need to do to get them."

"Kai."

"It's *Friday night*," he snapped. "No balloons Friday and Saturday nights, Mitzi. Someone's sending off balloons illegally."

"Maybe there's a delayed reaction."

"Does that mean that there are sixteen dead Passengers too?" I asked. Mitzi stumbled and I reached out with a hand to catch her, but she waved me away, looking pale.

"People would have to notice sixteen *other* dead people. Not to mention, the entire Council doesn't send off sixteen balloons in a week! It doesn't matter. We're getting answers. We're going to the workshop." Kai's strides shortened so he walked with twice the speed. Mitzi and I followed behind him but he drew away, even from us.

Mitzi said under her breath, "Just follow his lead. If he gets out of control, I'll knock him out at the workshop. We don't need another body on the streets right now."

By the time we got to the tunnels, Kai was far enough ahead of us that we could only hear his footsteps echoing. He sounded lonely, all the way up there by himself in that head of his. I began to shiver. The cold caught up with me, and in the dank, dark of the tunnels smelling like rotting spring air, it sank to the center of my bones. I shook, stuffing my hands into my armpits and grinding my teeth together against the shriek that sprang to my tongue.

A glint of light burst in the tunnel…and disappeared again. Kai beat us to the workshop. Mitzi cursed and looked over her shoulder. I waved her on, so she sprinted to the end, calling his name even though it echoed behind us and ahead of us in the tunnel, alerting everyone to our presence. Once in these tunnels, Kai's hands had been all over me and we had kissed standing on the rails. Today couldn't be farther from that moment.

I found the door, much to my surprise, and opened it tentatively. Inside, Mitzi chewed the ends of her hair, blocking Kai from my line of sight. I could hear his voice, gentle and soft. I shut the door behind me as quietly as possible, looking around the eerily quiet workshop. Where did they all go when they weren't in the workshop? Why wasn't anyone here?

I made my way to Mitzi and Kai, who sat holding his sister's hands. The girl looked exactly like Kai, but with long, pretty dark hair that fell below her shoulders. Her eyes bounced everywhere but on her brother's face. She tried to tug her hands free from him more than once, and he held on tight both times.

"Sabina," he murmured quietly, and then he said something in a language I didn't recognize. She flinched, hiking her shoulder to her ear, scrunching up her face tight. She shook her head.

"Use German, Kai," Mitzi said. "She understands more German. I know you don't like that but..."

Her voice trailed off, but Kai nodded and said in German, "Bean, where's Aurora? Why are you here on a Friday night?"

"Aurora's on the streets," said Sabina, and then she jerked violently. "Let me go go go. Go, Kai, go."

"I don't want to go," he said a little too harshly, and tears filled Sabina's eyes.

"Kai," I whispered.

His shoulders slumped. "Sabina, are Ashasher or Aurora doing something they shouldn't be doing?"

"They're working," Sabina told him, her eyes going to the ceiling. "Fixing the world."

Kai reached out and cupped his sister's cheek. I sucked in a breath at the tenderness in his face as Sabina's eyes settled on him. He said, his voice low and sincere, "We're all fixing the world, Sabina. We all want it to be a better place, right? Yes, some of us have better paths. You know how when you're walking outside, you can walk on the sidewalk or the street? Some people are walking in the street. They're going to get hit by cars. And they're going to get people in trouble and a lot of people hurt. More than them."

Sabina's eyes flickered from Kai's face to the ceiling. "We're all fixing the world."

"What are your teachers doing on the streets tonight, *chey*?" asked Kai.

Sabina's whole body vibrated violently. "Can't tell you, can't tell you. Fixing the world. Go, go, Kai. The dissonance between two balloons and the genetic markers for magical transference create a sequence of events that alter the indefinite integral of the *f* of *x*. The disruption of the continuity causes..."

She rambled on until Kai leaned forward and kissed her forehead. She closed her eyes, and we all held our breath as she fell silent. Kai said, "It's okay, Sabina. I'm not mad at you."

"Do you promise me?" she asked, breathless.

"I promise you forever and always," he said, and stood up. "Can you do a favor for me? Don't look at me like that. I'm not going to ask you to break a rule."

Sabina smiled at the floor. Her smile reminded me of Kai, so quiet and unsure. "What do you need?"

"For you to go to the bathroom for seven hundred and twenty seconds," he said. "Precisely. Can you do that for me?"

"Okay," she said and stood up, wrapping her arms around his neck. She said something to him in the strange language he'd used at first, and he replied in the same language. It must have been their mother tongue.

She disappeared into a room, shutting the door behind her. Kai said, "Mitzi, watch her. Ellie, come with me."

Neither of us argued. He seemed less manic now that the only person in the workshop was his sister. I followed him up the metal stairs that clapped beneath my shoes. I ran my hand along the yellow railings as we walked around the curve of the library overlooking the workshop area, and then Kai jimmied a door between two bookcases. He held it open and gestured me through first.

"Ashasher and Aurora share an office," he said quietly.

I stepped through cautiously, but saw only a messy desk and books stacked to the ceiling. A big, fancy desk made out of bright, polished red-colored wood with ivory knobs and handles sat in the middle of the room, lit by a giant overhead chandelier. The room felt like an aboveground study in a fancy mansion. It didn't feel in the least like I was beneath ground in a former subway station turned magic balloon workshop. Except for all the drawings of balloons scattered over the desk.

Kai turned over papers on the desk and said, "We're looking for anything with an equation."

I began to go through the piles of papers with him. We worked in silence, turning over sketch after sketch of balloons in different angles (who knew there were angles to balloons?) with only words written on them ("hopeful," "maybe," "promising"). Kai folded and stuck a few of these in his back pocket, but he shook his head and tossed most of them into a different pile. There were no equations written down. We opened drawers and pulled books down from the shelves, looking for answers.

What answers, I don't know. Just something. Something to explain what was happening, I guess. And I guess that Kai thought Aurora and Ashasher, one of them, had to be the one behind it now. I couldn't exactly disagree, but G-d, how could they? How could it be them? Ashasher was so kind, and Aurora really believed in saving people. She had been doing it so long. But no one else was here, other than their student, Sabina, and there were *sixteen* dead people on the street because of balloons.

Kai held up a handful of papers. "A lot of stuff here. It's hard to understand but…" and then he held up a single black feather. Ashasher. "Only he can remove the feathers. He doesn't shed them."

We stared at each other for a good long moment. It couldn't be him. It was just a feather. Perhaps he'd used it as a bookmark. But I'd barely seen him since I arrived, and whenever I came to work on the maps with Aurora, she said Ashasher was working. Could he be working on the rogue balloons? Was he working alone?

"Kai," I started to say, then fell silent. Below us, Mitzi said something and Sabina answered her. Seven hundred and twenty seconds were up.

Kai tucked the papers into his back pocket and said, "Maybe this will slow them down. Or maybe it's the evidence Felix needs. Come on, let's go."

We ran down the stairs, and Kai kissed his sister's cheek as he grabbed Mitzi's wrist. "We're out of here. See you later, Sabina. Be safe."

"You be safe," she said, and as the door shut behind us, I realized that was the most sane and hopeful thing she had said the entire time we were there. It wasn't particularly comforting.

We trotted through the tunnels at a steady clip, climbing up at the abandoned Potsdamer Platz station platform and climbing out the stairs, breathless and staying low to the ground as we slipped out of the death zone under the cover of darkness. With police sirens blaring and the sound of more and more coming closer, we stayed in a quiet street, hiding beneath a tree.

"Mitz, go home. Ellie and I are going to find Felix," Kai said.

"Ellie will come with me," Mitzi said calmly.

"What?" I looked back and forth between the two of them. "Why aren't we all going together?"

Splitting up at this point seemed like a really terrible idea. In every movie, splitting up was how people died.

Kai shook his head. "You are wearing absurd shoes, Mitz, and you stand out more. Someone has to be home in case Aurora stops by for some reason. I need Ellie with me. Felix won't play nice unless she's with me."

That sounded plausible. I shrugged and nodded when Kai raised an eyebrow at me. Felix had been a bit short and cold when I met him. I could imagine him being very difficult with Kai.

Mitzi glared at Kai for a good long moment and then said, "Fine. Don't you dare get Ellie killed."

"I'm taking her with me to prevent exactly that," Kai said. He twirled one of Mitzi's teal locks around his finger and then tugged on it. "Pretend to have faith in me."

"I don't, and I'm not pretending," Mitzi said. She shot him a glare as she hugged me. "If he's an asshole, just run home."

"Deal," I whispered back and let her go.

Kai took my hand, holding the papers with the other hand. "Come on. I know where he is."

For no reason at all, Felix was waiting for us in a park in an affluent neighborhood far from the wall. He sat on the back of a park bench, tall, his tattoos lit up in the streetlights, and completely at ease with standing out in the middle of the night. He stood up as we approached and nodded to the lights and screech of sirens whipping by us and going toward Phantasma.

"Thought you might have been involved in that," he said calmly.

Kai handed him the papers and the feather. "Sixteen dead bodies this time. Found these in Ashasher and Aurora's office."

"I know," Felix said, frowning. "The Volkspolizei got to the bodies before I did. That's going to be a disastrous amount of paperwork. All from the future."

"Varying times," I told him, feeling Kai's surprise through his hand in mine. "A few from the early nineties, a few from early two thousands, a few from around my time. Why didn't any of them survive?"

"I think sharing blood with Garrick must have protected you," said Felix slowly. "I suspect, though I cannot prove it, that he died when the balloon tried to jump through time. The jump killed him, not you. A balloon couldn't travel without a person, which means we have sixteen dead Passengers too. Somewhere."

"And it's likely because of something Ashasher or Aurora is doing," Kai said, his voice rough.

Felix shook his head. "It's hard to imagine two of the people who invented balloon magic being sloppy in their mathematical equations. Evidence is paramount. The accusations are serious, you understand."

But he was flipping through papers anyway, like he almost already believed us, even without the evidence. He handed them back to Kai. "This is not enough. I need real proof. What else?"

"That's what we have. Sixteen dead people, sixteen dead Passengers somewhere, and all of those papers," I protested. "How is it not enough?"

"I want a new safe house for Ellie," Kai said, skipping Felix's protest and deliberately not looking at me. "One safe from even Mitzi and me. I'm not going for more evidence and risking any more until you take her out of this."

"No." My voice stayed calm, even though my insides trembled. If he thought that would keep me safe, he was wrong. I couldn't imagine staying inside again, but staying inside indefinitely without him and Mitzi? I couldn't. I wouldn't. I'd leave the house. I'd climb out a window. I didn't care. I wasn't going to stay a prisoner like that.

"If we're caught or tortured, or if someone we think we trust is behind this and asks us where you are, I don't want to know," Kai said, staring ferociously at Felix who stared back at the two of us, his facial expression placid, as if he'd expected this fight.

"No. Don't ask me to be isolated and alone again. I can't…I won't lose you and Mitzi just because of some madman."

"Ellie." Kai's voice cracked in the middle.

My hands curled into fists. "I am a person, Kai. Not a thing. You can't put me where you wish and hide me without my consent. You can't move me around without any input from me. You can't—"

"Please," Kai said, turning toward me. "We're trying to keep you safe."

It took me a moment to gather my thoughts. Between his eyes, and the complexity of the emotions swirling in me like a hurricane gaining speed over warmer waters, I needed to close my eyes and pick my words carefully. "Please do not keep me safe at the expense of my sanity."

No one spoke for a moment. My heartbeat echoed in my ears, and when I opened my eyes, Kai had his covered with his hand, like that alone would be enough to ask G-d to protect us. Felix studied me under his hooded brow, playing with his bottom lip, thick arms crossed across his powerful body. I wanted to believe that with Felix on our side, no one would hurt me. No one had come after me. They had only pulled through more people who hadn't survived. Maybe I wasn't special. Maybe I was just lucky. Just an anomaly.

"I cannot move her to a safe house if she won't go, Kai," Felix said at last. "You know better than most that the Zerberus cannot take people against their will, even if it is in their best interest."

Kai flinched. I had no idea what Felix was talking about, but it was clear that Kai knew. His shoulders slumped. He said, "We're running out of time. Whoever is doing this is getting bolder. Maybe it's not Aurora, and maybe it's not Ashasher. Maybe someone's planting papers in their office."

"Not bolder," Felix said, shaking his head. The python on his arm moved, I swore. "Desperate. They're panicking. They're getting sloppy. And that's exactly how we're going to catch them."

"It's going to be someone I know, no matter what," Kai said, his voice breaking again. If we were alone, in the kitchen, I'd reach for him. But we weren't alone. We were on the street in the night with police sirens wailing in the distance.

Felix's shoulders sagged a little, and he sighed. "Likely. But we can't think about that right now. What we need is evidence. I cannot ask the Zerberus to strip someone of magic without evidence. I need a confession, or papers that have a name *and* say "time traveling" on them. Or, to witness it. I'm sorry. That's what I need to get the Zerberus to move on either Ashasher or Aurora."

I tried to imagine the raven-feathered man and his kind voice and his strange cadence killing people out of desperation. Or making balloons badly because he wanted to alter time for some unknown reason. Or quiet Aurora, who seemed to care so much for her students, for her people. The Aurora out of Saba's stories, the girl in the purple dress at the fence who wanted to share in his stories, the girl who brought him a red balloon when he needed it most.

It was the empathy, I realized, that kept me from believing ill of them. Could empathetic people kill?

Kai sighed, echoing Felix, and shook his head, his hair momentarily obscuring his face. "Scheiße."

Felix smiled a little, the corner of his mouth tipping up just enough for me to see under the glow of the streetlamps. "That's one word for it. We're going to find who's doing this, Kai. And we're going to keep Ellie safe. But I can't promise it won't get worse before it gets better."

"How do you know?" I asked suddenly. Kai startled, as if he had forgotten I was standing there.

Felix watched me with his eyes that caught every cut of light. "This is what I do. I bring people in for the Zerberus. Usually it's people"—he glanced at Kai—"with unusual talents. But sometimes it's people who stray outside the guidelines of balloon magic."

"You kill them," I said.

Felix shook his head. "No. I bring them in. We try them. And if they're found to be guilty, we strip them of their magic."

"Most commit suicide after that," Kai added quietly.

Felix's eyes glinted. "That's their choice. You know as well as I that one can live a good and meaningful life without magic, even in the face of incredible darkness."

Kai nodded. I reached out and slipped my hand into his, glad when his fingers laced between mine, and he squeezed my hand. I squeezed back.

"We should try to find the dead Passengers," Kai said, but he sounded exhausted, and some train stop beyond sad. Despondent, maybe.

Softly, I said, "No, Kai. Leave that to Felix. We should go home."

"Find me if you find anything more," Felix said. "It's better if the focus isn't on you so much. I'll try not to put you in danger. Kai, is she…?"

I blinked, but they weren't talking about me. Kai shook his head. "I don't know. I am afraid to talk to her. It's hard when she—"

"It's fine," said Felix, his voice soft, as if he were trying to comfort Kai without ever touching him. "It's probably wise not to trust her right now."

"Good night," Kai said, cutting the conversation short.

"*Gute nacht*," said Felix, and he saluted us in his own peculiar way, three fingers to his lips, before walking off into the dark.

We waited until the dark swallowed him before we went home. The walk was dark and quiet, Kai's fear heavy in the air around us. It took up all the air. I looked up at the sky and thought about an alley full of red balloons and dead-quiet bodies.

Silently, I said the Mourner's Kaddish for them, saying the last few lines aloud. "*Oseh shalom bimromav, hu ya'aseh shalom aleinu: v'al kol Yisrael. V'imru, Amen.*"

Kai startled me when he echoed, "Amen."

Chapter Twenty-Four

DAYENU

Łódź Ghetto, Poland, April 1942

Benno

Our wedding invitation, the relocation notice, came a week after Passover. We had done seders in secret, and for the first time in two years, I sang the Four Questions, usually reserved for the youngest child of the family. I had taught them to Ruthie years ago, just when she should have started school. Her birthday was during Passover. It had always been a special week for her, and she loved singing the question: *Why is this night different from all other nights?* I chanted the Hebrew, thinking the night wasn't different at all.

But it was different. Rebekah's father was still at the ghetto and he hugged me, just as a father would a son. And in the basement of one of the buildings, there were twenty-four of us, six times the legal number to be gathered. I imagined us back in Egypt, slaves hiding and whispering ancient prayers in secret. I imagined us being taken away by Pharaoh's army, executed in front of everyone to send a message.

And then, when I thought about it, when I heard my mama whispering her part of the Haggadah, sounding tired but hopeful for the first time since she lost her husband and her daughter in the same two-week span, I thought I'd like to send that message. I knew we weren't supposed to seek martyrdom, but if it came looking for me, I'd accept it. I'd die for this cause.

Last year, when we were celebrating Pesach in relative freedom, we only sang a few stanzas of "Dayenu." But this time, Chaim Eiderman, who led the service, said we'd sing all fifteen parts.

His voice was hoarse, and he was bent over, his knuckles broken and cracked, his black coat hanging around his thin shoulders, but over the light of the candles, he said, "G-d bestowed fifteen gifts upon our ancestors. May he repeat the miracle we witnessed in the land of Mitzrayim here in Łódź."

The first five stanzas of "Dayenu" were about God freeing the slaves. The second five were about the miracles God performed, and the final five were about being with God. Chaim taught us all of them, painstakingly, one by one, risking his life and our lives the longer we were down there, but every time we whispered *Dayenu*—"It would have been enough"—the knots in my chest unraveled a little bit further. When we sang the last line, *Ilu hichnisanu l'eretz yisrael, v'lo vanah lanu et beit hamikdash— Dayenu!* I cried.

I wept like a child.

It would have been enough.

It would have been enough.

That night, I lay in bed for hours, staring at the ceiling. Why hadn't a miracle happened here? What had we done wrong? Had the Jews in Egypt asked themselves the same thing? Did they also think God had abandoned them? Had it only been Moses, the speech-impaired shepherd, who had brought back their faith, wrapped up in their hope for freedom?

Is that what faith is? The tangible hope for freedom? Was I a bad Jew, a poor practitioner of faith, because I no longer believed that I would be free? That I believed God had forsaken us in our greatest time of need?

When I dreamed, I dreamed that I woke and the sun was shining, hot enough that the mud dried up in the ghetto, and when the bread truck came, it had a loaf for Mama and me both. When we went to work, our supervisor let us out early, without penalty, just because the sun was shining. As I walked home through the streets, Rebekah came out of her father's house and slipped her tiny, warm hand into mine.

"They took you away," I said to her, bewildered, looking around for someone who would come to take her away from me again.

She said, "They let me come home, because she's coming."

"Who's coming?"

Rebekah smiled. I loved her smile. Her teeth bit her bottom lip, like she was afraid to be too happy. "She's going to lead us out. She'll part the Nazis like the Red Sea."

And as we walked, others came out of their houses, everyone dressed in their Shabbat clothes, all clean and washed up. People were singing "Dayenu" and holding hands. A few people linked arms, running, laughing, and shrieking, straight down the middle of the growing crowd. My mama came out of the hat-making factory and walked next to Rebekah and me.

She said, "Do you think Ruth and Papa are waiting for us? Do you think Ernst is?"

I wrapped my arm around her shoulders and said, "Yes."

I don't know why I felt so sure, but I did. Wherever Rebekah and the others were going, whatever was happening, it was a miracle. My sister and my brother would come back to me, and my papa too. We were going to leave Łódź, walk through the fence and the guards, and then the fences would close around them, electric and barbed, wrapping them up, jailing them, just like the sea toppled the Egyptian army.

When we reached the fence by the cemetery, the girl from the other side stood in a huge gap in the fence. She wore her purple dress, and her dog sat at her side. She held in her hand a red balloon, just like the luftballon Ruthie and I saw from the train.

We walked toward her and she said, "Benno Hirsch. Dayenu."

Waking up made me want to die.

Chapter Twenty-Five

CONNECTING THE DOTS

East Berlin, German Democratic Republic, May 1988

I couldn't sleep. I couldn't stop moving. If I stopped moving, I was pretty sure I'd fall apart—and I didn't have time to fall apart. None of us had the time, but I was the only one teetering on the edge. If this fell apart, if the balloons were bad, then I had to get Sabina out. But how? And I couldn't leave Ellie and Mitzi behind. Not after everything.

Ellie and I didn't talk the whole way home, and when we got there, Mitzi was sitting on the bottom step, a beer in her hands, her eyes flat and vacant. I probably shouldn't have let her check all those bodies. Mitz didn't fall apart. She just shut down like a goddamn border crossing in protest.

I paced the living room, staring at the papers on the floor. *Not enough evidence,* Felix had said. But this was all we had.

I rubbed my face and then stopped, trying to rearrange the papers with my mind and find any clue to attach Aurora to the broken balloons. Or the not-broken balloons. It took me a few hours that night, long after Ellie had tired of watching me from the couch and had retired upstairs to her bed, to realize that there were two components to preventing what had happened tonight from happening again.

First, we needed to find evidence connecting the balloons to one of the Schöpfers.

Second, we needed to find motivation. Was it deliberate, or was it accidental? If it was accidental, how was the magic going so wrong? If it was deliberate, what was the intended purpose of the balloons? Why was someone releasing balloons so late in secret? Why were the balloons undocumented?

The more steps I took back and forth across the room, the more questions I had. There were no easy answers. The sketches told me nothing. Aurora, if it was her, was playing her cards close to her chest. If it was Ashasher, my gut told me we'd never catch him. He'd end us with one of those feathers of his, or he'd be out of the country with all the evidence as soon as he knew we were on to him. They could both lie through their teeth and I'd believe them. We'd all believe them. We'd never had cause to doubt them before now.

Like Felix, I realized that it could only be those two. They were the only two Schöpfers who were experienced enough to write new magic, magic that wasn't invented, magic that was only theory—and illegal theory at that. They were the only two Schöpfers willing to risk their jobs too.

Ashasher had once fought tooth and nail for a Passenger who was denied on the grounds that she was an unaccompanied minor. He sent her over the wall—I ran the balloon—anyway. I got in trouble, but he got censored for a whole month. He lost out on helping four people over the wall for that one little girl. I asked him if she was worth it, and he said he could never know the answer to that, but he could sleep at night and that was enough.

I didn't have enough information to solve the problem in front of us. And that didn't matter anymore. We were out of time to collect information. The problem was snowballing, and we needed to figure out how to stop it before we had thirty-two dead people on the streets next week. For a brief moment, I considered burning the whole damn workshop. But if the equations were on Aurora or Ashasher's person, then that'd do no good at all. Almost all of the balloon supplies were in the workshop, but the Council, with Aurora and Ashasher at the head of it, wouldn't be so inefficient as not to have backup balloons and writing utensils elsewhere. The Stasi could burn the workshop as well as I could.

For a heartbeat, I thought about that too. About telling the Stasi. I'd be lauded as a hero and be granted immunity forever. I might even be able to keep Sabina safe. But no, I couldn't. I didn't give a fuck about the Schöpfers, but they kept all the records of our Passengers. I couldn't do that to the people who were applying and had applied and were just waiting for a balloon. I couldn't turn them into the ghosts of East Berlin.

"I need more information," I whispered. It kept coming back to that.

"Want to know what I think?" Mitzi asked, scaring the shit out of me from the stairs. She sat there, wrapped in a blanket. I wondered how long she had been there. She stood sleepily and shuffled into the living room, carefully stepping over my piles of paper. We stood shoulder to shoulder, eyeing the mess. "I think that we have all the information. We just haven't put it together yet."

"Where is it?" I asked.

Mitzi shrugged, her arm moving up and down next to mine. "I don't know. In our heads."

"They taught us everything, Mitz," I said. When I said that to Ellie and Felix, they didn't seem to get it.

But now Mitzi turned to me, and I knew she understood. Her mouth tilted up, tight in the constraints of her sadness. "Yeah. Weird, isn't it? Like, I don't know. I've been running balloons for four years. And we've done two years together, all underneath someone who is betraying everything we were taught to hold dear."

"I don't hold them dear," I said. "They're keeping Sabina safe, that's all."

"Are they?" Mitzi asked.

I flinched and said, "You don't know what you're saying."

"You're serious? Of course I know what I'm saying, Kai. I'm saying that you were trying to keep Sabina away from people in Zerberus who wanted to pry open her brain and people who think she's fucked in the head. She was supposed to be safe here where the Zerberus barely notice the Schöpfers, but we ended up under the magnifying glass of the Zerberus in the most danger-ous city in the world. You think she's any safer here now than she was in London? What are you smoking, and where can I get some?" Mitzi's eyes flashed like a storm, and each word punched home a little harder than the previous one.

I scrubbed at my face and sighed. "You think I should take her out of here."

"Before it gets bad," Mitzi said softly. "If there are more bodies, the Stasi will put a curfew into effect and make traveling really difficult. You can get out now."

She was right. Sabina and I didn't have East German papers. We had visas stapled to our UK passports. We should have been getting them renewed every thirty days, but given that we lived here now, the Schöpfers used a stolen stamp to keep them up to date. It wouldn't be a problem for us to leave. And yet. I didn't know what I wanted to do. What I would do. I sank onto the couch and Mitzi sat down next to me, throwing her blan-ket around my shoulders. We leaned against each other, heads touching, and stared at the piles of papers.

"Just something to think about, Kai," Mitzi murmured, touch-ing my knee with her fingers. "If something happened to her, you would...God, Kai, could you do it? Could you survive it?"

There was no question. I shook my head. "Where would we go?"

"Get out. Far away from anywhere with these fucking balloons. A cottage in the Swiss mountains. Don't let her write magic. Tell everyone she's sick."

"She's not sick," I said. "That's the best part of being here. No one calls her sick. No one says that she'd be better off dead because her brain's so different, because her blood lets her do magic. They just let her be herself, Mitzi. How can I take her away from that?"

"Because whoever's doing this might kill her to punish you if you get too close to the truth. I can look for it. What are they going to do to me if you're gone?"

I turned my head and kissed the side of Mitzi's head. She was too good for me. Mitzi was the only one who never called me racial slurs in class. She was the only one who would be my partner when I was done training. And I wasn't scared of her. Her bark was much worse than her bite.

"Are you going to sleep tonight?"

I shook my head against hers. "I can't."

"Okay," she said. "I'm going to make us some tea. Sugar?"

Chapter Twenty-Six

THE LETTING GO

East Berlin, German Democratic Republic, May 1988

Ellie

The morning after all the dead bodies and balloons in the street was eerily quiet. I came downstairs to Kai passed out on the couch under a pile of papers and Mitzi asleep at the table, drooling onto one of the sketches. I carefully moved it out from underneath her face and put the kettle on the stove. They wouldn't sleep too long, not with the sunlight pouring through the front windows, creeping steadily closer to Kai's face. They'd want tea when they woke.

I sliced bread and popped it into the toaster and straightened all of the papers, figuring if they were in such a mess underneath Kai and on top of him, they couldn't possibly be in a particular order. I stacked them on the coffee table and dragged it back into the middle of the living room.

The kettle whistled, and Kai jolted upright on the couch, wide-eyed and alert. I stepped away from him, holding up my hands. "Just the kettle."

He slumped forward, pressing his face into his hands. "I thought it was the Stasi. I thought they'd finally come."

I wanted to touch him. I didn't know where we were after last night, and now wasn't the time to figure that out, but I didn't know what to do with the need clawing at my bones. The need that said the way to comfort him was to reach out and touch him. Not even kiss him or any other kind of touching other than my fingertips on his cheeks, absorbing the bloodshot from his eyes and the tired circles curling from his tear ducts toward his cheekbones.

I placed one of my paper doves next to him and he smiled, picking it up without seeing it. When his fingers touched it, the wings stopped. When I touched it, the wings beat to the rhythm of my heartbeat. Mitzi never picked them up. She said she didn't need to know what would happen.

"Thanks," he said softly, his eyes trained on the paper wings.

Sponge, he had called me. I understood now. I wanted to absorb it all, take it away from him, so he could be the mirror to the world. He was so bright sometimes. He only reflected back at the world what existed. In this much darkness, he was reflecting dark. I saw the shadows in the irises of his eyes and my heart beat faster, sweat gathering in the lines of my palms.

I retreated to the kitchen and slid the kettle off the stove, silencing the awful noise, but my eardrums vibrated even in its absence. Kai dragged himself into the kitchen and sank into a seat at the table. He hesitated, opening a hand to me, and I stepped toward him, unsure of what he was asking. But he only looped his arm around my legs and rested his head against my hip bone. I put a hand on top of his dark hair.

"You slept well," he said.

"One of us had to," I said, smiling despite myself. "Did you find anything?"

"No," he mumbled. "The toast is burning."

He wasn't wrong. I had to untangle myself from his arm to free the bread before the smoke became too much of a problem.

I dropped two more pieces of toast into the toaster and leaned against the counter.

Kai put his head down on the table, staring at Mitzi. "She has this miraculous ability to sleep through anything. Why couldn't she share that with me?"

"It's a family trait. One of my many gifts," Mitzi said, her eyes still closed.

"Put it on your résumé," I said. "Employers love that."

Mitzi grinned. "Spoken like a true capitalist. Always thinking about how to turn something into a rung on the ladder."

I had been sarcastic, but maybe Mitzi was too. I couldn't tell sometimes. I tossed two pieces of toast on a plate and slid it to her first, making Kai's face twist into false wounded pride. Mitzi barely lifted her head as she grabbed the toast and ate while half asleep.

Kai got the next two pieces, and then I sat down last. He reached over, stole one of my pieces of toast and, before I could cry foul, buttered it and returned it to me. "You don't have the patience to butter toast without breaking the bread."

"That's some sort of weird innuendo, isn't it?" Mitzi muttered.

I rolled my eyes. "How is that possibly innuendo?"

Kai pointed a knife at Mitzi. "Your mind is exactly as dirty as I thought it was."

She grinned at him through a mouthful of toast. "The day my mind surprises you, Kai, is the day pigs fly."

"Darling," he said, shaking his head. "It'd take more than flying pigs to surprise me."

"Ellie and I are going to head out to check the next Passenger," Mitzi said suddenly, glancing at me. I nodded before I even knew what I was doing. Like we'd planned this. I didn't want to be stuck in the house, and after Kai's overprotective streak last night, that was a possibility. Maybe Mitzi knew that.

Kai frowned but didn't say anything against it. "I'm going to see Sabina."

"And snoop," said Mitzi.

He shrugged. "Maybe. If it's empty. Hit and miss on weekends over there."

Mitzi gestured to my plate. "Eat up. We're getting out of here."

I tucked a piece of toast into my pocket and shoved the plate back at Kai. "Done. Ready. Let's go."

"Eager, eager," he muttered, but began to eat the remaining toast as I went upstairs to dress quickly for the outdoors. He waited for us in the front hallway, dressed with a hat tugged down over his ears, making him look younger this morning. He caught me as I passed by him for the open door. His lips pressed against my cheek, warm and quick. He said, "Be good out there. Be safe."

I studied the veins of gold in his eyes, searching for something he wasn't telling me. But his gaze was steady and clear. "We will. You be safe too."

He didn't say anything to that, just let both of us out first and then locked the door behind us. A few blocks north, we parted ways. Kai and Mitzi exchanged a few quiet, tense words out of earshot, but both of them looked relaxed as Kai headed toward the workshop and Mitzi and I turned to head east across the city, far away from the wall.

For a long time, we walked in silence and I didn't mind. The warmth of the late-spring air tickled my skin, and it felt good to be outside in the sunshine. I compulsively checked for my papers, just in case we were stopped. Mitzi kept checking over her shoulder the first few blocks, but the farther we got from the house and the wall, the more she relaxed.

Then she finally said, "We don't have a Passenger." As if feeling the weight of my glance shifting to her, she added, "I just figured while we could go outside, we should. The radio guys were rattled by all the deaths, even though they're being covered up pretty well by the powers that be. *Radio Glasnost* doesn't know about us, but they'll report the deaths as suspicious. Everyone will know. And I…You have to understand me, Ellie, but I suggested to Kai that he take Sabina and get out of here. I don't know if he's going to be there when we get back. I wanted to give him the chance to leave without worrying about good-byes."

The most words Mitzi had said to me in one breath this whole time, and they were to tell me that Kai might not be there when I got back to the house. I almost stopped and I almost turned around and I almost ran back to the house, just to say good-bye. Almost. Almost. I had always been an almost girl. I almost had straight As. I almost had a boyfriend. I almost had a date to prom. I almost didn't go on the trip. I almost didn't end up here.

Kai, with his golden-and-green eyes and his gentle, warm mouth. Kai, with his kindnesses when I was just a time-traveling stranger in his midst. Kai, singing as we walked. Kai, on the rooftops, sounding hopeful. Kai, in the tunnels, sounding lonely. I was the girl with the red balloon who shouldn't be in the black-and-white world of Walls and fear and lies. He was a kaleidoscope boy born at the wrong time in the wrong place, too bright for here, too much for everywhere else. We were the almost rights together.

And now he might not be there when I got back. I understood immediately why Mitzi had done what she did though. And I guess I could understand where Kai might be warring between protecting his sister and doing his job. If she was in danger, of course he should choose her. Of course he should take her out of East Germany to wherever she'd be safe.

"I hate this place," I whispered, stopping in the street. Mitzi stopped to face me, and I couldn't look at her, at my own misery mirrored in her eyes, under the fringe of her ridiculous hair. This was my pain. Anger built in me, pouring from the knife to my heart, dripping everywhere. I squeezed my hands into fists.

"I hate this place. Nothing good comes from here. Nothing."

"Ellie," Mitzi said, sounding nervous. She looked around, but I didn't care who heard me.

"It's so incomprehensible. Why am I even trying to help? Why does any of it matter? It always comes back to people being evil. And you know what, Mitzi? A lot of evil people are your people."

Mitzi's eyes flashed, and she stepped toward me until our noses nearly brushed, so close I couldn't focus on her anymore, but I couldn't make myself step away. "Yes, of course, this is because we're in Germany and I'm German. How could I forget? How could I forget that you and Kai have this strange, distorted tunnel vision when it comes to history and my country? Ellie, I'm sorry about what happened to your grandfather and his family. But I wasn't there. It wasn't me."

"I'm not asking you to shoulder the blame. Just look around and say that it happened and it was because average people couldn't stand up to power. And it happened again, didn't it?" I snapped.

Mitzi's voice sizzled with anger. "I spend most of my days helping people to the other side. To a place with freedoms. That's what I do. I believe that on the other side of this, I'll be here to make my country a better place. A place where anyone can be anything. You can be self-righteous some other time, Ellie Baum, but not to me. Not right now. I'll never compare our suffering now to the Holocaust, but I'm not my grandparents."

I knew how Germany was in my proper time period. It was a better place for a lot of people, but right now, it still seemed awful. I didn't know what was right. If Mitzi was right or if I was right. I didn't know if I could blame Mitzi for what she couldn't control. Maybe not. And maybe my words had been twisted and wrong, but I didn't know how to explain the knot in my chest. That history felt like it repeated itself, and the perpetrators were always familiar.

But Mitzi wasn't in my head. Mitzi was still here, still hearing my inability to articulate everything tangled inside me. She pointed straight at me. "I'm not apologizing to you, Ellie Baum. And I'm not apologizing to Kai and Sabina Holwell. You are from the outside. You can leave—yes, you. We told you we can get you to West Germany and you can be safe, even if in the wrong time. And Kai is leaving.

"But I have to stay. I am queer, in East Germany, surrounded by outsiders who do not understand that I—and my country-men, all these *volk*—are clinging to resilience. Stop telling me this is the only evil place on earth. Stop telling me that I am evil because of where I am. I've forgiven the people around me because *I must*, Ellie. You cannot move forward to do good with-out reconciliation. I believe that. You can keep your judgments. I am only trying to help."

She didn't ask for my forgiveness, and I wouldn't have offered it. She didn't apologize, and neither did I. But I nodded, and she stepped away from me. We walked together all over the city in silence. We both got ice cream on a *platz* and mean-dered through to a park as it began to rain. We sat on a bench and fed the pigeons until we had no more toast. We didn't say anything more.

There was nothing more to say.

When we got back from the walk, the house was empty. Kai was gone. The dishes were done and the table wiped clean. The papers on the table were gone.

There was a note, scribbled on a piece of paper in Kai's tight handwriting.

E,

M told you, I'm sure. I am still glad it was you. And you're the only time traveler I've ever said that to.

K

M,

You have always been the best of the best. I'll see you again.

K

Mitzi and I stood in the emptiness of the house until it swelled up inside me, bursting at the dams of my chest and leaking through the spaces between my ribs. I went up to my room and shut the door, flopping face-first on the bed.

He was really gone.

Kai was gone, and Mitzi and I were still here in East Berlin. One of us was in the wrong time period. Someone was using bad magic on balloons that were killing people, and there was just her and me to figure it out now.

For the first time, I believed I might be here for good. That I might not get home. I might now be an East German citizen, like my fake papers said.

And I'd be stuck here without Kai. I didn't cry right away, not until I came down the next morning and he still wasn't there. I tried not to cry in front of Mitzi, but once the tears started, I didn't think I could stop. Mitzi bought us chocolate, and we watched terrible East German television while breaking off tiny corners, neither of us willing to take a big piece. I fell asleep with my head on her shoulder.

Chapter Twenty-Seven

TRUST ME

Łódź Ghetto, Poland, April 1942

Benno

Mama and I wrote a request for relocation back into Germany, where we hoped to find Ernst. Where Mama hoped that she'd find Ernst. She had started talking about finding him like that'd be the miracle we were all waiting to occur. I didn't say anything, just like Papa hadn't said anything when Mama thought Ernst would be here in Łódź, waiting for us, when we left Berlin. I just kissed Mama's head and helped her write the letter.

Our request was denied.

Everyone's requests were denied. A woman down the hall had a baby, but the baby wasn't named on the relocation for the family. She requested a delay on her relocation until the baby was old enough not to need her. Her request was denied too. I didn't know what they expected the baby to do. No, that was wrong. I did know what they expected the baby to do. Die. They didn't care. They didn't care at all. We took up space for people moving here, so we needed to be moved, just after I'd finally started to believe I could survive the war here.

Our relocation date was my birthday, but I didn't say anything. There was nothing to make a fuss over this year. I turned
seventeen, and so many people would be forever the same age.
Ruthie's hair ribbons were still under my pillow, and on the last
night, I remembered them and tucked them into my pocket.

We lined up at the trains. The sun shone brightly, just like in
my dream. It was so bright and warm that I took off my jacket,
laid it over my elbow, and stood there in my shirt that used to
be white and my Shabbat trousers, waiting with Mama and our
relocation notice. Mama leaned against me, quiet but fearless. I
didn't think she was resigned. If anything, Mama seemed more
determined than ever. She told me the night before that we
wouldn't be pulled out of our rooms like screaming cats. We'd go
down there and hold our heads up high. We'd take whatever was
put in our path.

"You're never given anything more than you can handle,
Benno," she told me as we took our bags to the trains.

She used to say, "God never gives you anything more than
you can handle."

God was absent even from Mama's mind now.

She said, "It'll be a fresh start. Maybe I'll get the same work,
and you did well building furniture. Perhaps they'll let us take
the same jobs."

I said, "We could survive like that."

And she smiled, and then she reached into her pocket and
took out something, pressing it into my hand. "Happy birthday,
Benno. My darling boy."

I never found out where she acquired a lump of sugar, but
there it was, in the palm of my hand. I thought I might cry. I
hadn't seen or tasted sugar in weeks. I didn't want anyone to see
it, or take it away, or shoot my mother, so I slipped it straight into
my mouth, lifting my face to the sky. The sun melted over my
skin, the sugar over my tongue.

Nothing more than you can handle.

"Benno," said a familiar voice. I opened my eyes, and the girl in the purple dress was there, standing in line. She smiled at me, but it didn't reach her dark eyes. She lifted her own wedding invitation. "I didn't want to forget."

No one else seemed to see the girl. I looked at my mother to see if she saw this well-fed, rosy-cheeked girl in the clean dress standing among us like a beacon where she did not belong. But no one turned their heads. Mama just watched at the fence as children were sent off without their parents and loaded onto a train. I couldn't listen to them anymore.

I looked at the girl and then closed my eyes. Figment of your imagination. You're hungry. You're hallucinating, Benno, I told myself.

We loaded onto the trains, and the doors slid shut, shrouding us in darkness. I felt a cool hand slip into mine, and I stiffened as the girl whispered, "Benno, do you trust me?"

Mutely, I shook my head.

She said, "Benno, you must trust me."

Then she told me a story of a girl born in Poland to a wealthy family. But she was strange and difficult, and they locked her away for years before sending her to an institution. But then she wrote her way through the locked door, just kept writing until the words glowed on the paper and the lock melted away, falling from the wood like it had never existed at all. When her family saw her, they called her a witch and ran from her screaming. But she wasn't the only one. She found a few other people whose words turned golden on the paper, and with them, she began to learn what her hand could do with the power of a pen, what her blood could do when it was used as ink.

She whispered to me, "Benno. My gift, our gift, is freedom. We set people free."

I closed my eyes and shivered as the train rolled along the tracks, and then, all too soon, the train came to a stop. I heard someone shouting in German, and the girl's hand tightened around mine.

She said, "You must trust me, Benno."

I didn't say anything back, but my heart hammered in my chest.

Chapter Twenty-Eight

PLOTS HATCHED ON ROOFTOPS

East Berlin, German Democratic Republic, May 1988

Ellie

I stayed in bed the day after Kai left. I lay on my side, making paper doves out of old newspapers. I thought when I got up eventually, he'd be there, but he wasn't. When I finally dragged myself down for something to eat that evening, just Mitzi was waiting for me. She silently handed me my coat. I just put my hands through the sleeves and buttoned it as I followed her out the door. We went north, parallel to the wall, back to the rooftop. I hadn't been there in more than a week. It took my breath away again to stand against the chimney and look out over West Berlin, with all of the twinkling lights.

"I know you aren't going to forgive me," she said quietly.

"It's not your fault," I said after a long pause. I sighed and bumped my shoulder against hers. "It's right. Sabina's more important."

Mitzi slipped her arm through mine and said, "To Kai, she is. And that's enough for me."

"You were in jail once, right?" I asked, remembering the first time I met her.

She snorted. "Yeah. Kai got me arrested. He did *not* get me out. I'm the one who flirted my way out. Remember that because he lies about that all the time. It's a long story, honestly. I don't worry about getting caught anymore."

"Stasi or rogue Schöpfer," I laughed, not missing the part where she assumed I'd see him again. My chest was too tight to dissect that right now. "Take your pick, right?"

Mitzi winked at me, untangling our arms. "There you go. Nothing to do but laugh and go about your life at this point."

She sat down cross-legged, and I walked to the edge of the roof, entranced by freedom, by the West being so close and so unfathomably far away, until I heard the clatter of glass. Mitzi shook out a bag full of nail polish with a flourish, and I squealed loud enough that I had to cover my mouth, and we both giggled until there were tears in our eyes. Maybe it was just a matter of perspective, but honestly, I didn't think I'd ever be that excited about nail polish.

"I can't tell you how I got hold of this," Mitzi said mischievously.

I turned the bottles over in my hands. At home, Amanda and I would paint our nails together. Now I was here painting my nails with Mitzi. It felt like forever since I'd done all the mundane things of my life, like grocery shopping or getting a haircut. I never thought those things were important before, but that was because I had them. Now I didn't and I missed them.

I missed putting on makeup and playing with colors. I liked painting my nails. Amanda and I used to paint each other's nails after Shabbat services on Saturdays. I hadn't gone to Shabbat services in three months either. My heart ached a little bit when I thought about that.

I picked up the gold. "This would look amazing on you."

"Are you kidding? Like I need to stand out any more. You should do the gold," Mitzi said, gesturing to her hair and picking out a no-less-eye-catching magenta. "Besides, I want it to clash with my hair, not complement it."

I traded the magenta in her hand for lime green. "Mission accomplished. Gold star for me."

"Gold star?" Mitzi turned over the nail polish in her hand and gave it an appreciative nod.

"A reward system for little kids. You get a sticker when you meet a goal," I said and picked up the magenta. I lifted it against my hair. "Does it clash?"

Mitzi made a face at me. "Of course not. Your hair is amazing."

"Your hair is *teal*."

She uncapped the polish. "True."

I wanted to see Mitzi when the wall came down. Maybe I'd still be here. Maybe I'd cross with her on that night, just to say we did. As much as I wanted to go home, my heart fluttered in my chest as I thought about history being made in front of me.

Mitzi watched me draw a line of nail polish down her thumbnail. "Sometimes when I sit up here, it's like a simultaneous fuck you to my state and a penny in a wishing well to West Berlin. They're screwed, you know. They're this tiny island of hope in a sea of sadness. That's a lot for any city to carry."

"The other side of the wall is covered in graffiti and art." I painted the nails on her right hand first. "I think they're carrying it just fine. They know exactly what they are."

"That must be nice." Mitzi's voice fell into wistfulness. "To know yourself as a collective and as an individual. Sometimes I think about applying for a balloon myself."

"Blow on this." I traded her right for her left hand. "Why don't you?"

"My family's here," she said, and I dashed the paintbrush across her nail. "Ellie!"

"It's not dry. It's fine." I rubbed at her finger with my thumb. With the sunset behind her, Mitzi took on a strange, unnatural glow, her pale skin almost jaundiced in the light, her hair tiger-striped around her face. "I came anyway."

"Maybe you were always supposed to come. Maybe when you go back, you'll remember everything that happened here," she said slowly. "Maybe as our time progresses and you're born, you'll feel like you have to come here. Maybe this always repeats."

I finish her pinkie finger and release her hand, recapping the nail polish. "Do you think it's a loop? Time?"

"I don't know," Mitzi said, smiling a bit. "I must have slept through my physics class. When you know balloons can carry people over the wall, you start to think that physics isn't the be-all and end-all."

She had a pretty smile. Not the same type of smile that she had on her face when she was grinning and goofy and bouncy. This one wasn't a smile for me, or for anyone else. I think it was the first time I saw Mitzi smile to herself.

"Your turn," Mitzi said, picking up the magenta-colored bottle. She turned it over. "Oh my God. Nail polish colors are the best."

"What's that one?" I asked, picking up the lime. "This is Limerick." It took me a moment, but then I burst out laughing, bending over and holding a hand over my mouth to control the volume. "That's genius. But it only works if you know English. Mitzi, where'd you get these?"

"Not telling. This one's called Flirt with a Stranger," Mitzi said, wiggling the magenta bottle at me. "That sounds like an excellent idea."

I smiled a little, my stomach aching a little for Kai. I wondered if he was over the border already. I wondered if they were out of Germany, well into the land of the free. I wondered where they'd go. I didn't want to ask Mitzi. It was better, I thought, if we didn't know.

"I need your help," Mitzi said quietly. "I need a distraction in the workshop. I want to check the office and see if there's anything Kai missed. He might be gone, but it's not like the dead time-travelers just left with him."

I didn't hesitate. "Whatever you need."

Which was how, once our nails dried and the sun had fully set on the Iron Curtain, I ended up hysterically crying on the floor of the workshop with Aurora trying to calm me down. Meanwhile, behind us, a slip of a girl with teal-blue hair slid up the stairs. I tried not to look at her while I mopped up my tears and talked about my homesickness, how angry I was at Kai, and how alone I felt.

"I'm never going to get home," I cried, leaning into Aurora. She stiffened, but I didn't relent. "Do you think it was Kai? Is that why he left? Did he mess up the balloons?"

"I don't know," Aurora said after a long pause. "I didn't think Kai's understanding of magic was that in-depth, but I suppose it could have been, given his sister's genius. But Ellie, you must know that we are doing our best to make this time livable for you."

I wiped my tears off the back of my hands. Not all of this was invented, but maybe that was why they were buying it so easily. "Livable is a low standard."

Her voice was so sad. "I know. We're trying, Ellie."

Behind her, Mitzi reappeared on the second level, her jacket a little puffier. She had the papers then. I scrambled to my feet and said, "I think maybe I just need to take a hot bath."

"Yes," Aurora said with evident relief. "A hot bath cures a great number of ills and broken hearts."

"Something about the steam," I stammered. She stared at me and then Mitzi appeared, taking my arm with a sympathetic smile on her face. "Okay. Thank you for listening. Bye!"

"You were great up until the end," Mitzi muttered in the tunnels. "But it doesn't matter. We got the papers. Let's go."

And back into the tunnels we went.

Chapter Twenty-Nine

CULPRITS WITHOUT CAUSES

East Berlin, German Democratic Republic, May 1988

Ellie

We spread the papers out in the kitchen, piles after piles of paper that tumbled onto the floor, where we didn't bother to pick them up because we'd run out of room to put them. The floor was as good a place as any. We sat there, sipping tea and trying to sort through papers, while the sun rose and crept in through the windows. Exhaustion lingered deep in my bones, but I didn't think I could sleep if I tried. For once, I felt like I was doing something.

Mitzi had just stood to make another pot of tea when someone started banging on the front door. Mitzi and I both stopped moving, our eyes meeting across the kitchen. She hesitated and then grabbed a knife off the table and gestured to the small pantry in the kitchen. "Hide."

We ducked into the pantry, and Mitzi pulled the door shut tightly behind us. She shoved boxes against the door while I crawled into the back. I found the rat poison I'd found the first time I hid in here and wrapped my hand around it again. Mitzi scooted next to me and gripped my hand. This time, I could feel the paper dove's wings in my pocket, trying to move without any room. I breathed in.

"If they come in..." she whispered, and then the banging on the front door increased, making us both flinch. She cleared her throat and spoke faster. "If they come in, Ellie, you need to let me do the talking. If you can escape, go to the workshop. No one wants you dead. They don't know what we did. You can blame everything on me."

"They won't take you," I hissed. "Mitzi."

She shook my shoulder. "Promise me you'll let me take the blame if they come for us."

I didn't want anyone to take the blame for me or what was happening. Kai had already fled, and now Mitzi was preparing to be arrested. They'd never let her go if they got her. So many people never came back when the Stasi got their hands on them. How could this be any different?

The lock turned audibly and the door opened, creaking as it went. Boots in the hallway. I thought about praying, but my mind spun too hard to reach for any words. I pressed my forehead into Mitzi's shoulder, and she ducked her head.

Footsteps, quiet and slow across the living room. Into the kitchen. Then a pause before the person spun and ran, taking the stairs two at a time. Above us, doors opened and slammed shut. More than just the bedroom. Every closet was checked, and with every door that slammed shut again, Mitzi and I shook harder in the back of the pantry. It was only a matter of time before they'd check the kitchen. They were searching the whole house.

Footsteps pounding down the stairs. A chair knocked over in the kitchen. My throat closed tight, and I shook so hard that I bumped a soup can off the shelf behind me. It hit the floor with a thunk and rolled away from me. Mitzi hissed softly, but it was too late. The footsteps stopped.

This is it, I thought to myself wildly. This is where this unfathomable adventure ends. In a pantry in a kitchen in the wrong country in the wrong year. I held on to Mitzi. She was all I had left.

The pantry door rattled as someone yanked on it. But the inside latch held. In the dark, we could only see the boots crossing the thin line of light under the door. The door shook again.

"Mitz? Ellie?" A warm, familiar voice, trembling like the door. "Open up."

My first thought was that it was a trap, but Mitzi didn't have that thought. She dropped my hand and stumbled to her feet, flipping open the latch on the door and shoving it open. Light poured into the dark, blinding both of us temporarily.

"What in the name of..." she said. "You should be in Argentina by now."

Not Stasi. Not Stasi at all. I dropped the box of rat poison and pulled myself up on the shelves around me, pushing past Mitzi as Kai said, "We were at a Zerberus safe house, waiting for a way out. Felix said you found more papers, and I realized I couldn't leave, not until I saw this through," and I threw my arms around him.

He caught me, burying his face against my neck. He exhaled slowly, his body vibrating with intensity under my hands. I could hear his heart slamming around in his chest, loosed from a cage and wild. Slowly, I felt him unwind beneath the heat of his body against mine.

"You're here," I whispered into his chest. It reminded me of how he was on the dance floor of Phantasma. "Where's Sabina?"

"I sent her back. I had no other option. Felix might be okay, but the Zerberus at that safe house wanted her to come with them." He shook his head. "I told her to tell them I just got jittery because of Felix being Zerberus. I'm sorry. I thought when I came in that they'd taken you two."

"You should leave," Mitzi said, but the force wasn't behind her words this time. Kai reached out with an arm and pulled her into the hug. We stood there for a moment, just the three of us holding on to each other in the face of the impossible task of unwinding an invisible path of untraceable magic. Then Mitzi leaned back and said, "But you're here now. We should get to work."

Kai gestured to the papers behind him in the kitchen. "Clearly I can't leave you two unsupervised. You turn into thieves."

"You were looking for something like an equation. But what if it's not an equation?" Mitzi touched each of the piles. "We took everything. I'm sure Aurora will notice papers missing eventually, and Ashasher, whenever he comes back from wherever he is. I've been thinking about it, and has anyone seen Ashasher in the workshop other than that one day?"

We all shook our heads, looking around at each other. I could count on one hand the number of times I had seen Ashasher. But I saw Aurora every day that I sorted maps. None of it meant anything, unless it meant everything. My head spun.

Kai stared at the papers and said bitterly, "All those years of ignoring Sabina and shushing her when she talked magical theory. Biting me in the ass today."

"Do you think she'd translate for us?" I asked, peering at the page. The equations looked like gibberish without any numbers. I blinked, suddenly remembering math class at home. I hadn't thought about home in a long time.

"No, I don't want to involve her," Kai said shortly. "These are her teachers. I don't trust either of them right now. We found that feather, Ellie. At least we know where Aurora is right now. Ashasher could do anything."

His hands curled into fists on the table. Without looking at each other, Mitzi and I each covered one of his hands with our own. His head bowed, and we all stared at the papers meaninglessly for a short time. Then I took a deep breath. "We're wasting time again. Come on."

All day, the three of us sorted the papers from Aurora and Ashasher's office into four different piles: equations; notes from unknown theory books; Ashasher's notes; and Aurora's private scribblings that sometimes made sense and sometimes didn't, at least the ones we could read. Half of them were in Polish. As we went along, we tried to tease out what Kai called the two-pronged problem. We needed to find proof in these papers that one of them was the culprit behind the rogue balloons, and we needed to find out why. I doubted that Felix cared if we found out why, but Kai seemed to care.

He handed me a scrap piece of paper. "This doesn't have anything useful on it."

I frowned. "Why are you handing it to me?"

He lifted an eyebrow. "Make a dove. We could use one right now."

So I pressed and folded and made a tiny paper dove that sat in the middle of the table, wings rising and falling, and we did all breathe deeper.

I measured the time by the number of times we refilled the kettle and made new tea. I didn't understand the magic at all, so I sorted the theory from the diary entries. Ashasher's handwriting was abysmal. Maybe he couldn't see through all the feathers. Whatever the reason, none of us could read it.

Aurora's handwriting in her theoretical notes was tidy and neat, as if she knew others would see it. Her handwriting in her diaries was atrocious, and the words switched between German and Polish. It was close enough to looking like Yiddish that I wished my grandfather had taught me the language he spoke with my grandmother. I only vaguely remembered her. She passed when I was little, but when they spoke just to each other, they used Yiddish. My grandfather didn't speak a word of German after he moved to New York. Not a word.

"They just..." I shook my head and cleared my throat. "I

don't know. It's hard to imagine that either of them is the culprit. Maybe they didn't mean for it to happen."

"Good intentions mean very little when the bodies start piling up." Mitzi passed something to Kai. "Familiar handwriting. Not Ashasher."

He grimaced. "Sabina."

"Sometimes good intentions are understandable," I said.

"Sometimes," Kai said without looking up, and though there was no malice in his voice, it sank its teeth into my soft skin. "I think you forget that whoever did this is the reason you are here. You are not with your family. Somewhere in time, Ellie, you are a missing person."

"Kai," Mitzi murmured, her dark eyes fluttering over to me. In the dim light of the kitchen, she almost looked apologetic.

Kai blinked up at me and reached over, touching my hand with his fingers. I pulled away from him, turning my shoulder slightly as I pretended to read a paper. "Ellie."

I took a deep breath, and then let it out. My eyes caught a word and I straightened up, leaning forward. "Kai."

"I'm sorry—" he began to say.

I shoved a paper at him. "Shut up. This. I think I have it. I don't know whose handwriting this is—maybe Sabina's—but whoever it is, they're trying to go *back* in time."

"Back?" he repeated, taking the paper and frowning at it.

I leaned over and pointed out the lines, reading them aloud as I went. I didn't know all the German, but it wasn't necessary. The idea was clear as day. "Pulling someone from the past something-something would prove the something-something…reverse the equation."

"Pulling an individual from the past, particularly in the nineteen thirties, would prove the potentiality to reverse the equation to send someone back into that time period." Kai translated the line properly. He put the paper down. "It's Sabina's handwriting. I know my sister's a genius, but she couldn't do this without help."

"Look through all the papers," Mitzi said quickly. "Look for anything about the past."

We shuffled through the papers and couldn't find anything in Aurora's handwriting and, despite our best efforts, still couldn't read Ashasher's. Kai sat back and said, "Process of elimination."

"Ashasher," said Mitzi grimly. "If it's not in Aurora's notes and it has to be one of Sabina's teachers...It has to be him."

"How is he getting it so wrong? Why do people keep coming from the future?" I asked softly. "I thought he was the mastermind behind most of this magic."

"I read the physics about time travel after Ellie came," Mitzi said lightly. "Time's as much of a dimension as space. Like Ashasher says, space-time is like a fabric. But you can only go forward in time."

"Those same books will tell you magic doesn't exist," Kai told her. "And you and I know differently."

"But our magic, even if it's unbelievable to others, does subscribe to rules, doesn't it? We use mathematical equations to write magic onto balloons to account for the weight, height, and genetic markers of a Passenger. We use blood to make sure that only that Passenger or his family members can use the balloon," Mitzi argued.

"So the balloon can only go forward, but when the magic is disengaged," I said slowly, "like by finding a Passenger, then it returns to its previous dimension."

"I'm not a physicist but that makes sense to me," Mitzi said. "Travel to the future means you'd have to be going closer to the speed of light. Or I guess, since the time between Garrick and his balloon disappearing and you appearing was a few hours, it was probably at the speed of light. Physics took the balloon forward, but magic brought you back."

Kai rubbed at his face. He hadn't shaved in a few days, and he seemed more exhausted than either Mitzi or me. "So no matter what Ashasher does, he's not going to send a balloon back in time."

"Not unless he's smarter than the physicists from my time and your time," I said, shaking my head. "But if his motivation is strong enough, then it probably won't matter."

"Then what's his motivation?" Kai asked at the same time that Mitzi said, "Then how do we stop someone who doesn't care that the science doesn't support him?"

I shake my head. "I don't know. I think he has to be arrested. I think Felix will have to do his thing."

"Do his thing," repeated Kai slowly. He shook his head a bit. "That's a strange turn of phrase, but I guess you're right. We can only all do our things."

"Can Felix even get past the feathers?" Mitzi looked between us, her eyes widening as I was sure mine were. "Ashasher killed Garrick and all those other time-travelers. Maybe it wasn't the balloons doing it at all. Maybe it was Ashasher and whatever he can do. Maybe Kai just beat him to you, Ellie."

"And how many more do we not know about?" I asked softly because it didn't seem like anyone wanted to consider the possibility that I wasn't the first one. I was just the first—and so far the only—to survive. And maybe I was lucky. Maybe Mitzi was right. Kai had just reached me before Ashasher could kill me.

Kai shuddered. "We've been working with a murderer. My sister. My sister's been training with someone who's killed people. Oh god. I have to go. Sabina...Bean...I sent her right back to them."

"Stop," Mitzi cut into his thoughts and mine. She tucked teal hair behind her ear and reached out, closing her hands over his. "Kai. Look at me." It took him a moment, but then I watched him lift his eyes to hers. His face emptied of emotion again. I'd seen this before. He couldn't stay present. I didn't know how not to stay present. If I didn't cling to the facts, then I'd drift away. But none of this felt real.

"We don't know all the information," Mitzi said. "With the Volkspolizei presence by the wall because of the bodies the other night, I think it's safe to say Ashasher won't send any balloons over the wall tonight. They don't know that we know, so Sabina's safe. We can't go in there alone. We need backup. We'll find Felix in the morning."

Kai gripped her wrists and whispered in a hoarse tone that cut through me like a rusty knife, "You're positive."

"We can't go in there. They don't know we know," Mitzi repeated. "Ashasher isn't going to hurt Sabina. He doesn't know that we took the papers. He's threatened, but he isn't going to follow through without proof."

When he nodded, I exhaled slowly and gestured to the papers on the table. "But then, what about this? What do we do with this in the meantime?"

The safest place turned out to be between my mattress and box spring. We agreed that Ashasher wasn't likely to think that I'd be involved in stealing anything from him. He still called me a child. He still thought I was innocent. And it'd be hard for him to report the papers stolen without divulging their contents.

Kai sat down on the edge of my bed and covered his face with his hands. I sat next to him, leaning into him just enough that he had to feel me there. I didn't know what else to do. Mitzi watched him, biting her lower lip. Then finally Kai let out a long breath. "At least we know now."

Mitzi's smile was sad. "There's that."

She went downstairs to make dinner, and when I stood to follow her, Kai caught my hand. He whispered, "Wait. Stay. Just for a little bit."

I sank back onto the bed next to him and leaned my head against his shoulder. He turned my hand over in his, running his fingers across the lines of my palms. I shivered, and I could feel his smile through his cheek against the top of my head.

"Ashasher was the one to offer Sabina sanctuary. They'd keep her a secret from the Zerberus, train her to keep her magic safe, and protect her from the others back home. I didn't want to believe he was part of this. I still don't know how to believe this," Kai said, his voice rumbling and loud, like the beginnings of a thunderstorm creeping into this room and just this room.

I closed my eyes, relishing the calluses on his fingers running over the soft skin of my wrists. "Who is he?"

"I don't know," admitted Kai. "He speaks German and English, both with accents. Aurora told me once that he was Romani, like me, but he doesn't understand a lick of Romani when I speak it, so I can't help but doubt that. He's been here since they began to build the wall. He just arrived and formed the Council. Aurora was one of his first recruits. She was one of the first ever to use a balloon to help someone escape. She and the first Schöpfers were smuggled around Europe to concentration camps to help people escape. She's Polish, but her German's so good now that you barely notice. I didn't at first."

The silence that sank over us made me queasy. Kai and I could be a lot of things together, but the honesty left me feeling raw and exposed. He looked too thoughtful, too curious, and I didn't want him to redirect that on me. There were questions hanging in the air between us, and I wasn't ready for them.

"Want to hear a terrible joke?" I asked him instead.

"Always," Kai said, his voice lightening, though it seemed more for my sake than it did genuine.

I pretended to start a joke and then paused, shaking my head and covering my face with my free hand. "No, no. Never mind."

He pulled my hand free of my face. "You already said it was terrible. You can't back out now."

"No," I protested. "Jokes about German sausages are just *the wurst.*"

It took him a beat, but then Kai fell back onto the bed, laughing so hard that Mitzi yelled up the stairs to find out if we were okay. I shouted back that everything was fine, grinning as I looked over my shoulder at Kai. My feet kicked merrily in delight at his happiness. Kai reached up and tugged me by my elbow. I lay back on the bed next to him as his laughter faded, and then rolled up, and faded again. He took my hand and laced our fingers together. In the sunlight filling the room, I studied his dark skin against mine, the way his hip fit in the curve of my body. Two different worlds, two different times, and yet nothing felt so right as here, the quiet warmth of the room, the lingering happiness from his laughter hanging in the air, his thumb gliding against my skin.

He rolled over, his first kiss gentle and light, a warm summer breeze against my lips. He whispered against my mouth, "I promised you that we'd get you home, Ellie. I haven't forgotten that. We know that time can go forward. Before Ashasher's arrested, we'll make him write you a balloon home."

I started crying then, which was exactly the wrong thing for that moment. There's nothing worse than kissing someone you really like and then promptly bursting into tears. But Kai didn't seem to mind. My tears didn't freak him out, and he didn't leave or get awkward. He tugged me closer to him, wrapping his arms around me, and stayed there until his shirt was damp with my tears and I had calmed enough to hear his heart beating against my ear again.

"Come on. Whatever Mitzi's cooking smells good. We have a long day ahead of us tomorrow," Kai whispered, rubbing his hand up and down my back slowly.

Tomorrow, I might have to say good-bye.

Chapter Thirty

VISIT FROM THE POLICE

East Berlin, German Democratic Republic, May 1988

I didn't think I could sleep, but my body couldn't stay awake. Not two nights in a row. I fell asleep on the couch, whispering back and forth with Mitzi again about why Ashasher had done what he did, and what Felix might do to him. Sabina, Sabina, Sabina. Thank god she was too in her own head to be a part of this. Mitzi fell asleep too, my head on her lap, because when Ellie woke us in the morning, wide-eyed with her finger to her mouth, both of us jerked awake at the same time. Fists pounded on the door.

"*Polizei!*"

Ellie's blue eyes, wide with terror, grew impossibly wider. She shook as I grabbed her hands. "Papers, Ellie. Get your ID card. And get rid of those damn doves."

God, I fucking hoped Ashasher had done his homework with her papers. What if he'd planned for this too? What if Ashasher screwed up her papers in case he had to play this card? My mind raced through different scenarios, and none of them ended well.

Ellie ran up the stairs as Mitzi brushed back her hair and

tucked it under a hat. If they were going to give her shit for having blue hair, I'd get shit for being brown-skinned. We were both at risk when I answered the door.

"Good morning," I said to the two policemen on the steps. My heart snapped in half with the stress. All I could think was, This is how Ashasher's getting us back for taking the papers. He called it in to the Volkspolizei. He's going to get one or all of us arrested. "Can I help you?"

"We need to search the premises for an illegal person," the Volkspolizei said. "Let us in."

I didn't argue. *He'd played the card.* Ashasher thought I'd do anything to keep Mitzi, Ellie, and Sabina out of jail. And he wasn't wrong. But right now, he was making me pick between them. I remembered Felix telling me that he knew I'd be loyal. *To a fault.* Have I always been this easy to play? I gestured for the officers to come into the house and followed them, babbling about how it was just my half sister, Marie, and her friend from school. We all had work permits and college enrollments. There were stacks of books in Ellie's room and the room Mitzi and I shared when we were there. That should be enough for them. It had to be enough. Ellie had papers. As long as Ellie's German papers held, that was enough. My hands shook, and I tried to hide that as they walked through the house, opening the closet where Ellie once hid from Ashasher, checking the bedrooms.

To Mitzi and Ellie, one of the police said, "You've had no one else here?"

Mitzi shook her head. "No, sir."

"Where does he sleep?" the police asked, pointing at me.

I blinked. The house had two bedrooms. It was clear that Mitzi's clothes were on one bed and Ellie's on another. Ellie was paler than I had ever seen her. She was shaking hard. My hands itched to go to her and smooth away the wrinkles on her forehead, the way her eyes bounced around the room.

Mitzi didn't miss a beat. "With Eleanor, if he's lucky. Some nights she makes him sleep on the couch."

One of the police snorted and said, "Women."

I shrugged and gave him the only smile I could muster which was a small, wan one, like I couldn't agree more. He shook his head at my ID card and spat out a word that chilled me to my bones, a racist slur I hadn't had hurtled at me in ages.

"No. I am Romani," I said without thinking. He didn't care about language and what he should, or shouldn't, be calling me. But what was I supposed to do? Let him say that word just because he could?

The room stilled. Ellie's mouth pressed together in a thin line. Mitzi shook her head slightly at me in warning. If they wanted to call me racist words, then they could. I'd have to let them right now. Everyone's safety depended on it. The two police exchanged looks, and for a long time, I could only stare at the puke green of their uniforms and see myself hanging from a ceiling, bloodied to a pulp. Going into a Stasi prison meant one was unlikely to return. Especially me. Some things were constant in Europe. The treatment of Jews and Romani was reliably awful.

By the stairs, the policeman interviewing Ellie broke the silence by saying, "Baum. Jewish."

Ellie's chin lifted slightly as he turned over her papers. "I am just a student."

He nodded and handed her papers back to her. He quizzed all of us about what we were studying and where we were working. Ellie was just a student, for now, and she came across as young enough. Thank god it was a Sunday. She remembered where she was supposed to be going to school, according to her papers, and I could have kissed her for that. They doubted that Mitzi and I were related until Mitzi smoothly insinuated that our mother was a troubled woman.

She shrugged. "Our mother isn't here. We didn't ask. We didn't need her. She's damaging."

It was the right answer. As the police left, I heard one of them say, "A Jew and a Gypsy. Sounds like the beginning of the end. Sure we can't arrest them for that?"

I stiffened, waiting for them to come back and arrest me for being Romani and Ellie for being Jewish—and then, then we'd have a problem. But I shut the door behind them, and they got into their car, pulling away a moment later.

Mitzi shoved me hard, and I grabbed her wrists. "I wasn't thinking! I know! I know."

"Think *better*," she snapped. "They're going to come back now. You mouthed off to them. Congratulations, idiot. You're under surveillance."

"You've never been called that word in your life, Mitzi. Don't you dare tell me how I should or shouldn't react to it," I hissed, releasing her and pushing her back.

"I don't care. You're missing the point. I don't care. I care about keeping everyone safe. And if that means you have to hear that word again, I don't care." Mitzi poked me in the chest, her eyes flashing dangerously. "Our job requires us to be under the radar, Kai. You are now on the radar. Tell me how you're doing your job right."

"Our job? It's dead," I yelled back at her. "We found out last night that one of the two people we run balloons for has been using them to kill people. Our job is dead. There will be no more balloons after this, Mitzi. Nothing matters."

"Everything matters, Kai. You're wrong. There will be balloons. One bad seed can't ruin it all," Mitzi spat back, digging her finger farther into my sternum. I grabbed her wrist and dug my fingers into her pressure points. She gritted her teeth and then spat at my face.

"Fuck!" I swore and wiped at my face with my free arm.

"Stop it, both of you," Ellie said, pulling on a coat. She pulled her hair free of her collar. Her face had regained none of its color. Her fingers shook as she did up the buttons. "Kai, come on. We need to find Felix. Now. You both are missing an important point. If Ashasher sent the police here as retaliation, then he knows it was us. He has Sabina."

Time stopped. My blood froze in my veins, slicing me open from the inside out, and I stared at Ellie. *He has Sabina.* Bean, Bean, Bean, for whom I'd do anything. So busy fighting with Mitzi over a fucking word, and my sister's in the hands of a madman.

"I'll get the papers," I said, needing to move. My heart began to wake back up as I ran up the stairs. I hid the papers inside my coat and zipped it up, making sure they were secured in the interior pocket. When I came back down the stairs, Ellie was scolding Mitzi.

"I'm serious, Mitzi," she was saying. "It's distracting from what we need to do, and that's get Ashasher arrested. Have your existential arguments about racist terms and what's tolerable tomorrow. Today we're busy."

Mitzi shook her head. "Of course you'll take his side."

Ellie made a face at her as I slipped quietly down the stairs. "It's not sides. There are no sides here. Are you coming with us?"

Mitzi frowned at my shoes. "No. You two know Felix. I don't want to be the wrench in the plans. He has to trust you. And besides, someone has to be here. They'll be suspicious if they come back and we're all gone."

"Ready?" I asked, surprising both of them. Mitzi's eyes skipped past me, and she set her mouth in a thin line. She was still pissed at me. Ellie glanced at her and then at me. She nodded, and we both stepped out into the sunshine.

In the street, I took her hand and Ellie sighed, leaning a little against me as we walked. People's eyes followed us. I'd never noticed that before today, but maybe I was being paranoid. I murmured, trying to keep my voice as soft as possible, "Are you okay?"

She shook her head slightly. There was nothing to say to that. I didn't know how to make her feel better. I didn't know much about Ellie, really, when I thought about it, and I'd never felt that ache of helplessness so much as then, walking toward the café to find Felix. I thought Ellie understood me a great deal more than I understood her, and I didn't know how that could be. That she could have known yesterday how badly I needed to laugh, even over a bad joke, and how sometimes I just needed to feel another person next to me. She read me better than I read myself, and I realized I only knew her middle chapters. I didn't understand what made her tick, and I didn't know where she was going.

And if she left today, I'd never know her. It was the worst, realizing that she could leave and I'd never know her again. Our paths could never cross in the future. I'd be—look, I did the math on how old I'd be when Ellie came to Berlin in her time, and it wasn't pretty—and we'd just be two lines that intersected once. I didn't want that, but I couldn't ask her to stay. She couldn't stay. It fucked with everything for her to stay. She didn't belong here, and maybe, in her time, she was a happier person. Maybe she had a boyfriend there, and maybe she was free. Here, she was stuck in a prison state. How could she want to stay?

If I had the opportunity, if Sabina wasn't in the picture, would I travel to the future?

In a heartbeat. In a fucking heartbeat.

I'd get out of here, skip all the messy stuff in the middle of life, and get straight to knowing who I was and what I wanted out of the world. I'd leave in a heartbeat.

Not without Sabina though. Not without her. And maybe not without Mitzi, though I was still pissed at her.

"*Da ist er,*" Ellie said, bringing me back into the present.

This present, anyway. The idea of multiple presents hurt my head.

Felix sat at the café, sipping coffee and tilting back in his chair. He nodded to us as we sat down across from him. I took the papers out of my coat and put them on the table in front of him. "It's Ashasher."

"Interesting. That explains why Ashasher's been absent lately, doesn't it?" Felix mused, taking the papers calmly, as if he had expected them. I steadied myself against the sudden panic that Felix was in Ashasher's pocket. If he was an informant, he knew everything. We had given him everything.

But he shook his head, turning over the papers. "This is… He did his research. I assume Sabina's transcribing for him? I can almost understand enough of how this might work. But why?"

"That we're not sure about. But the balloons can't go back. Instead, the balloons are being sent forward because that's how time works. You can only time travel forward, not back. The magic in the balloon activates when someone on the other side is grabbing the balloon, and then the balloon is returning to its original dimension," explained Ellie, her explanation in German almost free of stumbling blocks.

Felix looked up at her, his eyes light and crystalline. "What else?"

Ellie's eyes shifted to me so I said heavily, "He has Sabina."

"Ah," Felix said softly.

"So we're going to arrest him, right?" Ellie asked, leaning forward. "Before anyone else gets hurt."

To our surprise, and then shock, Felix shook his head. "I have to review the evidence first and verify that you didn't tamper with it. I'm sorry, it's procedure. When I can verify with my boss that everything here is from Ashasher, then I'll go ahead with the arrest."

Shock was the least of the emotions that flooded me, filling up the empty spaces of my chest so that I couldn't breathe. My lungs had no room to move with that much anger and betrayal. Next to me, Ellie was so motionless I almost thought she was dead. Felix had the grace to look a little guilty.

"That's not what we thought would happen," I said as calmly as I could manage. My hands made fists on my lap. "We risked a lot for this. Ashasher sent the Volkspolizei this morning. It could be the Stasi tomorrow. And Felix, you know my sister's at risk. He's always used her as the threat against me."

"I know," Felix said, looking uncomfortable. "I don't make the rules. I just follow them. Look, I doubt he'll make a move before then. He's not reckless. Mad, perhaps, but not reckless."

"That's bullshit," Ellie said.

In English.

Heads turned toward us and I reached for her, but she was already standing up, her chair toppling to the floor in a silencing clatter. Waiters stopped on their way to the table. Ellie took a deep breath, spun on her heel, and began to run out of the restaurant.

"Scheiße." I went to follow her, and then glared over my shoulder. "You fucked up, Felix. Fix it."

He opened his mouth to say something, but Ellie was already down the street and out of sight. I was going to lose her, so I left without hearing what he had to say. Whatever it was, it was less important than keeping Ellie from doing something absolutely fucking insane right now. And what was she doing? Running down the street, dodging cars and soldiers and people? That was insane. Staying under the radar was completely useless now. We were on the radar. Ellie apparently wanted to be the very loud and obvious blip on the radar.

I followed her through the streets, losing sight of her and then catching her again, her blue skirt disappearing around corners. A policeman tried to catch me, maybe thinking I was chasing the girl for terrible reasons, but I escaped him and ducked down an alley, cutting between two streets, hoping to catch up with her. I knew where she was going. And sure enough, at the entrance to the tunnels, she stood, waiting for me, tears streaming down her face as her hands gripped the rusty gate. I had the keys. I stumbled to a stop, catching her face between my palms.

"I'll come with you," I told her. "Please don't run, Ellie. Not from me."

She nodded, her forehead touching my mouth. I closed my eyes and fished the key out from the chain around my neck. I unlocked the gate, and we stepped into the dark together. This time, we ran along the rails as fast as we could. We were out of time. Ashasher would have known how slow the Zerberus would work even when we brought them evidence. He would have us dead before they could act on anything. And Ellie needed to get home. Today. Today. I didn't break promises I made.

"Kai," Ellie said. "I'll do anything to keep anyone else from getting killed. Anything."

Me too, I wanted to say. Instead, I just opened the workshop door.

Chapter Thirty-One

THE GIRL WITH
THE RED BALLOON

Chełmno, Poland, April 1942

Benno

When we unloaded from the train, German guards greeted us. One of them shouted for us to line up and we did, Mama's hand tight in mine. In the daylight, the girl was gone again. A hallucination, but her words stuck to my blood, slowing it in my veins, steadying me. *Trust me, Benno.* Did I trust her? I didn't know her. I didn't know anything other than that she might be a mentally disturbed girl. But then, she didn't know me either. She might be risking her life to help me. If she's real, I thought to myself.

"You will be assigned work and fed soon. Here, unlike at Łódź," said the guard, standing up on a box in front of us, "you will be fed for the work you produce. But first, you must be cleaned and disinfected. We do not want disease here."

Long ago, we had stopped worrying about privacy. At the muzzle of a gun, I cared even less. We were divided into men and women before we stripped and headed into trucks to the showers. I hugged my mother before we parted ways, just in case. I whispered into her ear, "I love you. I won't leave without you."

Her fingers dug into the bones of my back. She whispered back, "I love you."

As we began to get onto the trucks, the girl appeared again, still in purple. Her hair was loose this time, a wild mane around her face, and she reached for my hand. "Benno, now!"

I didn't think. I took her hand, and an electric shiver went up my arm. Hand in hand with the girl, I walked away from the trucks and the other naked men, past the guards and toward a warehouse next to the tracks. I stared around in wonder as we walked through the crowds without a single person turning their heads. *Impossible.* But though I waited for the guards to shout and start shooting at us, not a single one seemed to notice me missing. Not a single one seemed to see us.

"Where are we going?" I asked the girl.

"I am giving you a balloon. It'll carry you straight into a Polish resistance camp. They're expecting you. They'll get you out of Europe. You aren't safe here. You need to go south, go to Palestine."

Last week, I, with twenty-three others, had whispered, *Next year in Jerusalem* at the end of the seder. Today, a girl who had somehow made me invisible was telling me that I needed to go to Palestine.

I whispered, "I'm already dead, aren't I?"

She shook her head and handed me a long wool overcoat. Too warm for the weather, but enough to cover myself. "No, you're very much alive. The trucks are rigged to kill. They turned the exhaust back into the cabins."

My veins froze, and my fingers stopped fumbling with the buttons on the overcoat. I turned away from the girl to look at the trucks where I could see people gathering, loading into them in hopes of a shower, of getting clean, of work and food. *Mama.*

"We have to go back." I managed to make the words come out of my mouth. I pulled the girl back in the direction of the trucks. "My mama. Mama. She doesn't know."

"We can't go back, Benno. We can't go back. She's already gone," said the girl in the purple dress.

"Mama!" I screamed. Not a single head turned. "Mama!"

Panic seized my veins, and I fought against the girl. She was younger than me, but she had clearly eaten good food lately. I was weak from hunger and malnutrition, and though I was taller than her, no matter how hard I fought, she continued to drag me along the side of the warehouse. My breath stuck in my throat, and my vision turned black. The girl's palm collided with the side of my face.

I gasped, blinking, and watched her untie the string of a red balloon from the handle of the door on the side of the warehouse. A red balloon, like the one Ruth and I had seen. She said, a little unkindly, "We do not have time for your emotions or any heroics. I can only save one life today. I chose you. You have all your stories, and you're young still. Benno, you and I, we'll change the world. But you must trust me. Take this and do not let go, even if your arms hurt, even if you're afraid of heights. Do you understand? Until it lands, do not let go and do not look down."

She handed me the string to the red balloon. It floated in the sky, like this was nothing more than another spring day, another sunny day. Like *happiness*. I stumbled backward, away from the girl and against the wall of the warehouse. I sank to the floor and held my hands over my face. *Mama*.

"Take the balloon," whispered the girl. "Don't let their deaths be in vain."

I held out my hand, and she pushed the balloon string into my palm. My fingers wrapped around the string, and the balloon began to lift me off the ground, straining my arms and shoulders. I didn't have the strength to tighten my muscles and hold on, so instead I dangled like an empty potato sack. My arms, thin and weak from hunger, shook, but I didn't let go. I did not let go.

When we arrived at the Łódź ghetto, I was sixteen years old and Ruth was five. My mother was forty-six, my father forty-eight.

When I left the Łódź ghetto, I was seventeen years old and Ruth was five. My mother was forty-six, my father forty-eight.

When I die, I will be an old man. My teeth will no longer work, and my eyesight will fail me. I will no longer hear anything, much less the distant memories of German and Polish and Yiddish. My mind may not recognize anyone around me. I will lose myself to the murky waters of time and age.

But even then, I know that I will always know that my sister is five. She will always be five. Even now, when I am old, her hand in mine is soft and clammy, fat and unsure in anything but its grip around my hand. A child's hand. Her dark curls stick to her cheeks and get caught in the collar of her jacket.

The balloon carried me free of Chełmno. Dayenu.

The balloon carried me to a Polish resistance camp. Dayenu.

They snuck me south across mountains and through the Nazis' backyard. Dayenu.

They found me a boat to Palestine. Dayenu.

They saved my life with a magic balloon. Dayenu.

They saved me. Dayenu.

And I never learned the name of the girl with the red balloon.

Chapter Thirty-Two

BURNING BRIDGES

East Berlin, German Democratic Republic, May 1988

Ellie

The workshop smelled like scented candles and coffee, a combination I might have found comforting in any other time because it almost smelled like home. Not today. Not now. Not with Sabina standing on a table in front of us, a noose around her neck, hands tied behind her back.

My eyes tracked upward, following the rope to a steel beam crisscrossing the ceiling above the upper walkway, and dropped back down to Sabina, her toes curled around the edge of the table. Next to me, Kai stopped dead in his tracks when he saw her. I didn't know what to say, but I didn't have to say anything. Sabina shivered and shot a glance sideways at Aurora sitting next to her, writing on a piece of paper. As if there weren't a girl ready to hang beside her.

Ashasher wasn't anywhere in the workshop. Just Aurora, and she wasn't trying to get Sabina down from the table.

Aurora.

I looked to Kai, but he was staring at his sister, holding a finger against his lips as he tried to edge closer to the table. I had to distract Aurora. Maybe she wasn't the one who put Sabina up there on the table with a rope around her neck. Maybe she wasn't behind all of this. Maybe she too felt like she was chasing ghosts.

"Where's Ashasher?" I whispered. "Where's everyone else?"

Aurora glanced up, and her eyes were wide. "He isn't here. I'm surprised it took you this long, Eleanor. And I wouldn't walk any farther, Kai. I sent the other Schöpfers elsewhere, of course. Out on errands, for fresh air."

Kai stopped, rocking on the balls of his feet as Aurora shifted the table and Sabina whimpered. I couldn't tear my eyes away from the woman with the raven hair on the other side of the table. We didn't have proof it was Ashasher. We only knew Aurora's papers didn't contain notes about the past, we couldn't read Ashasher's, and Sabina transcribed for someone. But now that I thought about it, I'd never seen Sabina with Ashasher. And Aurora was out that night I found the first dead time-traveler. She could have sent off a balloon before she ran into me.

It was Aurora. It'd always been her.

The woman who saved my grandfather killed people to try to go back into time. The person who saved my grandfather and thus helped me be who I am was the person responsible for where I was. For what had happened. For me being a missing person in my time. My heart cracked, crumbling around my lungs. I couldn't breathe.

I took a step forward, and Aurora placed her hands on the edge of the table. Sabina wobbled, her feet inches from the edge. Behind me, Kai's voice cracked. "Ellie, please."

Sabina began to cry, and Kai made some sort of strange warbling noise and said something in Romani.

We wasted so much time. All that time. Being unsure, being unwilling to see what was right in front of us. The purple scarf from that rainy night that Kai and I saw two people send off an unscheduled balloon. Her presence the night the next time-traveler arrived, dead. All we knew was that a Schöpfer was doing the damage, but of course it had to be her. Of course. Who else would have been brave and bold enough to circumvent the rules as the one who brought a balloon to a boy in a death camp all those years ago? She never believed in rules. She'd always worked outside them. What made her brilliant at her work had also made her the Schöpfer who went rogue.

Aurora, with her beautiful hair swept back perfectly, like she'd walked off the cover of a Brontë novel. Aurora and her quiet, precise voice. Aurora, the girl who had worn a purple dress and brought my grandfather a red balloon. Aurora, the girl who had saved my grandfather's life but killed his nephew decades later with another balloon. A life for a life, an eye for an eye... Aurora would see the whole world blind.

"But you saved my grandfather's life. He had the first balloon." The words I meant, the words I really wanted to say, wouldn't come out. *How could you kill? You were saving lives.*

Aurora looked up at me, her absurdly light and bright eyes tired. She nodded slowly and said, "I wasn't supposed to give him that balloon. We weren't using the magic yet. I didn't know if it would work, but the trains kept coming to Chełmno and people just kept dying. I thought since he was young, smart, and strong, he might survive."

"He did," I said. "He escaped south and then to Israel. He moved from Israel to the United States with my grandmother in 1952. He told me about you. You were the girl with the red balloon. The girl in the purple dress with the red balloon." We'd never talked about the details. She thought my grandfather's cynicism the heart of his resilience, but what was at the heart of her rebellion?

"I'd already learned how not to be seen. It'd been the first part of my magic I'd conquered, so I found it fun to stand out against a world that had gone so gray. There wasn't anything happy about that world, you know. We were the magical counterpart to the Zegota. The Polish government in exile founded the Zegota to help the Polish Jews. There were so many. And then poof, there were so few. Where did they all go? How did they kill so many so quickly?" she whispered, like she was remembering.

I wondered what she and my grandfather would do if they sat down together. I think they'd cry. I didn't know how to hold my hatred for her and all the deaths she caused and my gratitude that she'd saved lives in the Holocaust. She was someone we'd call Righteous Among the Nations. Could we call someone who later went on to become a murderer a righteous person?

Then she bent her head. "But never mind that. I've figured it out. How to stabilize the magic. And I knew you were coming, though I'm surprised you brought Kai. I'm sorry that you'll have to die tonight, but I can't have anyone too close on my heels."

"Where are you going?" I asked. Kai edged forward in the corner of my vision.

"Now, now," Aurora said, turning toward him. "I don't want to kill your sister if I don't have to."

"Stop," he whispered, voice hoarse. "You said you'd protect her. I trusted you."

Aurora flinched. "I am trying to right a wrong. Sometimes there is collateral damage. Sabina is collateral damage." She glanced at me. "You are collateral damage. You're proof that not every balloon must kill someone. When the Stasi come for you, it will be because you wrote your own death certificate."

The closet. The rat poison. "I won't be taken by the Stasi. The Zerberus have all your papers. They know what you did. They don't need to know why. Even if we don't live, you will be arrested. They're going to strip you of your magic, Aurora."

Her eyes shifted down to the paper. "I will die for a cause then. I will die knowing that my path is the right one. I told your grandfather once that I'd tell the stories his people couldn't tell if they all died."

"But they didn't all die. Hitler and the Nazis lost. And the next evil will lose too. Evil's always done by people who believe they are in the right," I said, stepping toward her again. Her hands reached for the edge of the table, and I shook my head. Whatever I did, if I kept her arguing about moral ambiguity, she paid more attention to me than to Kai. Every time, he edged forward, a little closer to his sister. "You don't need another body on your conscience, Aurora. You don't want that. You're not a murderer at heart, are you? You want to save lives."

"You know nothing, child," she said, her fingers closing around the edge of the table. If she pushed the table, Sabina would fall. "You think I don't know how to write those balloons from my memory? I've written dozens. I'll write more. I'm going to write them until I get what I want. Those papers that Kai took? They're only half of what's necessary. And I have copies."

I stopped walking right next to one of the candles. "You're not trying to go forward in time. You're trying to go back in time. What? To kill Hitler?"

"Who wouldn't kill Hitler? But you're wrong if you think that's all. I'd rescue Benno's mother," Aurora said, her voice trembling. "I could have, but I didn't, because I didn't know how. But now I do, you see. I have all the magic, and I know how to write more than one balloon at a time. Think of all the knowledge we have now. Think about how we can change lives. Save lives, Eleanor."

I stilled. My grandfather's mother. He never talked about her, but she survived Łódź with him and died at Chełmno. I'd found her name at the United States Holocaust Memorial Museum in DC last year. My grandfather sat *shiva* for her every year, even though he shouldn't. Not anymore. Jewish law actually said he should move on, but every year, the week of her death, he sat in his house in the dark, and he said the Kaddish over and over again.

Aurora whispered, her voice carrying in my silence. "Eleanor, I'd rescue her. And I'd rescue Ruth. Because I knew she was sick. He asked me for medicine, you know. He told me stories about people who were braver than I was. But I know more now. I want to right wrongs. Wrongs I did out of ignorance and cowardice."

"Ellie," Kai said. I glanced at Sabina, at the sheen in her eyes. From tears or from whatever world her mind had taken her to, I wasn't sure. She had to stay present though, if we were to get her out of here. Kai could get her out, I realized, and I could stay and deal with Aurora.

I swallowed. "It wasn't cowardice. You were a little girl. Like Sabina. Let her go."

Aurora's smile shook me to my core. It was sad and hopeful at the same time. "I was your age. Wouldn't I be a coward now if I didn't try? If I knew I could do it."

"You're killing people to save people," I countered. "How does that make sense? How do you justify this?"

"Let Sabina go," said Kai, his voice rising again. He was two long steps away from the table. Almost there. "Aurora, she's just a girl."

"I'm not letting her go, Kai, because I need her for the science. Because once I have the science down, I'll be able to save more lives than I lost along the way." Aurora sat back down. "Just sit there and wait, and when I'm ready to go, we'll trade. My escape for your sister's life."

But Sabina's legs were beginning to tremble. She couldn't hold that position much longer, and if she collapsed, she'd hang herself. She wouldn't even need Aurora to yank away the table. Kai began whispering to her in a steady stream of Romani, the language lilting over his tongue. But she only sagged farther, the rope indenting her neck.

"Sabina," I said, choking on her name. "Stand up."

"Yes, dear, stand up," said Aurora absently.

Kai's hands were fists at his side. I had to do something before he tried to get to his sister. Aurora could still hang her faster than we could cut her down. I didn't even know how we'd cut the rope off her. My voice sounded desperate now instead of steady, and I didn't even mind. "Aurora, let her go, and you can spend all night telling me how you're fighting science. Science can only take us forward in time, not back."

"I'm getting closer," she retorted. "The last body the other night was from 1991. I am closer."

"Closer is not enough," Kai said. "Aurora, I'd like to kill Hitler too. And everyone who hurt my people. And if you had the science down to an art, if it were possible, I'd volunteer to do the deed myself. But you can't. You won't. You'll only kill people for a pipe dream. Guilt or no guilt."

"Your family died at Łódź, and Auschwitz, and Bergen-Belsen, and Ravensbruck, right alongside her family," snapped Aurora, her eyes flashing. "We'll never know how many Roma died in the *o baro mudaripen le Rromenge*. You don't even have a word for it, boy. Your people believe in collective amnesia. She..." She gestured to me. "At least her people understand. Collective memory is more powerful than collective amnesia. Without Hitler, Germany would have never been divided. Without Hitler, we'd have no East Germany. Without Hitler, we'd have no Stasi. Do you see? Because of Hitler, we have so many more deaths than just the war. Kill Hitler, save the people I should have been able to save, change the world. It's so simple."

It was never that simple. I knew that now. And I knew we were going in circles. I had everything to lose—Sabina, Kai, and my way home—but secrets weren't among them. "And if you wait eighteen months, Aurora, the wall comes down."

Even Sabina seemed to focus at that. I continued on, never lifting my eyes off Aurora. I had to get her out of here. I had to get rid of her ability to continue this experiment. I had to keep her from killing Sabina. All at once. We were never going to agree. She was never going to give up unless all her research was gone. Unless she couldn't continue.

"The wall comes down in 1989. Germany is reunited as one Germany a year later. By the time that I come to Berlin," I said, stepping a little closer to the candle on my left. It was one of the tall pedestal ones. Next to it sat a box of matches. "Germany is one of the most powerful, peaceful, and respected countries on earth. Without ever resorting to militarization."

No one breathed for a beat, and then Aurora shook her head. "It does not negate the deaths that came before this."

"Nothing will negate them," I said. *Or the ones you caused, Aurora. What's the difference? We'll never know all their names anyway.* "I don't want them negated. I want to remember my grandfather's family who died in the Łódź ghetto. I want to know that the Holocaust made me who I am—and not just because my grandfather's a survivor. I don't want more people to die. I want to believe that World War II is the reason we haven't had another world war. I want to believe that we're all here for a reason, and what we have now, and all that history behind us, is important and meaningful even when it's terrible. Even when it's sad."

"You'd rather me let his family die."

"They're already dead." I swallowed back tears. "They've been dead. You can't change that because of your conscience. We can't change the past, Aurora. We can only try to do better in the present and the future."

I saw her pushing the table at the same time that I moved. I knocked the candle to the ground and it shattered, glass everywhere, the flame nearly going out before it caught hold of all the papers on the ground. Aurora screamed as the table shifted and Sabina's feet came off the edge of it, the weight of her dropping against the edge of the noose. Kai lunged forward, shoving the table back underneath his sister's kicking feet. She stumbled, and he climbed up to her.

"Ellie, leave her!" he shouted at me over his shoulder as I leaped forward to follow Aurora. "Eleanor!"

Grabbing the matchbox off the floor from where it had fallen next to the candle, I struck another match and threw it on the ground. I tracked Aurora around the tables and toward the chalkboard. The fire began slowly, but everything inside the workshop was paper and wood. The fire crackled and burned, the smell of smoke overwhelming the scented candles. I stepped in the shards of the coffee mugs, my heart pounding in my chest. Aurora moved ahead of me, grabbing for important documents and throwing books at me over her head.

I dodged one and ran after her, past the burning workshop tables and the active balloons, waiting for blood and magic, past the chalkboard with my name on it and ideas on how to get me home. Past the active cases of Passengers waiting for freedom. Aurora worked her way up the metal stairs, her heels clanging with every step, as she headed for the offices and library. There had to be another exit.

Stop, drop, and roll, my instincts told me as the fire licked at my feet on the stairs.

Burn it to the ground, my heart said.

"You're destroying the only chance to change history for the better!" Aurora cried. "You foolish, stupid, simple-minded child!"

My heart ached when I dropped another match. If she was right…What if she was right? What if she could prevent all those deaths—my grandfather's family, my family, Kai's family, not just the Holocaust but the war and all the men and women who died in it, the Cold War, the division of Europe and the Iron Curtain…No. There was nothing that said she could do it. I struck another match and left it by the library of books in the loft that overlooked the workshop tables. I couldn't read the titles anymore, not through the smoke that rose, clogging my lungs.

I tried to strike another match, but it snapped between my shaking fingers. My throat burned. Too many people died here, forever missing from their lives in their own times. Me, stuck here. I clung to my thoughts, a mantra running through my mind. *You cannot erase a wrong. You can only make it right in the present and the future. Killing people to save people isn't fair.* I'd snapped the last match. I crumpled the empty box in my hand and stood up again, covering my mouth and nose with my hand to guard against the smoke. It wasn't much help.

The room blazed hot and fierce. Below me, Kai had Sabina down and halfway to the tunnel door. He yelled my name, and I ignored him. She was just going to keep doing this, just keep *killing people* in pursuit of something unattainable, unless everything she had compiled was destroyed. I had to make sure it all burned.

In her office, Aurora filled a box with books and papers. She didn't look at me as she spat out, "You've destroyed forty years of research. It'll take me years to fix this. You are the only Jew in the world who would say that a few dozen lives were not worth saving the lives of six million."

"Ten million, and more, if you count soldiers on all sides who died," I corrected her. "I hope it all burns. I hope you never get it back. If you had exact science, then maybe I'd have a different answer. But you don't. You just have death in hopes of saving lives."

"That's how progress works, you insipid child," Aurora said. She shook her head and pulled at a bookcase on the far left wall. It swung open, revealing an escape. The fire crept across her carpet. I couldn't breathe in the smoke, and I coughed. She said over the blaze, "Some people must die so others might live."

"I can't…I *won't* accept that." I doubled over, trying to bring air into my lungs. The room spun, burning at the edges of me.

"You are a foolish child. Benno would hate you for what you've done. You could have saved his family, and you made the decision not to," she said, and then she stepped through the tunnel and pulled the bookcase closed behind her. I grabbed at the shelf and pulled with all my weight, but it moved just an inch and caught. Locked.

Below me, the workshop was entirely ablaze, the room filling with thick, dark smoke as the fire consumed everything in sight, all the good and all the bad. The smoke curled up through the holes in the metal grated pathway I stood on outside Aurora's office. A fire in front of me, between me and that passageway. The entire workshop on fire beneath me, between me and the tunnel passage. Kai and Sabina were gone, safely into the tunnels.

Me and a fire.

Decades ago, my grandfather was a seventeen-year-old boy who survived Łódź on luck and health and hard work, and then he was sent to Chełmno, from which almost no one survived. He survived Chełmno because a teenage girl named Aurora gave him a magical balloon so he did not die in a gas chamber and his body was not incinerated. No one breathed in his ashes.

It seemed so fitting that I'd die here in a fire, that smoke would be the last thing I breathed in, underground in a tunnel beneath my grandfather's former city, divided by a Wall, death on one side and art on the other. It seemed so fitting. My eyes stung, blurring with tears from the smoke scissoring through them, and I closed them, coughing. I sank to the floor, burying my face in my skirt, trying to breathe.

You'll pass out first, I told myself. You won't burn alive. The smoke will make you asphyxiate. You'll just pass out. You won't feel a thing. It'll be okay.

A hand touched my shoulder and shook me. A damp cloth pressed against my mouth, and someone hauled me to my feet by an elbow. I stumbled along, inhaling a hand and damp cotton.

I tripped and fell against the wall, screaming as the heat, conducted along the metal walls, burned through my sweater.

The stairs. Someone was shoving me into the fire. I shook my head and tried to push the person away, but fingers dug persistently into my arm as I was shoved one step at a time down into the inferno. I sobbed as the heat grew intolerable, so hot I couldn't breathe, so hot I smelled nothing but my hair, burning. Books, burning.

If you give a girl a magic balloon, she will burn down the world.

The sound of metal wrenching against metal. The walkway. It was melting and coming down on us. And then cold. Cold. Cold. A shock against my hot body as I stumbled toward the clear, cool air, gasping and stumbling. I fell to the ground, and then I heard the metal again. A door. I lay, shaking, on the damp ground, and then a hand touched my face.

"Ellie," whispered Kai, his voice hoarse and shaking. "Eleanor. Breathe. Just breathe."

I'd burned everything. I burned it all. No one else would die, just like I told him, and now, no one in the past had the opportunity to live. And I had burned my own way home. Somewhere in there, Aurora must have had the balloons and the way of sending me home. She was too methodical not to think of the reverse equation. It had either burned or she'd taken it with her, and now I was trapped. I couldn't say anything. I couldn't do anything but shake in the cold tunnels.

Kai left Sabina and me in the tunnels, returning to find Ashasher, Mitzi, and Felix frantically searching for all of us. The fire in the workshop was noticeable. The smoke came up through manholes, and sirens wailed through the city. The police would be in the tunnels soon. Ashasher carried me out, and his feathers, swirling like a hurricane, were the first things I saw when I opened my smoke-dried and burned eyes in the day. I couldn't cry, but I wanted to sob.

Ashasher didn't tell me I had done the wrong thing. When we got back to the house, he carried me upstairs and let Mitzi take care of me. He just said, "Brave girl. Brave girl."

I closed my eyes again and listened to Mitzi as she cried and talked to me in German I was too tired to translate, a cool cloth against my forehead. My body wouldn't stop shaking, even when I ordered it to stop. To stay still. I just wanted to be still.

I wasn't brave.

I had been so afraid.

Chapter Thirty-Three

AFTERMATH

East Berlin, German Democratic Republic, May 1988

Unraveling the events of the day took hours, and considering that Aurora had nearly succeeded in hanging my sister, and Ellie had set the entire workshop on fire, it was the least of my concerns. But once Ellie was home safe and Sabina was upstairs, detoxing under Mitzi's watchful eye from whatever concoction of drugs Aurora had given her, Ashasher and Felix sat me down in the kitchen and demanded to know what had happened. So while Ashasher treated the burns on both of my hands, I told them.

They wanted to know which came first, the candle or Aurora trying to kill Sabina. I couldn't remember. In my head, they were all the same thing. The burst of flames across the floor, the burst of movement into my limbs to get the table back under my sister's feet so I could cut her loose. I hadn't been paying much attention. For some reason, I thought Ellie would be on my heels when I pulled the noose back over Sabina's head and pulled her past the growing fire to the tunnel.

When I turned around, the fire was moving—well, like a fire—like a goddamn freight train really, across the room, and Ellie was lighting more and more matches, like a girl possessed. Like a girl who had snapped off the branch of reality. I screamed for her, and she didn't even turn around. She followed Aurora right up those stairs and around the curvature of the pathway to Aurora's office.

When I went back in for her, the smoke was the killer. I made it to the steps. The soles of my shoes would still be on them. They melted right through, burning a grid onto the bottoms of my soles. I tore off my shoes when I finally got Ellie into the tunnel. She was breathing, barely, and alive. I didn't know what else to do. I couldn't carry her and Sabina out myself so I had to leave them behind to find help.

Felix, apparently unaffected by Ashasher's hypnotizing feathers, turned to him. "Aurora escaped the office but went into the train tunnels. We're still working to recover..."

"She's dead?" I interrupted.

"She didn't know the tunnels and the train schedule like you Runners do," Felix said with a shrug. "Or maybe she did. Maybe she knew we'd convict and cut her from her magic."

"But there are others we need to worry about now. Eleanor Baum," said Ashasher, "needs to rest. Setting fire to the equations and balloons might not have been the best decision..."

"Just because it wasn't the decision you or I would have made..." I said, standing up. I didn't know how to talk to him. In my head, he was still connected to everything that happened. He knew we'd thought it was him when we went to the workshop. We hadn't talked about it. I didn't intend to. "Doesn't make it a bad decision."

"Kai," Ashasher said, his voice stern. His dark eyes held mine. "Ellie's not in trouble, and I cannot judge her. I wasn't there. I was about to say that knowledge once learned cannot be unlearned.

Ellie is fine. However, the Council submits Sabina Holwell as a potential accomplice to Aurora's crimes to the Zerberus."

My stomach dropped out and hit the floor. I whispered, "She's a child. She doesn't know—"

"Sabina is not damaged. You brought her here to prevent her from being institutionalized or used for bad magic against her will because you did not believe she was damaged. She is more than capable of knowing right from wrong. We failed to keep her safe, and for that, we will submit ourselves as an entire community to the Zerberus as failing to protect a student and for endangerment of a student, but Sabina must also be investigated. She knows now how to make the rogue balloons, Kai. She has been trained to use blacklisted magic. We cannot ignore that."

I slumped. "And if she's arrested?"

"Unlikely," Felix said quietly. "I doubt we'll even strip her. I think we'll probably put her on probation. And she might not dislike that. I am afraid to find out the extent of abuse she suffered at Aurora's hands."

Everything inside me twisted clockwise, a lock sliding into place. I had failed everyone. Garrick. Passengers. Ashasher. Felix. Mitzi. Ellie. Sabina. I couldn't even keep Sabina safe. *Safe* was such a useless word. No one was ever safe, even when they thought they were.

"Kai," Felix said. "Take a few days. Just take care of Sabina. We'll come around eventually, but we have a lot of cleanup to do."

I remembered what Mitzi had said before Ellie and I left. "Will there be more balloons?"

"Not right now," Felix said, looking at Ashasher. "We'd like to have this Council back on its feet and sending Passengers to safety no later than the end of the month." He stood, shaking Ashasher's hand first, then mine. "Take care of yourself. And don't worry about the Stasi or Volkspolizei."

I had forgotten about them. "Why not?"

Felix smiled. "That was a problem. I handle problems. Take care, Kai."

When the door clicked behind him, Ashasher said, "I don't know if you'll ever forgive me, Kai, but I hope you will. I had no idea that Aurora…It's terribly hard to imagine someone you've known your whole life, someone you thought you knew very well, shunning ethics and morals to pursue a path so dark and treacherous that it nearly claimed the life of three, four young people. And she did kill people. *She killed people.*"

The wonder in his voice sounded genuine, and he shook his head as if he couldn't believe it. Ashasher and Aurora had worked together for twenty-seven years. I'd say that I couldn't believe he didn't know, but the grief in his eyes and his voice, the slumped shoulders of a man who always sat so squarely and so properly, resonated deep inside me. I was not the only one feeling lost and adrift at the moment.

I swallowed and said, "It wasn't your fault. I-I should have… I don't know where I went wrong. I don't know."

"Me either," admitted Ashasher.

I pointed at the ceiling. "I'm going to go check on them."

"Of course," Ashasher said, sounding sad and defeated.

In Ellie's room, Mitzi sat in the windowsill, a book on her lap, her eyes swollen from crying. She climbed off the sill, the book toppling to the floor, and wrapped her arms around me. I gripped her tight, pressing my face into her hair. She smelled so clean and fresh. No smoke. Her shoulders shook as she tried to keep the tears at bay. Her fists clutched at my shirt.

"I'm fine," I told her. Liar, I thought.

"Liar," she whispered against my neck. I smiled. "You're such a goddamn liar, Kai. I could have lost you today and I was so *fucking* mad at you."

I couldn't breathe. When I closed my eyes, I saw the fire. If I lifted my head, the smoke came back, searing the inside of my nose. "They're investigating Sabina. Aurora's dead. And every-thing's gone."

"Why did she do it?" Mitzi whispered.

My eyes found the girl asleep in the bed behind her. The long brown curls strewn over the white pillow. The burns on her face and arm covered in salve and bandages. Her lungs gasping and rasping with every breath. Mitzi had given her some sort of medicine for all the smoke she inhaled, but our medicine wasn't as good as it could be. I wondered if we could get a balloon for her to get into West Berlin. Over there, they could take care of her properly.

And I still didn't want her to leave. My selfishness felt like a black pit at my core.

I shook my head. "I don't know."

Mitzi stepped out, probably thinking I wanted to be alone. But I didn't know what to do, standing in the room with the sleeping girl who had burned down everything, who had nearly gotten my sister killed in the process, who had warned me before we went in that she would do anything to keep more people from dying because of the rogue balloons. She had warned me, and I hadn't listened. Because I hadn't thought she was capable of that.

And I hadn't thought Aurora was capable of circumventing law and ethics to pursue her own moral code.

Once, I'd thought I was good at reading people. At knowing people.

I no longer thought that. How could I?

I sat on the edge of Ellie's bed and rested my elbows on my knees, watching her over my shoulder. Her breathing changed, and she blinked open bloodshot eyes.

"Sabina," she rasped.

"Safe," I said, running my fingers over her hair. My hands were clumsy in the bandages, but I still managed to tuck her hair behind her ear. "Just rest, Ellie."

She reached up, lacing her fingers through mine. I let her.

For a few days, this was our routine. Mitzi and I played nurse to two girls. Mitzi helped them to the bathroom and cleaned Ellie's burns, and I sat with them, holding their hands and getting them water and food as necessary. Mitzi or Ashasher changed my bandages, and when Mitzi told me that there'd be scars, I didn't mind. Then I wouldn't see the scars from the fights in England anymore.

Sabina recovered quicker, medically, than Ellie, but refused to speak to me. I couldn't figure out if she was embarrassed or pissed at me, but it didn't seem to matter why. I couldn't find the answer because she wouldn't talk to me. She kept her hands over her ears when I came into the room. Sabina didn't talk much to Mitzi either, but at least she was talking. It was hard not to be jealous. Ashasher came by with food for us, but we didn't hear from Felix for a few days.

Then he came back to interview Ellie, who was still prone to coughing fits and slept more than she was awake. I was sitting in Ellie's window when Mitzi came up the stairs and opened the door. "Felix is here. To see Ellie."

I closed the book. Ellie's eyes were open, but she stared resolutely at the side of the bedside table. "Okay."

Felix stepped into the room, carrying a chair from the kitchen. He sat next to Ellie and turned on a tape recorder. He spoke in English, surprising me, and Ellie, I think. "I'm recording this, Ellie, for others. You're not in trouble. How do you feel?"

"Like crap," she said softly.

Felix said, "It'll take a while for your lungs to recover. You need rest more than anything."

She smiled, the first smile I had seen from her since before the workshop fire. "I'll stop running up and down the stairs."

When Felix asked her why she'd set the fire, Ellie turned away from me. "I kept thinking about all those people missing from their lives, how no one would ever find out what happened to them, about how their families would never have closure because their bodies were here, not there. That killed me. I couldn't...I can't, I can't stand that idea. Even if she was right. Even if she'd be able to save other lives, what about these ones?"

She paused to drink from the water Mitzi offered her, and then she slumped back onto the bed. She sounded weak when she said, "I didn't know what else to do. I didn't see another way. Your way was so slow, Felix. More people were going to die. She was committing genocide to prevent genocide. It didn't sit right with me. Besides, you're not supposed to mess with history."

She opened her eyes. "Am I terrible? What if she could have killed Hitler? What if she could have stopped the Holocaust? What if she could have saved my family?"

Felix sighed, setting down the tape recorder. For once, he looked thoughtful, and young, and like he was actually giving Ellie's question some thought instead of readying a glib company line from the Zerberus.

"I can't speak for your family, Ellie. I don't know if Aurora could have done what she wanted to do. I think she was extraordinarily arrogant about her skills, and you're right, many people would die in the pursuit of that magic. But I can tell you one thing. Hitler," Felix said, "came to power because of a multitude of reasons. The Holocaust happened not because of one person, but because of many people believing in an ideology promoted by a charismatic man at the right time and place, and millions of people colluding. History is not singular. Events do not happen in a vacuum. Altering history is far more complicated than the death of one man. If we knew how to go back in time and prevent genocide, we would. We'd have many more genocides than just the Holocaust to fix. History is riddled with deaths. We're all here because of ghosts."

Tears ran down Ellie's cheek. I brushed them away with the back of my hand. She turned her face away from me, and she might as well have stabbed me in the heart. She whispered, "I'm always going to wonder. I'm always going to regret."

"I'd think it strange if you didn't," Felix told her gently. "History and time are impossible knots. We'll never understand every moment that makes the next moment more likely. If we understood time, as both a metaphorical concept and a physical thing, then you'd be home by now, Ellie."

Sabina appeared in the doorway and I slid off the bed, walking toward my sister. I shut the door behind me. Sabina stood, rocking back and forth on her bare feet, picking at her lips while her eyes darted around my head nervously.

Even though I was tired of trying to take care of people who didn't want me to take care of them, I said, "You okay?"

Sabina stopped rocking, and her eyes met mine. She shook her head. She said, "No."

My heart stopped. "What's wrong? What do you need?"

She started to cry. Everyone was crying today. "I'm sorry. I'm sorry. I'm sorry."

I wanted to claw open my skin. I didn't know what to do with the tightness inside me. I didn't even have a name for it. I couldn't breathe, but I said, "You have nothing to be sorry for. I'm sorry I didn't ask more questions. I'm sorry you went through any of that."

She wrapped her arms around me, and I kissed the top of her head. I sighed and said, "You went with her sometimes, didn't you?"

A small figure trailing behind a taller one with a purple scarf. The night by the wall, the second illegal balloon after Ellie's. I saw, and I didn't want to see. Could I have saved lives too? Ellie wasn't the only one with questions. Sabina's arms tightened. "Yes."

I didn't say anything for a moment because I didn't know how to tell my sister I forgave her, even if what she did bordered on unforgivable. Then I said, "We'll be fine, Bean. You and me."

She whispered, "Do you remember, in England, when we used to ride the Tube from one end all the way to another, just to see the people? Vroom-vroom, gaps, and the clatter. The lights."

I nodded a bit. Her hair still smelled of smoke. "Yes."

"I want to go back there, Kai. I want to go home. This isn't home. I'm scared here," she whispered. It had been a long time since Sabina had said something so sensible and straightforward to me.

I closed my eyes. There wasn't a home for us, or if there was, I wasn't sure what it looked like. Sabina barely remembered what home was like for us when her magic spilled over everywhere. But it was controlled now. Maybe we needed to try. Ask for forgiveness. "Then we'll go home. That's where we'll go."

"Felix said he'd take me," she said. "If you didn't want to go. You're happy here."

"I'm happy with you, chey. You're my sister."

"If Ellie stays…" Sabina said, and then she shivered. "She used to tell me that I held you down. That you could be at university being brilliant, but I made you change everything."

It took me a moment to realize that she didn't mean Ellie. She meant Aurora. I shook my head again. "No, kid. She's wrong. I love you. If you want to go back to England, then we'll go back to England."

"I'm sorry," she said again, still holding on to me.

"I'm sorry too," I told her.

I was sorry for so much more than I knew how to say. Ellie held a good portion of the words trapped in my chest. I didn't know how to ask for my apologies back.

Chapter Thirty-Four

CHIMES OF FREEDOM

East Berlin, German Democratic Republic, June–July 1988

Ellie

It took me a few days to be able to walk around without coughing, but slowly, my strength returned to me. I showered on my own and rinsed the smoke from my hair gratefully. I slept through the night without waking, after night after night of nightmares.

I began to make doves again.

Kai and I talked, cautiously at first, and then he finally said what had been sitting between us since the fire. "I don't know if I would have done what you did." My heart squeezed in half, but then he added softly, "But you were willing to die in there, just so others didn't die because of Aurora's balloons. I don't know if I could have done that either, El."

I whispered, "You would have died for Sabina. That's about the same thing."

When all of the pieces of history and magic fell into place in my head, I closed my eyes against the incompatibility of two truths in my mind. "Aurora saved my grandfather."

"Yeah." Kai shifted a little on the bed, his feet cold against mine.

"And she killed people." We'd been over this so many times in the last few days, but it still confused me. After all the horrors of the Holocaust, how could Aurora ever want to see another person die?

"She did." Kai rolled over, propping himself up on an elbow. "Where are you, Ellie?"

"She saved Saba's life. I wouldn't be here, if it weren't for her. And I wouldn't be *here*, if it weren't for her," I said, mostly to the ceiling because it was too hard to look at Kai right now. My heart ached, like its four chambers were being torn apart.

"Ellie," Kai said, his voice low and warm against my ear. "You're making it hard for me to stay pissed off at Aurora."

I smiled a bit, letting my eyes close so I could only know him at the places where we touched: his forehead against my temple, our hands clasped between our hips, our cold feet bumping off the edge of the bed. "Time's twisty. I wouldn't be me, if she hadn't saved him. But I wouldn't be here at all. I wouldn't be missing either. Everything we do now…Will I remember this? If I ever get home, will I remember this?"

For a long time, Kai was quiet, and then he said, "Is it selfish to say that I hope you do?"

I twisted my fingers with his. My thumb ran over the thin bandages, knowing that beneath, his burns were still healing. "Most of the things we think are selfish aren't at all. We're just so conditioned to think that wanting things is wrong. We can want to be missed, Kai."

"I always want to be missed," he told me, his voice shaking, like this was a confession. I opened my eyes, looking at him so close that he was out of focus. "I miss my Passengers. Every single one of them. And sometimes, I worry that I only miss them because they're the only people to whom I was important."

I touched his cheek with my other hand and kissed him softly. "You're important to me."

When he told me that Sabina had been suspended and remanded to the London Zerberus for the next two years, I looked away and said, "So you're going to London."

"Yeah," he said, scooting closer on the bed. "Felix offered me a job with the Zerberus. Doing more of what he does. Fixing problems, not just running balloons."

"You'll be good at that," I said. I felt like I'd spent most of the last few days unable to look him in the eye. But if I turned to him, I'd cry. I had burned my only way home. I'd be staying in East Berlin until further notice. No one said that directly, but they didn't have to. Ashasher had looked through the paperwork we had given Felix and said that it was incomplete. He didn't understand enough of what Aurora had written to duplicate it. He told me this with clear remorse, but I understood. It wasn't his fault.

"Will it be weird?" I asked him. "Being so close to your family but not at home?"

His fingers brushed against the back of my neck, at the tiny wisps of hair curling there in the heat and humidity. "I'm going to try to repair that bridge. Sabina will be living with the Zerberus, but maybe I can go home. They didn't understand her before, but if we can explain to them, if her magic is under control..."

His voice trailed off, and I heard the unsaid words. *If they understand that everything I did, I did for her.* When I breathed in, I found something firm inside myself, an anchor by which to steady myself. "They'll understand, Kai. They'll be glad you came home."

"You could come with me...us," he corrected himself quietly. "Felix said that if you wanted to, he could get you out of here. Maybe the Zerberus in London will find you a way home. They're working on it."

I thought about London, speaking English, living in a whole new city again, a whole new world, all over again. Still the wrong year. Still the wrong time. Mitzi here, all alone. She was losing her best friend already. Everyone was always leaving Kai and Mitzi,

261

I realized. I didn't want to be one of those people who left. Mitzi wanted me to become a Runner with her, but my fingers itched for doves and the balloons. I didn't want to ask, not yet, but if I were to stay, then I wanted to do everything I could.

The cool early summer crept into hot, humid days, turning my room into a sauna. I sat downstairs more often these days with Sabina. We crept around each other, unsure, both very aware that we were unintentionally pulling Kai in opposite directions.

Almost two months after the workshop fire, Kai bounced back into the house and pulled me off the couch, turning me in a big circle, an overdramatic dance. I laughed, and then had a coughing fit. My lungs still hadn't caught up with how much better the rest of me was feeling. He pulled me against his side, steadying me as I sucked in a deep breath.

"Surprise. Ready?" he asked.

Sabina glanced up from the table where she was writing out more testimony to Aurora's manipulations. "Just tell us."

"Bruce Springsteen is playing. In East Berlin. *Here*. On *this* side of the wall," crowed Kai. "And we're going. Ellie, you think you can?"

I didn't care if I could. I was going. Mitzi, Sabina, and I laughed together for the first time as we dressed upstairs, letting Mitzi play with our hair and do our makeup. Glitter covered the floor, and I didn't even care. The city felt restless, an excited simmer building below the surface as thousands of people of all ages, but especially people our age, streamed toward the Radrennbahn Weissensee where the stage was clearly set up and we could hear the roar of people. Halfway down the street, Kai caught up with me and turned his hand over, offering it to me.

I slid my fingers between his, feeling the scarring skin on the back of his hands. My shoulders were already pink in the sun. My white sundress clung to my skin. The heat was almost as oppressive as the government, and I wished I had Mitzi's guts.

She had ditched her bra, declaring it unnecessary with a sundress in this heat.

Kai swung our arms between us. His enthusiasm was contagious. I rocked on my toes for a few steps, missing his cheek the first time but pressing my lips against it the second stride I took. He stopped dead in his tracks, tilting his head to kiss me. I reached up with a hand, curving my fingers into the side of his face and around his ear. Our lips tasted like salt from our sweat, but it might as well have been the tears that I knew neither of us would shed. He gripped my body through my thin sundress and pulled me flush against him. He kissed me hard, hard enough to bruise, hard enough to make the color rush back to my own cheeks.

People catcalled us. His eyes were wild and golden. "Pretend nothing's changing, Ellie. Like everything's going to stay like this forever."

I wanted to take that word and press it into every crevice in his body, every nick in his skin, every bruise he's ever gotten in his life. *Stay.* It lingered in the air between us and on the end of his tongue. I wanted to kiss him but sensed that he didn't want to be kissed. He wanted a reply. A promise. This promise I could make.

I ran my finger across his lips. "Yes."

When he kissed me again, I thought I'd combust there on the sticky streets of Berlin. It'd be worth it.

"Sponge," he whispered, and I smiled. "Soak this up. Keep it forever."

I wanted to stay soaked in his sweat and his love and the beat of this city so I made promises I couldn't hope to keep, and our clothing stuck together.

It didn't matter if we wanted to say anything to each other. The wild and loud crowd drowned out our voices. All three hundred thousand of us sang along to "Born in the USA" and over people's heads, giant white flags waved. Sabina and Mitzi joined a bunch of girls dancing. I leaned against Kai, watching them and swaying, entranced by Springsteen's voice, even all the way at the back. I couldn't see him, but it was enough to hear him.

When Springsteen sang "Can't Help Falling in Love," Kai pulled me into his arms and buried his face in my tangled curls, and we rocked back and forth in a sea of waving lighters. I didn't close my eyes. I didn't want to forget this ever. Sabina and Mitzi came back, whooping and laughing, spinning around us. We all fell against each other, laughing, and hot, and sweaty, and madly in love. In love with everything. With forgiveness. With the cusp of freedom within sight. With music. With a crowd of people fearless and in awe.

Chapter Thirty-Five

A WAY HOME

East Berlin, German Democratic Republic, July 1988

Kai

They repaired the workshop because the remaining Schöpfers needed somewhere to work. The work of using balloons to send people to safety in West Berlin continued because Aurora hadn't taken away with her the reality of East Berlin—that dissent was dangerous. Dissent continued to build, wild and free, and the government was fighting to hold on to control.

The city hummed with a frenetic sort of energy, the kind that came when people saw the light at the end of the tunnel and realized it wasn't the oncoming train. It was hope. The world was changing. We were along for the ride.

I raised my eyebrows at Ellie and found milk in the fridge, pouring it into my tea, which made her shake her head in disgust. "You're sure you want to come to this party? It's in the workshop. You know. The one you set on fire."

"Yes, I'm aware. And you should ask Sabina too. It'd probably be helpful for both of us," Ellie said.

I tried to kiss her, but she put her hand on my mouth and pushed me away. "Gross. The tea always tastes like ass when you put milk in it. It should be illegal."

"How do you know what ass tastes like?" I called after her when she ran up the stairs.

"Mature, Kai!" she yelled back at me.

I didn't mind. It meant that things were approaching normal between us again. Just in time for us to leave. Mitzi came downstairs and made the same face at my tea. "Gross. Is that what that was about? Girl has good taste. Except in men."

I stuck my tongue out at her. "You're going to watch over her for me, right?"

Mitzi washed her hands and dried them on the towel. "No, I thought I'd let her run over the city lighting things on fire."

"You're funny sometimes," I said, and added more milk to my tea, just to spite her.

* * *

The workshop looked brand new. They'd changed the entrance to be brighter and wider. No more yellow-covered metal. Everything was made of gorgeous wood and well lit. The books were all replaced, and unless you remembered it, like I did, you'd never know the room had been on fire. Chandeliers hung from the ceiling with tiny paper airplanes, Ellie's doves, and dozens of red balloons, and people milled around—Zerberus, Schöpfers, Runners, and Ellie, drinks in hand, laughing and talking.

Ellie stuck close to my side for most of it, until Sabina tugged at my sleeve. Mitzi took Ellie's hand instead and dragged her across the room to meet a few Runners. Part of me wondered if Ellie was going to become a Runner herself. A Runner, or a Schöpfer, though there wasn't much time left for a Schöpfer to be needed here in East Berlin. There'd always be somewhere that balloons were needed though, and while it made my chest tight, wherever that was, Mitzi would be there. And maybe Ellie too.

Sabina led me back out into the tunnel, the dark swallowing us. She cleared her throat. "Don't be mad."

Warily, I said, "Okay."

"It's really important that you aren't mad."

Spoken like someone who had done something really aggravating. All thoughts of what would happen after the wall came down slipped away from my mind. "Just tell me what happened, Sabina."

"I can write Ellie a balloon back to her time," she whispered. In the tunnels, the words echoed around me. They cut right through me and whispered something that felt a lot like hope into my veins.

I shook my head. "No. She won't do it. She's not going to kill someone just to get home. I know her."

Sabina paused, and then said, "No. I fixed the equation. I've been thinking about it, and I know how to do it, Kai."

"Don't," I said. "Don't you say that unless you mean it, Sabina."

"I do. I mean it. Felix will be so mad. It's against the rules even with the modification, but I know. I know I can. I figured out how to go forward in time without pulling anyone back."

Who was this hopeful, helpful, optimistic, rational girl? How long had I been missing out on her because Aurora was drugging her so I thought she was getting worse here and not better?

I said, "Why are you asking me?"

"Because," she said, her voice soft, "if you don't want me to say anything, I can keep a secret."

Worse than Aurora giving my sister drugs to make her seem fuzzier than ever was this. We kept tripping over these mental blocks, where Sabina looked at the world and saw it full of walls and gates, and gatekeepers and border guards. We stood in a tunnel by a ghost station, next to a magical workshop, and she wanted to know if I'd keep a secret, keep a possible way home from Ellie just because I loved her.

I tried to keep my voice gentle without patronizing her. "No, Bean. I'm not keeping this from Ellie. She deserves to know if there's a way home for her."

"Should I tell her?"

I shook my head. "I'll tell her. Don't tell Felix. I'll talk to him."

Her arms were around my neck in an instant. "I know I can write the balloon, Kai. Trust me."

I wanted to tell her I did, but I didn't. I just hugged her back, and we walked back into the workshop together. The brightness and the sound overwhelmed me for a second, and I had to orient myself in the new space before I saw Ellie by Mitzi, listening to some story Nicki was telling in the corner. I slipped up behind her and touched the small of her back with my hand. She turned immediately, looking worried.

"Hey," I whispered. "Can I talk to you for a second?"

She handed off her drink to Mitzi without a word and followed me through the party, weaving through the crowd and heading toward the door. I stepped into the tunnel, holding open the door for her. I checked my watch in the light, making sure we were safe from trains. We had a few minutes. I was cheating a bit, standing in the dark with her, but as soon as the door shut behind us, I immediately regretted it. I couldn't always read Ellie's voice. But I was getting better at reading her face. Now I couldn't see her.

"Kai?" she asked, her voice hesitant. "What's going on?"

Best to get this all out in one breath. "Sabina thinks she can write you a balloon home. She fixed the equation. She says no one will die."

For a few heartbeats, neither of us said anything. And then Ellie exhaled hard and said, "Do you think she can? For real?"

She said that a lot. *For real.* Like there was something for fake worth talking about. I reached for her wrist. Her pulse pounded against my fingers. She stepped toward me in the dark. "If she says she can, I think she can. She's...She's a prodigy. I wish she hadn't been Aurora's prodigy, but if it works out in your favor this once, is it so bad?"

Ellie trembled a little bit. "I…Oh my G-d. I don't even know what to say. I can't…I didn't think I'd go home."

"Do you want me to talk to Felix?"

It took a moment, but then Ellie said softly, "Yeah. I do."

In the dark, I didn't see her coming. But her mouth brushed against mine, like she was trying to find me in the dark, and kissing her seemed like an infinitely better idea than crying in the tunnels because this was much different than me moving to London and her staying here. She was leaving. She'd leave. And this time, I'd be the one staying.

But she kissed me like she did in the tunnels for the first time, with the quiet confidence that had carried her all these months in the wrong time.

I kissed her back like that confidence was contagious.

I wished it was. I wished we always absorbed the best traits of everyone around us. I wished that was possible. Maybe this world would be less miserable.

We didn't talk to Felix that night, or even the next morning. We were too busy trying to remember all of the curves of each other and imprint them in our memories. She asked me again whether she'd remember any of this when she went home. She asked me late at night in bed whether going home was worth losing all of these memories. Worth losing me. I splayed my fingers over her stomach.

"You said home was a fantasy," she reminded me, her stomach moving as she spoke.

"I lied," I said, kissing her smile. "I wish I had a home. I was jealous. I'm still jealous."

"You have a home," she whispered back, her fingers walking across my chest, across my heart. "Sabina."

I stilled and Ellie propped herself up on her elbow, leaning over me. Her hair spilled around her bare shoulders and brushed against my face, my shoulders, my chest. I imagined her face to be as still as it became when she was very serious, her eyes very dark blue.

"Maybe we're not always looking for home, but only how to make our home fit us better. Sometimes, Kai, I think you don't know how big your heart is. Maybe your home right now can't hold all of you."

I kissed her and then murmured, "It's killing me, Ellie. Not to ask you to stay."

"I know," she said, her voice just a hush in the dark. "But I don't think I'd be able to say no."

In the morning, I woke alone. Downstairs, Ellie and Sabina were bent over equations as Sabina explained the magic to Ellie. I made breakfast, the hum of their voices keeping me company, and I tried not to think of a world without that soft, American-lilted laugh. I tried, I tried, I tried.

Chapter Thirty-Six

GOING HOME

East Berlin, German Democratic Republic, August 1988

Ellie

I read once, and I wished I could remember where, that Brave was a place. You could just go there if you wanted. There were dozens of Braves, everywhere, all over the world, where ordinary people stood up to tyranny and oppression.

People marching on streets, or standing in squares, or camping out in the public eye. People standing in front of tanks, people laying garlands of flowers around the muzzles of automatic weapons, people linking arms. People who sat down when told to stand up. People who stood up when told to kneel. People who sang songs, people who asked questions, people who wrote, people who created art. People who played a cello in a city under siege. People who had done brave things before the time I was in, and people who had done brave things after I was there, and all of the people yet to come. Injustices are countered by acts of courage. We create Brave wherever we are brave.

You. Me. Kai. Mitzi. Felix. Ashasher. Sabina, doing the right thing.

What could change if we started to measure society's successes not in wars won but in moments in which we countered injustice? When good *did* win out over evil.

Kai and Sabina delayed their move to London so she could write the balloon with strict supervision from Felix and Ashasher. Our house turned into a makeshift workshop, and I loved it. The house was alive and busy all through August, full of theory and discussions about time and physics and magic. The debate about how much time had passed in my time came up again and again. Felix thought less time. Sabina thought time might have been frozen—I liked this theory—while Ashasher thought more time might have passed. They all wanted me to be prepared for any of those possibilities. Either way, Sabina regularly went on tangents about crisscrossing the lines of time and causing paradoxes. Only Mitzi and Ashasher could soothe her when she spun herself up, her eyes glazing over as if she could see the lines of time right there in the safe-house kitchen.

I overheard Ashasher telling Kai that paradoxes and something about the rules of changing futures and time and history were exactly why he couldn't seek me out in my time. Kai had stalked out of the room and slammed the bedroom door. He refused to talk about it, and for a few days, it was like the Kai I had first met in a dark alley. Distrustful and glowering.

But the night Sabina brought in a balloon and began to write on it at the kitchen table with blood she'd pulled from my arm that morning, he was quiet. We both watched from the doorway as Felix sat next to Sabina, peering over her shoulder. He'd make sure that her magic was true and untainted, not like Aurora's magic.

Kai's head ducked, his mouth pressed lightly to my shoulder as he slipped his hand into mine. "Let's get out of here."

He, Mitzi, and I went north to the rooftop. I hadn't been on it since that night when Mitzi and I had painted our nails up there. We climbed to the top and stared over the wall. None of us said anything, but we didn't have to. It was our last night together. Kai leaned on me from one side, and Mitzi from the other. I closed my eyes. I didn't need the lights of West Berlin tonight. Everything inside me was lit up, alive with love and regret. I wished there was a way to live in every time all at once, so I never had to lose anyone. So I never had to choose between people who loved me.

In the morning, I woke slowly, drowsily, surprised by how cold I felt tangled up in Kai. He always slept late, but lightly. I brushed my hands over his bare chest and he stirred, eyes flickering open and closing. He smiled a bit, then stilled, as if he remembered what morning this was. That it was not like any other morning when we lay there whispering to each other before joining the Space-Time Continuum Party downstairs. His arms forced their way around me on the warm sheets, and he dragged me tighter against him.

I murmured, "We should do something drastic, like cut off all my hair, just to find out if things stay the same when I cross back over."

Kai let go of me so suddenly I thought I'd said something wrong. He pushed himself upright on the bed, staring at me. "Six months here, and you think that *cutting your hair* is the most drastic thing you can do? Where have I failed you?"

I laughed and half-heartedly swatted at him. "Shut up."

"You're just distracted, thinking about getting your portable telephone back," he teased me. And then his face turned somber and he caught my hand, pressing it against his chest. "Do you want to remember this?"

I hadn't actually thought he'd want to talk about what would happen when I left, if it worked, if I returned to my own time. I scooted upright in the bed. "You know I do."

He watched me. "Even the terrible parts?"

"Even the terrible parts," I affirmed, thinking of the bodies in the street, the balloons, the fire.

He ran a finger across the skin between my underwear and my T-shirt. I shivered and my stomach tightened. He could barely keep the smile off his face. "And the not-terrible parts."

I rocked forward onto my knees and kissed him. "Especially the not-terrible parts."

I wanted everyone who had ever told me I was too young to fall in love to see the way he looked at me now, like he was committing me to memory. I wondered how I could ever explain this to anyone.

One time, I spent six months back in time. I fell in love with a boy who had no obligation to love a world that only gave him gray skies and loneliness. I fell in love with a girl who loves so fiercely that she holds the world together. I fell in love with a few good people who used their magic for good, and I fell in love with a few more people who used it questionably but whose hearts meant well. I fell in love with believing in magic.

If you give a girl a red balloon, she'll believe in magic and memory. If you give a girl a red balloon, she'll never want to let go.

Kai murmured, his eyes never stilling anywhere on my face. "I shouldn't ask this of you, but I need to, Ellie. Forgive me."

Don't ask me to stay, Kai. Please.

He whispered into my cheek, "I can't be there. When you go. I want my last memory of you to be here. Like this."

I wondered if I would have been able to see him off, if I had stayed when he was going to London. I understood then. I nodded, and then kissed him again. Because I loved him. Because I had to leave him.

I celebrated Shabbat for what I hoped was the last time in this time, in this safe house. The candles sat in the same candlesticks Kai had brought me that first week, and this time, Felix said the prayer along with me. We said the same words that all of the generations before me had said, that my grandfather had taught me all those years after a magic balloon took him out of

Chełmno. *L'dor vador*. Generation to generation. When the candles flickered out, dousing us into the dark of the kitchen, Kai pressed his lips to my temple.

Felix and Ashasher decided a few days prior to my departure that I'd leave from one of the parks, in the morning, to try to hope I'd land at a time of day that was safe. Sabina fretted still. There was a risk, she and Felix had explained to me out of earshot of Kai, that I wouldn't land exactly at the right time or day, or in the right place. Magic was an imprecise science. I said as long as my balloon didn't kill anyone like she promised me, I'd cope with whatever happened. It was worth the risk.

Mitzi, Felix, Sabina, Ashasher, and I walked to the park together, holding a handful of balloons. Mitzi held mine with a gloved hand, a Runner for me today. The others and their balloons were distractions for police. Behind me in the safe house, Kai lay in bed, his arm over his eyes. I left him paper doves covering my old room. He'd watched me fold them over the last few days, one by one, and not one of them fell out of the sky this time.

Mitzi's hand touched my arm, and I glanced sideways at her. She gave me a small smile. "Scared?"

"A little," I whispered, gripping her arm tight against me. It was a little bit of a lie. I wasn't scared at all.

"I think it's brave," Mitzi said a few steps later. When I looked at her, she was looking at the sky with a small smile on her face. For once, she wasn't wearing a hat, and her teal hair flipped around her face in the wind, obscuring her expression for a moment. "Maybe even braver than coming here."

"Coming here wasn't a choice," I reminded her.

"It was," she teased me. "You heard your Saba's stories. You knew what would happen. You were dying for an adventure."

"If I wanted an adventure," I said, laughing, "I'd take a balloon to Everest. Berlin in 1988? Maybe not high on my list."

Reaching the park, I had never felt stranger in my life. My heart felt light and my steps lighter. I was the happiest and the saddest I'd ever been. I ached for Kai, but I loved having Mitzi and Sabina and Felix and Ashasher with me. I wanted to go home and I wanted to stay. Mitzi's arm squeezed mine, and the balloons floated above our heads.

In the park, Felix turned to me and said, "Ready?"

I took a deep breath and nodded, stepping forward to hug him. He whispered, "You're never alone, wherever you are. You'll always be able to find one of us, if you need to. Okay?"

I hugged Mitzi and cried, because it was Mitzi. She kissed my cheek. "Be good and be sparkly and flirt with a stranger, darling."

"I love you. Take care. Be safe." I whispered, because even if it was a silly thing to say, it felt right.

I hugged Sabina too and wished her luck in London. She hugged me tightly and said, "Thank you for loving Kai."

There wasn't much I could say to that. I didn't know how to tell people they were easier to love than they knew. Ashasher placed his hands on either side of my head and kissed my forehead. "Good-bye, brave girl."

"Not yet, not yet," yelled a familiar voice.

I spun, my eyes frantically running over the crowd, looking for him. He was running across the park, his hair flying behind him, both dark and bright in the sunlight. I stepped toward him, my heart beating wild and erratic. *He came. He's saying good-bye.* He stumbled against me, wrapped his arms around me, and then kissed me, gently, fingers at the curve of my jaw and under my chin. My eyelashes fluttered closed, and it took me a moment to catch my breath.

"I'm your Runner," he said simply when I opened my eyes. "This is my job. Besides, it makes sense if your balloon is my last."

He handed me one of my paper doves. It'd been refolded from my creases, and I could see his neat handwriting on the paper, but I didn't want to read it now. I wanted to take it with me, home, where I belonged. I tucked it into my pocket, my eyes starting to fill with tears. Then he tugged two gloves out of his pocket and slid them onto his hands over the burn scars. He took the balloon from Mitzi and glanced at his watch. Then he looked up at me and said in that low, quiet way of his that sent shivers through my blood, "Ready?"

"Yes," I whispered back. An electric shiver ran through me.

Next to me, Mitzi said, "I say this to every Passenger, so Ellie. May your journey be safe and your destination full of freedoms."

"Now," said Ashasher, and the others released the balloons they were holding.

The red balloons rose against the fierce blue sky, slowly and then gaining speed toward the sun. I stepped against Kai, rising up on my toes. I closed my eyes when our noses touched. His heart beat against mine. Our lips trembled against each other.

"Good-bye, Ellie Baum," Kai whispered.

We kissed as I wrapped my hand around the balloon string and he let go.

Author's Note

One of my favorite authors, Madeleine L'Engle, said in her Margaret Edwards Award acceptance speech, "Often the only way to look clearly at this extraordinary universe is through fantasy, fairy tale, myth." This line has guided most of my writing and became my touchstone while writing *The Girl with the Red Balloon.*

To my knowledge, no one escaped death camps or ghettos with magical red balloons. No one escaped over the Berlin Wall with magical red balloons. But people did escape from both concentration camps and death camps, from East Germany and from other places of war and oppression. And they did not do this alone. People in places of war and oppression and terrible crimes face choices, and many ordinary people have made the extraordinary choice to save lives even at the cost of their own. As Kai says in the book, "People never mentioned in history books still made history."

So what is historically accurate in the book?

The Łódź ghetto was real. Approximately 204,000 Jewish people passed through its gates. About eight hundred remained in the ghetto when the Soviets liberated it on January 19, 1945, and approximately ten thousand Łódź residents survived the

Holocaust after being deported to camps, including Auschwitz. Few people escaped Chełmno, but one of the people I read about was an unnamed eighteen-year-old boy. Łódź also housed more than five thousand Romani people, almost all of whom were killed at Chełmno and Auschwitz.

The Romanichal, Kai's people in England, are very much real. And the Roma of continental Europe who died during the Holocaust, somewhere between five hundred thousand and 1.5 million, were real, as are the Roma who reside there now. Throughout history, the Roma have suffered horrifically at the hands of people in power, and they remain some of the most persecuted people in Europe. Benno uses the word "Gypsy" for the Roma as that was the only word then, but as Kai tells Ellie, the proper word for non-Romani people to use now is Roma or Romani.

After the immediate aftermath of World War II, Germany was carved into pieces for the Allied forces to control. The Soviet Union gained control of East Germany. As the world quickly moved into an arms race and the Cold War, East Germany became the demarcation on a map, and the Berlin Wall was more than just a way to keep people in East Berlin. It was a symbol. People tried to escape East Berlin into the West in a variety of creative ways, including hot-air balloon, hand-dug tunnels, train tracks in the ghost stations, hanging on beneath cars, hiding in trunks. Some of these were successful, and many were not. The fall of the Berlin Wall on November 9, 1989, became the symbolic end of the Cold War.

The world is not as black and white as I saw it when I first dreamed up a girl going over the Berlin Wall with a red balloon.

I don't have any answers. All the answers I found in the writing of this book led me to more questions. And I'm starting to think that the answering isn't nearly as important as the asking.

Be a sponge.

Acknowledgments

This book was a labor of love, an exercise in chasing the heart of the story through many drafts, many false starts, and several years. It's a book, not just a story in my head or on my hard drive, because of some really wonderful people.

Thank you, first and always, to Louise Fury, my amazing agent. Working with you has been my favorite adventure. Thank you for loving this book like I do.

Thank you to Wendy McClure, Jonathan Westmark, Alexandra Messina-Schultheis, and the entire Albert Whitman & Company team who brought this book to life with your own magic. If you made paper doves, they'd fly.

Thank you to Dr. Ian Hancock for his assistance with the Romani language. Thank you to my sensitivity readers for your advice and patience. Any mistakes in the story and text are mine alone.

Thank you to my high school teachers who probably knew I was writing books in their classes instead of taking notes, and to my Allegheny College professors, especially Professor Howard Tamashiro and Professor Susan Slote, who introduced me to elements of history, politics, and children's literature that led me to this book.

To my favorite guys: Stephen Mazzeo, my plot guru. I still don't know how we're friends, but it's kind of the best. And of course, Paul Krueger, my optimism proxy. You're the wurst, but you probably learned that from me. What's next?

This book would have never happened without my CPs. Thank you to Christina June, Rebecca Paula, Leigh Smith, and Rebekah Campbell for your incredible, unwavering and absolute support for my magicballoonbook, and especially Kai and Ellie. You are the best of the best. MTWBWY. I'm the luckiest writer in the world.

To Nita Tyndall, Tristina Wright, Michella Domenici, Marieke Nijkamp, Lindsay Smith, Nicole Brinkley, Sara Taylor Woods, and everyone who read *The Girl with the Red Balloon* over the last few years and offered their sometimes tear-stained notes. Thank you forever. Thank you to Meghan Harker, Blair Thornburgh, Dahlia Adler, and EK Johnston for their constant support and love and occasionally validating my righteous indignation.

Thank you to my family for their support, their early reads of this book, their respect and patience with my writing. A special thank you to my brother who read an early version of this book, offered notes, and to whom I dedicate every description of Kai and Ellie's eyes.

The Girl with the Red Balloon is, and was from the very beginning, dedicated to both of my grandfathers who passed before I began writing it. I would not be a storyteller without them. One of my grandmothers passed not long after this book sold, and her pride in me and my writing meant the world. I am eternally grateful for her love, guidance, support, and the books she gifted me as a child. May their memories be a blessing.

And thank you, reader, for picking up this book. For following Ellie into this world. For feeling so deeply like Benno. For fighting alongside Kai. For believing in the goodness of people like Mitzi. Be brave. Be a sponge. And remember, you too are making history each day. Let's make a history that lifts up all people, erases no one, and leaves behind nothing but hateful ideology.

KATHERINE LOCKE

lives and writes in a very small town outside of Philadelphia, where she's ruled by her feline overlords and her addiction to chai lattes. She writes about that which she cannot do: ballet, time travel, and magic. She not-so-secretly believes most stories are fairy tales in disguise. *The Girl with the Red Balloon* is her young adult debut.